Praise for Liz Allison's *The Girl's Guide to NASCAR*

"Liz has captured the reality of our business
like no one ever has before."
—Jeff Hammond, Fox Sports

"Liz Allison has seen the sport from every angle. I can't think
of a better person to give the ladies the inside scoop."
—Larry McReynolds, Fox Sports

"As a radio personality, TV host, pit road reporter and author,
Liz has found a way to tap in to a myriad of media arenas
while pursuing her passion in racing."
—George Pyne, president, IMG Sports and Entertainment,
former COO of NASCAR

"Liz's abilities are evident as she brings the
world of NASCAR into the homes of our fans."
—Lesa France Kennedy, president,
International Speedway Corporation

Praise for Wendy Etherington

"Wendy Etherington pens a delightful tale of love lost
and found again in *Full Throttle*."
—*Romantic Times BOOKreviews*

"Wendy Etherington's *A Breath Away* crackles
with energy and sexual tension."
—*Romantic Times BOOKreviews*

"These two together are dynamite."
—*CataRomance* on *Just One Taste…*

"Captivating Characters! A Sizzling Seduction! A Perfect Plot!
What more can you ask for in a romance?"
—BJ Deese, *Romance Junkies*, on *Sparking His Interest*

**Liz Allison and Wendy Etherington titles
in the NASCAR Library Collection**

No Holding Back

Also by Liz Allison

The Girl's Guide to NASCAR
(A NASCAR Library Collection title)

*NASCAR Wives:
The Women Behind the Sunday Drivers*
(A NASCAR Library Collection title)

Also by Wendy Etherington

Full Throttle (A NASCAR Library Collection title)

LIZ ALLISON
& WENDY ETHERINGTON

NO HOLDING BACK

H

HQN™

ISBN-13: 978-0-373-77263-6
ISBN-10:   0-373-77263-7

NO HOLDING BACK

Dear Reader,

Welcome to the Garrison family! As a reader of our series, you're now officially part of the GRI team.

Since we're both a bit racing obsessed and certainly believe in the power of happily-ever-after, the inspiration for *No Holding Back* came easily. The series is ultimately about family—a family who loves, laughs and cries together.

We had a great time sculpting our own imaginary NASCAR world. We've introduced most of the important players (though we hope to throw a few surprises your way in later books) and we're thrilled to take you on the 180-mph ride.

Make no mistake, the journey you're about to take with Cade and Isabel is a bumpy one. The Playboy and the Tough as Nails Girl whose only passion is her career don't fall in love easily, but they do fall hard—and forever.

Between Liz's years as a driver's wife, commentator and writer and Wendy's experience as a rabid racing fan and romance author, we've formed a team that promises to give you an inside peek into the NASCAR world and the relationships of the people who live and love there. We can be reached at www.lizallison.com or www.wendyetherington.com or P.O. Box 3016, Irmo, SC 29063.

Let's go racing—and romancing!

Liz and Wendy

This book is dedicated to our husbands, Ryan and Keith, who keep our engines fired every day.

NO
HOLDING
BACK

CHAPTER ONE

"CADE, JOHN HEPNER'S ON the phone!"

Involuntarily, Cade Garrison's hand jerked, causing his Sharpie marker to smear a jet-black line across the publicity photo he was autographing. Great. NASCAR's chief cop calling? "I haven't done anything," he called back to his sister.

Lately, anyway.

"He didn't say you did. I think he wants to congratulate you on Saturday's win."

Wary, Cade capped the marker and walked across his office, where he was spending the afternoon autographing fan memorabilia. He peeked around the edge of the door, eyeing his sister, Rachel, at her desk as she typed on her PC. "You sure?"

"I *think,*" she said, flicking him an annoyed glance.

"Mmm." He didn't think he could take seeing his name attached to a violation of NASCAR rule 12-4-A (actions detrimental to stock car racing) or hear the "you need us a lot more than we need you" speech again. It had been rumored that a continuous betting pool circulated the racing body's offices

in both Daytona Beach and Charlotte, with everyone plotting and profiting on the next time he'd
face disciplinary action.

"Don't be such a chicken," Rachel said. "What
can he do to you that he hasn't done already?"

"I'm not chicken." He'd marched back across the
office and had picked up the phone before he realized she'd easily goaded him into answering. What
had ever possessed him to hire his sister as his manager?

*She's saved your butt a million times and still
loves you.*

Oh, yeah. There was that.

"John, how are you?" he said into the phone with
false cheer.

"I'm good, Cade. I just wanted to congratulate
you on your big win Saturday."

Unaware until that moment that he'd been
holding his breath, Cade dropped into a chair with
a sigh of relief. "Thank you, sir. It was a team effort."

"And the press conference went well, I hear."

"You were there, sir?" Cade asked, his voice rising.

"No, but I heard."

Of course he had. A driver couldn't sneeze in the
garage without somebody noticing it, and—if the
driver was him, anyway—reporting it. He used to
laugh off the scrutiny, but that was before his fall
from grace. In the aftermath, he was all too aware
of every move, gesture and comment he made. "My
sponsor was pleased," he said neutrally.

"And we all know how important that is, don't we?"

Refusing to give in to the disappointment that flowed through him, he rolled his shoulder. He'd made a mistake. One he'd definitely paid for. "Yes, sir."

"Good luck at Nashville."

"Thank you, sir."

Almost immediately after he set the receiver in the cradle, and before he could wipe the bead of sweat rolling down his face, his sister called to him again. "Some woman named Mandy is on the phone!"

"Who's Mandy?"

"Brunette. Five-seven, a curvy one-fifteen."

He darted to the doorway and glanced around the meticulously neat office. No curvy brunette. Other than his sister, anyway. "She's here or on the phone?"

"Phone."

"Then how do you know what she looks like? I don't even know who she is."

"Neither did I, so I asked."

"And she told you…"

"Brunette. Five-seven, a curvy one-fifteen."

He searched his memory for Saturday at Dover. After his amazing win—his first in eighteen months—he'd slid out of his only slightly banged-up Go! Energy Drink Chevrolet, stood on the window frame and was showered with soda and Busch beer by his team. TV interviews, hug from Dad, hug from Rachel and crew chief, more beer, some of which *might* have reached his mouth. Press conferences one and two followed, then some champagne…

Back to his motor coach in the driver's compound. Remote control car racing? More champagne? The details were fuzzy for some reason.

He'd woken up with a headache on Sunday morning—how had *that* happened? He'd bummed around his motor coach, gone to the garage, then watched the NASCAR NEXTEL Cup Series race from the Budweiser suite. Everybody was full of congratulations, and with the beer company being the sponsor of the entire series he raced for, he'd *had* to toast them with a bottle of Busch beer. Or two. But surely he'd switched to ginger ale at *some* point.

"I'm drawing a blank," he said finally.

"Your brain's just having a hard time seeing through all the champagne bubbles." She paused, her fingers stilling on the keyboard. "Or maybe it's the suds."

"Cute. I talked to a lot of people this weekend, but a curvy brunette wasn't one of them. Though, there might have been a blonde…."

"I thought you'd sworn off women after that weird chick chased your golf cart through the infield at Charlotte."

He waved his hand. "That was last week, Rach."

Still, with John Hepner sending spies to his press conferences, it might be wise to lay low the next couple of weeks. He needed to concentrate on build-

ing momentum from the win. No one ever said getting back into the NASCAR NEXTEL Cup Series
was going to be easy and without sacrifice. "I should
probably pass on Mandy."

Rachel raised her eyebrows. "You think?"

Ignoring her sarcasm, he scowled. "Why don't
you try using the intercom instead of yelling every
time I have a call?"

She grinned. "I like seeing you run to the doorway."

"Well, I'm not doing it again."

"Right."

"And tell Mandy I'm busy."

"Whatever you say, boss."

He was halfway across the room before he spun
and darted back. He peeked around the door just as
Rachel picked up the phone receiver. "But get her
number just in case."

Satisfied he'd done his virtuous deed for the day,
he lost interest in signing publicity photos. Who'd
want them, anyway? (Other than Mandy and possibly that blonde who was pleasantly fuzzy in his
memory.) He was the black sheep. The outcast to
his perfect, three-generations-of-successful-and-
upstanding-racing family.

Somehow, no matter what he did, he was sure
he'd never measure up to their successes. He'd sure
never get the attention his NASCAR NEXTEL Cup
champion older brother, Bryan, did. And he'd been
retired for more than two years.

But then brilliant, responsible, stalwart Bryan had

never punched out his primary sponsor's son on pit road, been severely punished by NASCAR—good-bye fifty championship points—lost his bid to make the Chase and the top ten in final championship point standings, lost his sponsor, nearly been fired by his father, then been given a gracious reprieve by driving the Garrison Racing NASCAR Busch Series car.

Cade, on the other hand, had to plead guilty on all counts.

Before last August, he'd just been the mischief-maker in the family. He loved life, women and parties, which—occasionally—led to minor trouble. These days he'd been forced into therapy for his emotional outbursts. (Of which there had been—count 'em, folks—one.) People looked at him with pity and doubt. Sponsors scattered like cars during a wreck at Talladega.

Making amends definitely sucked, but he supposed it was time he paid his dues like everybody else. He'd sailed into this sport with a famous last name, a smile, an attitude and a bit of talent. He'd spent two years in the NASCAR Busch Series, winning the championship one year, coming in third the next. Following his brother's retirement, he'd been promoted to the NASCAR NEXTEL Cup Series car, where he'd spent two years, finishing seventh, then the unremarkable twenty-first following his "outburst."

Yet all the family's hopes and dreams for the future rested on him. His grandfather and father each had

Championship titles; in fact, his father had two. After his father retired from driving, he'd started his own race team, allowing Bryan to come along and break the family records. Bryan was always going to be the one to carry them through the next generation. All Cade had to do was smile and wave in the background.

But then, in one crazy moment, everything had changed.

And not because of a race. A few years ago, Bryan had been heading to a sponsor event when a tractor trailer jackknifed in front of him. With his driving experience, he'd managed to maneuver his car to a safe stop on the side of the road. But other drivers weren't so skilled. His car was smashed, along with his right leg. Bryan's career was over, and it didn't take long for the family to turn their attention to the only other racer they had.

Rachel walked into his office and dropped a box on his desk. "Sign."

"The box?" he asked, looking blankly innocent just to be difficult. As the baby in the family, he'd worked this move to perfection by the time he was six months old.

His sister rolled her eyes, which were a pale blue and matched his own. But while many a lovely lady had told him his were "sparkling" and "sexy," Rachel's were nearly always serious. "The *contents*, race boy."

"All of them?"

"Oh, please. There are half a dozen cars, some T-shirts and hats, a small stack of pictures and a couple of teddy bears."

"That'll take *hours.*"

"Then you need to get moving, don't you? There's another box after this one."

Heaving a tired sigh, he leaned against the desk. It was nearly three o'clock, and he'd made plans to meet friends for drinks at six, but if he didn't start complaining now, Rachel would have him working until past seven. "More? How can there be more? I thought I was the *un*popular guy in this family."

"No, sweetie, you're the *notorious* member of this family."

He picked up a yellow-and-red model car from the box. It was a mini copy of his last NASCAR NEXTEL Cup Series ride. Talk about cruel. "It hurts, Rach."

"I'm sure the fans will feel your pain as you climb into your hundred-thousand-dollar custom-built Corvette, drive to dinner with a smokin'-hot blonde centerfold, then end the night in your multimillion-dollar house on the lake." She smiled wanly. "Life is tough, yes?"

"Come on. I appreciate my fans."

"Then act like it." She strode purposefully toward the door. "By the way, if you skip out on Mom's Monday-night dinner again, you're going to get a call."

"I've got plans!"

"I suggest you reschedule."

"Ugh." Cade collapsed into his executive chair. He cast a tired look at the stack of photos, cars, T-shirts, caps and other assorted merchandise for him to sign.

He loved his job, he really did. NASCAR fans were the most loyal in the world. They cheered him and supported him, and even the ones who thought he could be too wild at times bought his and his sponsors' merchandise, came to the races and shouted his name at appearances.

Grannies made him quilts. Moms offered to find him a wife. Young women flashed him smiles—an especially nice perk. Guys tipped their hats. Young boys admired his driving. He owed everything to them. Their loyalty—even when he crashed out of a race—never failed to astound him. They were his people, and he belonged to them.

Besides, what other choice did he have? Get a real job?

He shuddered.

So, he signed and signed. And signed. When his mom called about dinner that night, he totally caved and said he'd be there. She always ate early, so he could make her happy and still meet his friends at the club later.

Ever since his parents' unexpected divorce nearly two years ago, he, Rachel and Bryan alternated running interference between his mom and dad. His dad's life was racing. Always had been, always would be. His mother had supported them all as best she could, but the life on the road, the time and energy commitment, and the obsession with better performances and besting stronger competition every year weighed heavily on her. After Bryan's forced retirement, she'd hoped they could step back from racing, just be a regular family.

But no once else wanted to step back. They wanted more and more. They wanted championships and trophies. They wanted to beat the best every week. Giving up their driving life force wasn't an option.

His parents had parted. He, Bryan and Rachel had been left in the middle, trying to understand, yet never really coming to terms with the split in their once close-knit family. Even with their unusual profession, they seemed so normal, so bonded.

When he pulled his Corvette into the driveway of his mother's house just before six, his gaze automatically slid to the far-right window, the one that had been his bedroom growing up. These days it was a homage to a collection of figurines, whose pastel, smiling, cherubic faces frankly gave him the creeps.

Everything had changed since those idyllic childhood days. The adventure of going to the track and playing football in the infield compound with the other drivers' kids was in the past. Now he raced against many of those guys. And as he'd grown older, he'd become more aware of the pressures his parents must have felt for decades. The tension was bound to boil over eventually. Which it did—eating away at their marriage.

They couldn't ever forget their family was a business. Balance sheets sometimes took precedence over feelings and affection. Racing results replaced family time. The dirt track on their country acreage where they'd once had picnics and family races had gradually lost its appeal to the big tracks. The excitement of simply qualifying had been replaced by the need to finish well, to win and win it all.

He wouldn't trade his family for anything, but something was missing. Either in himself or in their bond as a whole. And he had no idea how to find it.

But firm in his role as the family playboy, he was smiling as he walked in the door. "I could go for a seriously thick burger," he said as he strolled into the kitchen.

His mother—her highlighted cap of blond hair curled to glossy perfection underneath her jaw, then tucked behind her ear—cast him an affectionately annoyed glance over her shoulder. "We're having chicken casserole."

Cade hid his disappointment and kissed her cheek. "I can hardly wait. You need help?"

"Not from you, sweetie." She smiled. "No offense."

So his prowess on the track had never translated to the kitchen. Not the greatest shortcoming in life. Shrugging, he walked into the family room.

Parked on the sofa and staring at the TV sports

report, his brother held a glass of iced tea in one hand and the remote in the other and didn't glance up. Cade headed down the hall leading to the garage and snagged a bottle of water from the fridge.

After he twisted off the top, he settled onto the sofa next to Bryan. "Anything interesting?"

"They mentioned your win as if it was the most miraculous event in a decade."

"Oh, yeah?"

"'Former NASCAR NEXTEL Cup driver and member of the legendary Garrison family finally finds his way into Victory Lane after eight billion starts.' You know the drill."

It hadn't been *that* long. "They mention you?"

"Sure." Bryan hunched his shoulders. "'Perhaps company president and former NASCAR NEXTEL Cup Series champion Bryan "Steel" Garrison is on to something. Has he finally managed to control his wild sibling? Will this upbeat mood survive? Can the Garrison boys really hope to add to Mitch Garrison's legacy?' As always, Dad takes the victory laps, and I take the heat."

"*We* take the heat, and he's earned those laps."

"Yeah." Bryan rubbed his temples. "Yeah, I know. I just get tired of explaining it over and over."

Cade nudged his brother's shoulder. "I'm going out with some friends later. Why don't you come with us? You work too much."

"I'd rather work."

Bryan had recently gone through a bitter divorce,

and no one in the family seemed to be able to break through his wall of resentment. Personally, after going through that mess, Cade figured he'd be drowning himself in women, not work.

At thirty-two, Bryan was still young. He had the Garrison square jaw, dark brown hair and pale blue eyes that matched Cade's own with enough similarity that they'd often been mistaken for twins when they were teenagers. But these days the prematurely silver threads clearly marked Bryan as the older brother—and the one who handled stress with the least amount of grace.

With Rachel in the middle, Cade supposed they seemed like bookends of the perfect family to many. But then no family was perfect. Least of all his.

Shaking aside the troubling thoughts, Cade again focused on his brother. The guy was good-looking, wealthy, hardworking and eligible. Now that Bryan was back on the market, he ought to have chicks crawling all over him. And he would—if Bryan ever stopped planning, working and strategizing long enough to look around at the curvaceous scenery.

But the guy just wouldn't listen to reason.

"Come on, man," Cade said. "Everybody misses you."

A hint of a smile crossed Bryan's lips. "They've got you, don't they?"

"Two's better than one."

"Sorry, bro."

Ah, the ladies they could attract with their older-younger-brother deal. It just made Cade's heart break.

"I'm going to Dad's after dinner," Bryan added.

"Oh."

In addition to his brother trying to handle the media pressure and living up to their father's legacy, their parents' divorce had divided the family on many levels. Bryan, with his love and passion for racing, had taken Dad's side. Rachel, with her understanding of racing, but her frustration with things she saw as obsessive, had taken Mom's.

And Cade? Well, he was caught somewhere in the middle. Understanding both sides. Frustrated with both sides.

Rachel strode into the den. She halted at the sight of Cade and clutched her heart. "Working all day, plus on time to dinner? You're going to lose your standing as the rotten kid."

Cade levered himself off the sofa. "We wouldn't want that. I'll just go."

She pushed him back down, then she sat next to him. "Thanks for signing everything."

"We should be caught up by now."

"Now we're only six months behind." She reached across him and swatted Bryan's leg. "What are you brooding about today?"

Bryan cast her an annoyed glance, then focused again on the TV. "I'm not brooding." He snorted. "What a ridiculous word."

"Old-fashioned, maybe. But apt. Look up *brood*

in the dictionary, your picture is right there. You and Heathcliff's."

"Who?"

"From *Wuthering Heights*." When Bryan still looked blank, she waved her hand. "Never mind. You should be in a good mood for once. A big win, no scandal, no fines or lost points."

"We've got Daytona coming up in a few weeks, and I don't like the wind-tunnel results."

Cade frowned. His crew chief had told him his car was looking good for the big July night race. "Hey, I thought we were—"

"Not your car. Shawn's."

Cade clenched his jaw. That car was his, too. At least it used to be. After his blowup last summer, Shawn Stayton and he had swapped rides. Now Shawn was the one who raced on Sunday. He was teammates with the legendary champion, Kevin Reiner, who drove the other Garrison Racing car.

Cade was on the outside, fighting each week to prove he deserved a second chance, that he could handle the competition and pressure of the NASCAR NEXTEL Cup Series, while Shawn became the beneficiary of his father's smiles and words of encouragement.

"How awful," Cade said dramatically. "All's not well in the 86 car with the golden boy?"

Bryan's eyes chilled. "Cut it out, Cade."

He wished he could put aside his resentment. Cade had brought on his troubles himself, and

Shawn wasn't a bad guy, but dealing with family always made things more extreme, more personal. "I'm gettin' a beer."

He'd nearly reached the kitchen when he met his mother in the doorway.

She held up a casserole dish between her oven-mitt-covered hands. "Let's eat."

Cade abandoned the idea of a beer, since his mother didn't allow bottles or cans at the table, and instead helped her carry the rest of the dishes into the dining room. By the time they'd said grace and begun to eat, he'd managed to shake off his bad mood.

Eternal optimism. He supposed it was the curse—or maybe it was the blessing—of being the family joker.

"Hey, can Shawn take my place at Thanksgiving dinner, too? Then I could go to Hawaii for the holidays."

"Absolutely not," his mother said, her authoritative glare sweeping everyone. "We're all going to be together this year. Aunt Sue is coming over with her kids, and we're going to have a nice, big family day."

"Is there any particular reason we're already planning Thanksgiving?" Bryan asked. "It's June."

"Because if Mom doesn't start nagging now, we'll find a way to squirm out of her big party," Cade said.

His mother shook her head. "I don't understand

why it's such a big sacrifice to spend one whole day with your family."

"We spend our whole day, nearly *every* day with one another. Personally, I could use a break."

"You'd rather spend Thanksgiving with strangers?"

"Absolutely." He grinned. "Especially if they're curvy, bikini-clad strangers."

"Well, too bad," Rachel interrupted. "This is important to Mom, and you're coming."

Cade stuck out his tongue at her.

"Good grief," his mother said. "You two still act like you're twelve."

Rachel rolled her eyes. "*He* certainly does."

"Just because you're jealous of my youth and vivaciousness, while you're turning into an old maid…"

Rachel tossed a dinner roll at him.

Cade's mother turned stark white. "Rachel Leigh Garrison, have you lost your mind?"

"I've had it with him, Mom! I may have to work with him, but I don't have to take crap about my personal life."

"What personal life?" Cade asked.

From across the table, Rachel glared daggers at him.

"Don't say *crap,* honey," their mother said, patting her daughter's hand.

The fact that he'd rendered Rachel speechless satisfied Cade for the moment. He said nothing and chewed his chicken. After the hard time she'd given him earlier in the day, she had to expect he'd get her back.

However, he recognized the need to back off. Cade couldn't run his life for more than ten minutes without his sister. If he didn't have her as his manager, an ally against his car owner and the company president—his father and brother respectively—he'd never have a moment's peace.

"I'm off," Bryan said as he rose. "Thanks for dinner, Mom."

"You're leaving already?"

He kissed her cheek. "My knee's stiffening up. I need to get in the whirlpool."

"You should at least stay to help with the dishes," Rachel said.

Seeing a spasm of pain cross his brother's face, Cade realized he hadn't spent the night brooding so much as trying not to betray how much his leg was bothering him. It seemed the pain of his forced retirement was growing worse instead of healing.

"I'll do his part," Cade said, rising from his chair and gathering the plates.

Bryan shot him a grateful look, then strode out of the room.

As Cade, his mom and Rachel headed to the kitchen, his mom cast his sister a worried glance. "Honey, you *are* going out on dates, aren't you?"

Cade bit back a grin as Rachel sighed in disgust.

CHAPTER TWO

"HOW'S YOUR BURGER?"

Isabel Turner shrugged, but smiled slightly for her colleague. She couldn't seem to work up an appetite.

"It tastes better when you actually take a bite," Susan Long added.

To keep her feisty friend quiet rather than feeling a real need to eat, Isabel bit into her juicy burger.

She and Susan worked as PR reps for Cumberland Atlantic, better known as CATL, a conglomerate of companies that spent the bulk of its marketing efforts in the world of the National Association for Stock Car Auto Racing—NASCAR to anybody who hadn't spent the past fifty years on a deserted island. And even they were probably familiar with the concept of racing on the beach.

"It's good," Isabel said once she'd swallowed and wiped her face.

For the infamous burgers at the Rusty Rutter—the Lake Norman joint that often lured wealthy homeowners, most of them part of NASCAR nation—Isabel should probably come up with a better adjective. As she made her living communicating and helping others do so effectively, her lackluster attitude was embarrassing.

She was off her game—no doubt about it.

"You're not still thinking about *him,* are you?" Susan asked.

Isabel scowled. "Of course not."

Susan dropped her fork and rolled her eyes. "Oh, hell, you are."

"I'm not," Isabel said, though she was.

"That's why you suggested coming here, isn't it? He and his buddies hang out here."

"I refuse to answer on the grounds of self-incrimination."

Susan shook her head, her bright red hair brushing her shoulders. "I don't know you anymore, I really don't."

Isabel didn't know herself, either. She was practical and—usually—professional. Any appetite the juicy burger managed to spark died.

He's forbidden.

"There are plenty of other men out there besides Cade Garrison," Susan said, her gaze reflecting her annoyance.

But none she wanted. None she craved and dreamed about. None who made her lose her breath and made her forget everything that was important to her.

He was a driver; she was a rep for a sponsor—as of this year, a competing sponsor. The only part of their relationship that was appropriate was the moments they exchanged greetings as they passed each other in the media-center hallway between track press conferences.

Nothing else was acceptable, yet she'd crossed the line once and often dreamed of doing it again, even eighteen months after their illicit night together. If she hadn't spent all of last year working on the company's NFL sponsorships—safely away from Cade—who knew what she might have done by now? She'd only been in proximity to him for four months, and she was already sweating like an addict in search of her next fix.

Needless to say, her loss of appetite was the least of her worries.

"He's forbidden," Susan said, voicing Isabel's own thoughts.

"I'm aware of that."

"So he's more alluring. We all want what we can't have."

"That's certainly part of it."

"You're risking your job."

"I haven't done anything." *Lately, anyway.*

Susan leaned forward and whispered. "But you *did*. Forget it. Forget him and move on."

All sensible and logical arguments, but Isabel couldn't make her heart—or her body—listen. Her career meant everything to her. It and her uncle had saved her from a none-too-pretty fate.

Her parents had been overloaded with problems—including lack of steady employment, drug addiction, bounced checks and petty thievery—that eventually led to jail time. They were directionless and not interested in their neglected, defensive, sometimes trouble-making daughter.

When she'd been turned over to foster care at age fifteen, the state of North Carolina had found her uncle—her mother's brother—and contacted him. Never knowing about her existence, her uncle was appalled by the childhood she'd endured and offered her a home with him and his family in nearby Charlotte.

With a boisterous personality and dedicated work ethic, John Bonamici left an indelible imprint on her confidence and personality. He'd nurtured her and adopted her, though she'd kept her own father's name to remind her of where she'd come from. He'd sent her to prestigious—and expensive—Davidson College, then helped her get a job with CATL after graduating.

As Isabel's uncle had moved up the ranks of CATL's executives, earning the title vice president of marketing, she'd been given more responsibility, as well. She'd vowed to rise above her humble beginnings and never cause her uncle to regret bringing her into his home. At the office and track, she worked harder and longer than everybody else. She wore her professionalism like a badge of honor.

Her night with Cade had been her one slip. Everybody was entitled to *one* mistake, right? Still, it had to be forgotten if she hoped to keep her job and her family's respect.

Now more than ever.

Despite enduring jibes of nepotism by some of her colleagues, this year she'd become senior PR rep. A lot of people said she was being groomed to take over her uncle's job when he retired in a few years.

"I know I need to forget him," Isabel said finally to Susan, the only person she'd dared tell about her night with Cade. "But, I—"

"But nothing." Susan squeezed her hand. "You could be a *vice president* soon. You want that job more than anything, don't you?"

She didn't hesitate. "Yes."

"Then no Cade."

"No Cade," Isabel repeated, hoping if she said the words often enough she'd actually begin to absorb their meaning. She waved her hand and picked up a fry. "You're right. Of course you're right."

Susan sighed in obvious relief. "You're just lonely. You work yourself into the ground, then go home to an empty apartment and memories that are better left in the past. Have you thought about online dating?"

"You mean dating online or finding somebody online that you actually date in person?"

"Cute. Very cute." Susan sipped her wine. "I mean *actual* dating. I find guys like that all the time."

"You find guys in line at the grocery store."

Susan grinned and flipped her hair over her shoulder. "Because I'm open. And smiling." She nudged Isabel.

Isabel forced a smile and pushed her empty beer bottle aside.

"Girl, you're as closed as a constipated clam."

"Oh, thanks. How flattering."

"You're beautiful."

Shaking her head, Isabel crossed her arms over her chest. She was ambitious and savvy.

"You're downplaying your Italianness. All that dark brown hair and chocolatey eyes…whoa, baby."

"My *Italianness?*"

"You know, like you guys have looks and great salad dressing."

"You're trying to piss me off."

"Better than depression."

"I might just call some of my Jersey relatives and have you taken care of."

"You don't have Jersey relatives."

"Sure I do. Somewhere way back, right after the Sicilians."

"Humph. Maybe. You *do* make a seriously awesome lasagna."

"My uncle does. I reheat his works of art. He keeps assuring me I have the pasta-making gene somewhere, though." She paused and brushed her finger down her beer bottle. "Along with the need for revenge."

Looking a touch nervous, Susan stirred her pasta. "You're trying to distract me from my point."

"You had one?"

"Yep. And it was good, too." She angled her head, considering for a moment. "You need to focus on yourself, what's best for you and your career. Tap into your inner Sophia Loren, and let those boys come to you." She sent her a mild glare. "Which they would do if you didn't live to intimidate them."

"I don't *live* to intimidate people."

"Oh, you know you do. You don't even have to say anything. You use that evil eye, and people jump to follow orders."

"The Sicilian eye, or the Jersey one?"

"You have two?" Susan asked with equal parts doubt and caution.

Isabel smiled genuinely for the first time all night. "If I so choose."

"You are one scary chick."

"And don't you forget it."

"Oh, crap."

Isabel glanced at her. "Hey, I was kidding about the curse thing—"

Susan waved her hand. "No, not that." She nodded and stared over Isabel's shoulder. *"Him."*

Of course Isabel knew who'd just walked in the door behind her, and as much as she wanted to turn, she didn't. But her heart rate picked up. "With who?" she asked.

"The usual—Dean and Jay."

Childhood buddies. They were cool guys and always supportive of Cade—even through the crazy

sponsor fight last summer. NASCAR, his sponsors
and the press had all barbecued him, but his friends
stuck by him and often stood in front of him, defending his outburst to anyone who'd listen.

Isabel thought those actions said as much about
Cade as they did his friends.

Stop.

She slid a fry through ketchup and reminded herself
that this idealistic view of Cade had to go. He wasn't
perfect by any means, but she'd elevated him to legendary status, rationalizing that any man who could
get her to risk her job had to be amazingly unique.

All last year she'd smiled fondly when she
thought of him, and then promptly ignored her pangs
of longing and went right back to work. But these
days her feelings were a jumble, centering around
her attraction to him, their forbidden past and
tension-filled present. She couldn't stop recalling
the awkward aftermath they'd endured by skipping
all the usual steps in a relationship and sleeping
together before they even knew each other, and wondering what she could have done to change things.

Her agitated emotions made her weekends at the
track difficult and caused her to squirm now beneath
Susan's pointed stare.

"Don't move," her friend said.

"Can I eat my burger?"

"You weren't so interested before."

"Okay, look." Isabel leaned forward and folded
her arms on the table. "Maybe I have a crush on the

guy, but I haven't lost my senses completely. I'm not going to jump his bones or fall at his feet, or even ask for his autograph."

Susan's gaze slid to hers. "Of course you're not. I'm sorry. He doesn't even see us, anyway. He's too busy checking out that blond waitress."

Isabel had reached for her burger, but she pulled back. "Thanks a lot. *Now* I want to look."

"She's not really all that hot. Big boobs, though."

"Not at *her,* you goofball."

Susan grinned. "He, on the other hand…"

Disgusted, Isabel tossed her napkin on the table. "Since you drove, I'm getting another beer."

She strode to the bar. "Michelob Light, please," she said to the bartender, who then moved away to get her beer.

"Hey, Izzy."

Irritated by Susan's teasing, she had to fight a jolt of surprise at Cade's voice. She turned and stared at him over her shoulder. Her heart thumped once, hard as a kick. "Why do you call me that? You know I hate it."

Unabashed, he grinned. "'Cause it makes sparks fly from your eyes."

"Five-fifty," the bartender said from behind her.

Isabel started to lay down a ten when Cade said, "Put it on my tab, Pat."

"No, I really—"

"It's not against the law for me to buy you a beer, is it?"

"I guess not." *But it's probably the only thing that isn't.*

She wrapped her hand around the bottle, and he laid his hand over hers. Her pulse leapt, and now she needed the beer to moisten her dry throat.

"Allow me." He twisted off the top, then handed back the bottle.

She tried to breathe normally.

It was one thing to see him on pit road or at a press conference, when he was in his driver's uniform and she was safe behind her NASCAR NEXTEL Cup hard card credential dangling from a neon-yellow lanyard, and make polite, *professional* conversation. It was entirely another to see him in regular clothes—ones those broad shoulders filled out quite nicely—and have his hand brush hers.

"Thanks," she said finally.

"My pleasure."

She made the mistake of meeting his pale blue gaze. Dear heaven, the man had eyes that would tempt a saint. Her stomach flipped over and her throat closed. She sipped her beer and prayed for a witty comeback.

"So," he began, "what's a nice girl like you…"

"Oh, please."

"Well, you're just standing there, looking like you swallowed a trout."

"I am *not*."

"Are, too."

"Am—" She stopped herself in time from sinking

to arguing like a third-grader. The man brought out the absolute worst in her. At least when he wasn't making her pulse race.

She rolled her shoulders. "I have a dinner engagement to get back to. Thanks for the beer."

He nodded toward a table of guys a few feet away. "You and Susan want to join us?"

"Ah, no. We have to get up early for work tomorrow."

"You're always working."

"So are you."

He said nothing for a moment, then nodded. "I guess I am. If you change your mind, the invitation stands." Smiling, he headed to his table, where several women had gathered around his buddies, obviously waiting for his return.

Isabel strolled back to her own table. She was proud she hadn't made an idiot out of herself, but she'd been abrupt as a result. Copping an attitude was a defense mechanism left over from her childhood. Some kids used humor, some kids pulled into themselves, and some kids—like her—threw the first punch.

Come to think of it, maybe *that* was why she and Cade connected so easily.

"You walked over there just so he could watch you strut in those jeans," Susan accused the moment she returned.

"I did *not.* I got a beer." She held up the bottle. "See?"

"A beer *he* bought."

"Who are you—the sponsor-etiquette police?"

Susan's eyes grew frosty. "No, I'm a friend. A friend who's worried."

Isabel hung her head. "I'm fine."

"You don't look fine."

"I am." Shaking off the worry and dread that had no doubt been passed on from some intuitive Sicilian ancestor, she looked up. "I appreciate your concern, but I'll get over it." She paused. "I'll get over *him*." It hadn't worked in eighteen months, but surely it would *eventually*.

Susan picked up her fork. "I know you will. Can we talk about something besides work and drivers now?"

"You bet."

They fell back on complaining about the traffic, the shoe sale at Nordstrom's and the drudging difficulty of exercising with a demanding job.

"We're still young, right?" Susan asked as they shared a hot fudge brownie.

"I guess so."

"Our metabolism hasn't completely shut down yet, has it?"

"I'm not sure. Even though I'm at the track every weekend—where the menu includes hot dogs, hamburgers and more hot dogs—I haven't gained any weight in years." She frowned over her bite of lusciously warm brownie. "But then I'm constantly running around. Or I don't have time to eat at all."

Susan goggled at her. "Who forgets to eat?"

"I do, I guess."

"That's not natural. But if you could bottle it, you'd make a fortune."

"I'll remember to eat—the next time I go to my uncle's and smell his marinara sauce. It'll make up for a few missed lunches."

"Mmm, speaking of bottling and making a fortune…"

Isabel angled her head, considering. "It's not a bad idea—John's Special Sauce. Maybe after he retires."

The waitress dropped by to refill their coffee, and Susan stirred in cream as she commented, "So the Cup Series goes to Pocono and the Busch Series to Nashville this weekend. Where are they sending you?"

"Both."

"Jeez. Really?"

"Roger Cothren's son is making his first Busch start, so we're using the opportunity to launch Mini Fudge Stars to complement Roger's Double Fudge Stars car." She rolled her eyes. She thought the plan was a little *too* cute, but she'd been outvoted. "Then there's a Cup Series press conference on Sunday morning about Bruce Phillips changing teams next year. We're officially following him to his new ride."

"Good grief."

"This is the last peaceful moment I'll probably have this week."

"Roger Cothren doesn't seem old enough to have a son driving."

"He turned eighteen a few months ago."

"I guess he'll have a primo engine."

Since his family's engine shop was legendary and patronized by dozens of racing teams, Isabel knew that was true. Could the kid drive? Maybe. Could he handle the pressure of driving in the big leagues and with a famous last name to boot? That was another thing entirely. "With Phillips changing teams, Silly Season has officially begun."

"Doesn't it seem earlier every year?"

"June's about average these days."

"Is he going to Baker?"

Isabel cast a quick glance toward the other side of the restaurant, where Cade and his friends were working on a huge platter of buffalo wings. Baker Racing and the Baker family were big rivals of the Garrison's. The animosity went all the way back to 1973 when Joe Baker bumped Mitch Garrison—Cade's father—out of the way to win the Season Opener in Daytona. Mitch went on to win two NASCAR NEXTEL Cup Series championships, but he never won that magical February race in Daytona Beach. The Garrison family always blamed Joe, and the prejudice had filtered down to the next generation.

"Yeah, he's going, but you don't know that," she said to answer Susan's question.

"They want a veteran to settle down those wild young boys?"

"They certainly *need* to settle them down, but

whether or not a veteran will do it is anybody's guess."

"It seems to me—" Her gaze darted to the two men approaching their table. "He's coming over here," Susan whispered urgently.

"You think I should get up and do a dance?"

"I think you and that smart mouth are headed for big trouble."

"Can you help us for a minute?"

Isabel looked over at Cade, her gaze shifting briefly to the bartender hovering just behind him. "With what?"

"A Blue Bomber."

She nodded toward the bartender. "He looks capable to me."

"He doesn't know how to make it," Cade said.

"You could tell him."

He grinned. "I don't remember, either."

"Probably because you drank three of them," she muttered.

"Probably."

"Shots aren't your specialty?" Isabel asked the guy behind Cade.

"I've never heard of this one."

Before Susan could work up a protest, Isabel levered herself out of the booth and headed toward the bar.

Some skills continued to pay dividends, she supposed. Bartending had certainly paid the bills at various times in her life, especially when she was in college and eager to pay her own way instead of relying on her uncle.

The work had been hard, sweaty, largely unsung. But she memorized recipes easily, she was fast mentally and physically, and she was good with faces—and names that went with faces, probably the reason she also excelled at communications and media relations.

Behind the bar, she surveyed the layout in a glance, then began building Cade's drink. By now, Cade's friends and Susan, plus a few other people, had followed the action. Unlike earlier, when she'd been pressed to put more than three words together talking to Cade, she confidently fell into a rhythm as she poured and explained the nuances of a complicated shot. She pushed two glasses in front of Cade and tried not to wonder why he'd requested this particular drink, or why now.

She recalled the role the drink had played in her and Cade's carnal mistake. They'd both been at the same lake party, with him celebrating a win at Homestead, the last race of the season. She'd wound up behind the bar as she often did at parties, since she got her fill of small talk at work. She'd made a variety of shots, and by the time the party had wound down several people needed a ride home. Since she'd stuck with soda, she volunteered to drive, and Cade's house ended up being the last on the route.

Fate or convenience?

She still wasn't sure, but there was no sense in

reliving the sleepy-eyed look in his eyes that had led her to his front door and beyond. She'd made a mistake and moved on. They both had.

Shaking aside the memories, she looked at him. "Ready?"

"You bet."

She dropped the shot glass in the glass with the 7-UP, the resulting fizz making the shot glass float briefly, allowing Cade to drink the contents.

Naturally, the crowd cheered.

There were more orders, which she complied with as long as each drinker had a designated driver. By the time she and Susan headed out of the bar, the manager had torn up their dinner check. "Not a bad deal," Susan said as they walked to the door. "Free dinner and a show."

"It was fun being back behind a bar."

"It's good to know you have a skill to fall back on in case CATL fires you for flirting with Cade Garrison."

"I wasn't—"

"I think I was the one flirting with her," Cade said as he appeared behind them and held open the door.

Isabel didn't look back as she thanked him. Another direct look into those amazing eyes and she wouldn't be responsible for her actions.

Susan waggled her finger at Cade. "No flirting."

Cade clutched his heart as if wounded. "Would *I* do anything improper?"

"Yes."

"Your lack of confidence is shocking."

"Just watch your step, mister."

Isabel observed this exchange with amusement. Cade flirted with any female breathing, so she didn't take his attention personally. She was pretty sure their attraction went both ways, but regardless of his lighthearted attitude, he would never do anything to jeopardize his comeback. Racing and his family's reputation meant too much to him, and he couldn't take another scandal.

"Can I at least walk you ladies to your car?" he asked. "It's dark, two women alone outside a bar…"

"And we need a big, strong man to protect us?" Isabel finished, making sure she added a touch of sarcasm.

"Don't you?"

"I think we'll manage," she said drily.

When they reached Susan's SUV, Cade opened her door, then strode around to the passenger's side. Though she'd already climbed inside, he reached for her seat belt. He said nothing as he pulled the belt across her body, his hand brushing her thigh when he pushed the buckle into the lock.

Isabel was glad she didn't have to respond, since she was holding her breath.

"Have a safe trip home," he said as he straightened.

"Thanks."

Their gaze connected for a brief moment before he backed up and shut the door.

"Girl, you are in so much trouble," Susan said as she started the car.

Isabel blew out a breath. "I certainly am."

CHAPTER THREE

"OH, DAMN," CADE SAID into his headset radio.

"Problem?" his crew chief, Sam, called back.

"Nah, just a close one." Cade drove into Turn Two of the wide, smooth, slightly banked, well-seasoned track, his adrenaline pumping, but his heart rate steady.

He'd been to the 1.3-mile concrete Nashville Superspeedway a few times in his career. And since only the NASCAR Busch cars and trucks raced here, he'd missed it during his NASCAR NEXTEL Cup years. For winning a few years ago, he had an awesome Gibson guitar trophy, specially designed by Sam Bass, and he knew that win had fueled his summer and helped him win the championship later that year.

There was no cooler trophy in racing, and he was itching for another one. "Car feels good. A little tight in the corners."

"We're due for a pit stop in less than twenty laps."

"Yeah. I'm cool till then."

Cade checked his rearview mirror as he rolled down the back straightaway. The line of cars behind him was longer than the one in front. Always a good sign.

The car felt great, and the team's chemistry was strong. The guys in the shop had worked their butts off for weeks to get the car ready—building the chassis, molding the frame, painting and balancing. The engineers ran tests and worked to improve the car's performance. The pit crew practiced daily. The marketing group and office staff dealt with sponsors and handled the business of racing. Hundreds of hours went into the cars and teams to build a successful operation.

But he was their face to the world. Everything he did or said reflected on them. A great deal of their success rode on his shoulders. Their hard work and professionalism kept his confidence high and ultimately improved his driving. It was a circle of trust and faith.

A trust he was sure he'd broken with one stupid swing of his fist over too many criticisms of his driving. Surprisingly, many of his over-the-wall guys, as well as shop guys, were willing to move with him to the NASCAR Busch Series. They'd defended him and stood by him, and he strove daily to earn back their respect.

When he managed to get back in the NASCAR NEXTEL Cup Series, he definitely wanted these guys with him. They'd gone down with the ship; they deserved to be around for the christening of the new vessel.

"Trouble, Turn Two," his spotter said. "Go high, go high."

As smoke billowed in front of him, tires screeched and cars spun, he drove to the outside of the track and mentally braced himself for the possibility of getting a nudge or flat out nailed. No matter how astute and eagle-eyed a spotter could be, sometimes the wreck twisted the wrong way, and a driver wound up in the middle instead of cruising by.

Thankfully, he cruised by.

The wreck changed the pit strategy, so he'd be coming in for changes as soon as the officials opened pit road, instead of the green-flag stop they'd planned several laps later. Rolling with the moment and altering strategies made the difference between a good team and a great team.

There were only fifty laps left, and they had been hoping to get to lap 120, save their tires, then a gas and go, hopefully pushing them into the top five. Currently, they were stuck in twelfth place. Not bad, but he wanted better.

"Let's get four," Sam said into the radio.

"Some guys will get only two," Cade said.

"Maybe, but we gotta lot of laps left."

As much as Cade wanted to get to the front, he knew Sam's advice was sound. Exiting the track, he pulled into his pit box under the number 56 yellow and blue Go! Energy Drink sign.

His gloved hands clenched the steering wheel as

his team went to work servicing the car. He drew deep and even breaths, readying his body for the moment the jack was released and he got the signal to pull away.

He longed to turn his head and watch the ballet that made up a professional racing pit stop. These guys practiced constantly, trained their bodies and minds like the well-oiled machines they serviced and still managed to offer him an *atta boy* when he saw them at the track or shop.

"Go, go!" the gasman yelled.

Cade jumped on the gas and pulled out into the tight pit road traffic.

"Nice work, everybody," Sam said. "We're tenth."

"Now, that's how it's done, boys!"

For the rest of the race they sailed on the same lucky star they'd somehow captured the week before in Dover. Cade passed the guys who'd only taken two tires. One car's engine blew. Other cars just seemed to part before him. Maybe some drivers were concerned he'd literally punch his way through to the front. Maybe his reckless rebel image could work in his favor.

"Three laps," Sam said in the headset.

In second place, centimeters from the bumper of the car in front of him, Cade wanted more. He always wanted more, but today he thought he could get it.

Heart pounding, he pulled to the outside as he drove into Turn Three. The momentum was with him, and he pulled past the other car. They inched forward and backward all the way down the final straightaway. The crowd was on their feet.

Cade held his breath as he crossed the start/finish line half a car length in front.

The crowd roared—in support or protest or just plain excitement. Cade took his celebration lap, did the requisite burnout, then pulled into Victory Lane.

For the second time in as many weeks, his team showered him in Busch beer while he climbed from the car. It was amazing to see the smiling, cheering faces of his friends and team, and even Bryan and his father looking up at him as he stood on the door frame and pumped his fists in the air.

Wiping beer from his face, he did the on-camera interviews, then posed for Victory Lane pictures with his team and sponsors and the coveted guitar trophy.

"Nice job, son," his father said, pulling him close for a quick hug as they headed to the media center.

"Thanks. The guys gave me a great car."

"But that was a cool move at the end. Learned that from your old man, did you?"

"Where else?"

Bryan, as usual, said nothing. They were an outspoken, boisterous family, so his older brother stood out in that he was the quiet one. Cade was more like their father than anyone—which led just as often to fireworks as it did to understanding.

But nothing ever felt as good as his dad's hand on his shoulder, both of them smiling as they pushed through the crowd to address the assembled press as winners again. And since interviews with his champion father and brother were more cherished than ones with just him, the reporters would no doubt be giddy.

When they rounded the corner of the building, he nearly stumbled at the sight of Isabel, holding open the door. He'd seen her briefly a couple of times over the past two days, but he'd pushed her out of his mind to concentrate on the race. Now he couldn't remember how to breathe. Her striking dark brown hair, the silky-looking strands falling just past her shoulders, her warm brown eyes and her barely-there smile always hit him in the gut.

"Congratulations, Cade," she said with a polite nod.

"Er...thanks."

"Mr. Garrison, Bryan." She extended her arm into the media center. "Heading to the press conference?"

"Ah, yeah," Cade said.

As if she knew he had nothing clever to say, as if she realized his brain had frozen at the sight of her, her smile widened. "While you were in Victory Lane, NASCAR let us bring Roger Cothren and his son Billy over to give their comments about the race. Do you mind waiting a few minutes while we wrap things up?"

"Not for a lady as pretty as you," Cade's father said.

Before Cade could scowl at his father, Bryan strode in front of him and waved Isabel inside. "I've got the door," he said.

Cade had been out-mannered and out-compli-mented by his brother and father. *He* was supposed to be the charming one in this family.

"Come on, son," Cade's father said, glancing back. "You're the one they want to interview."

"Yeah, right."

But his irritation was forgotten by the time he'd brushed by Isabel and inhaled her faint, mysterious perfume. In fact, he had to shake his head to focus on where he was and what he had to do.

Cade simply followed blindly in everyone else's wake as they walked through the reception area. Only a few muffin crumbs were left on the counter-top against the wall. Reporting must be hungry work. From there, they moved to the entranceway of the main media room, where the working press were as-sembled into four rows of desktop seating.

He found himself inhaling with ridiculous deepness to catch another whiff of Isabel's enticing scent. He felt ridiculous, like a dog with his nose in the air, trolling for a breeze full of somebody's backyard grill.

When they stopped at the doorway, Isabel turned toward them, her polite smile firmly in place. The distance she was carefully and purposefully putting in place only made him want to bust down that barrier. He *shouldn't,* of course, but that didn't make the need subside.

"They're wrapping it up," one of the NASCAR media reps said quietly to Isabel.

"How'd he finish?" Cade asked, welcoming any question or coherent conversation at this point.

"Twenty-first," Isabel said.

"Pretty good."

"We were pleased. The father/son, big cookie/ mini cookie promotion has gotten a lot of attention. Now, if Roger could just win tomorrow…"

"You'll get a big promotion?"

"I already did. As of February, I'm senior rep."

"Congratulations. I guess hanging out with all those football players worked in your favor."

"Yeah." Her eyes brightened. "But I missed racing."

And me? Did you miss me?

Thankfully, she turned her attention back to the press conference before he could ask anything that stupid, leaving him to watch Roger's son and remember his own first NASCAR Busch Series start.

Cade hadn't even finished. He'd gotten caught up in a wreck about halfway through that—thankfully—he hadn't caused, but had still done enough damage that he wasn't able to complete the race.

He still remembered his first postrace press conference—reporters whose questions ranged from sympathetic to probing to jaded and confrontational. He could hardly swallow as his father was asked whether this younger son could ever hope to live up to his father, grandfather and older brother. His father had assured everyone Cade would be the best yet, that he'd known how to race before most kids learned their multiplication tables.

Did his father now regret those confident words? Was he disappointed?

Though he'd never say so publicly, Cade knew he was. He knew it every time his father looked at him.

As he watched Billy Cothren's Adam's apple bob while he answered yet another question about what it was like to grow up in a famous racing family, Cade promised himself he'd take time in the upcoming week to call the guy and offer his support.

Of course he couldn't look at the drivers—seated on stools in front of the room—without seeing Isabel's profile out of the corner of his eye.

What was it about her that drew him?

There were a lot of things—her looks, her intelligence, her enthusiasm for her job, her love of racing and even her sarcasm.

He just liked being around her, and he chafed at the idea that their jobs kept them apart. Did that only increase her appeal?

Maybe. He was ornery enough, and she was certainly a challenge. But though he tried to blow off his attraction to her as just a passing thing, he suspected there was more.

It had been well over a year since they'd spent the night together, but it stood out in his mind as if it were yesterday. All last year when she'd been away from the track, he'd wondered if he'd ever see her again. His smile when she'd walked into the media center at Daytona had bordered on gleeful.

How had he let an entire year go by without contacting her? He'd called her once after their one night, but she'd told him flat out that she wouldn't risk her job by dating him. Still, before he'd punched his sponsor, and while she was handling CATL's NFL publicity, their relationship might have had a chance.

But he'd avoided her. Because he knew she wouldn't just be a girl he called to have a few beers and some fun every once in a while? Because a relationship with her might actually get serious?

Why had he asked her to make that particular shot at the bar earlier in the week? To remind her of what they'd shared? To see her reaction and gauge her feelings about him?

If so, he'd screwed up. She'd had little reaction beyond a flash of surprise. He wanted more. He didn't like pretending she meant nothing, but he knew—like virtually no one else—the dangers of giving in to an impulse.

As the questions to the Cothrens wound down, Isabel entered the room, standing beside the line of chairs used by the drivers. She called for one last question, then followed her drivers through the exit on the other side of the room.

A NASCAR rep led Cade, his father and brother to the vacated stools. "Next is our race winner, Cade Garrison, his father, Mitch, and his brother, Bryan."

"You've never won back-to-back races," a reporter asked. "How does it feel?"

"It feels great," Cade said. "It was a team effort.

The guys at the shop gave me a great car. We had fast pit stops all day."

"You took four tires, where some teams took two. Do you think that made the difference in the race?"

"Sam made that call, and I drove by those guys pretty fast, so yeah."

"Did you know the car was good enough to win all day?"

"It was a good top-ten car, but we caught some breaks and that last adjustment was dead on. It just flew, and we got to the front."

"Are you making a serious run at the Busch championship?"

"It looks like it."

The same reporter followed up with another question. "Did you not plan to?"

Not in the beginning. After a DNF at Daytona, and continuing to sulk about losing his former ride, he hadn't gotten too much accomplished. Once he'd gotten over his pity party and concentrated on his job again, everything improved. His attitude, the team's belief in him, even his relationship with his family.

Did he resent his father and brother for tossing him out of the NASCAR NEXTEL Cup Series? Hell, yes. But he also understood their family reputation was at stake. He understood he had to be "punished" in order to attract another major sponsor. Still, there was a small, personal place inside of him that wished they would have stood by him, not as his bosses, but as his family.

"I always knew this was a championship team. A lot of my guys from last year came with me, and their hard work has gotten me through the tough times."

Another reporter stood. "This question is for Mitch. If Cade wins the Busch championship, will you put him back in a Cup car?"

"We haven't made any decisions about Cade for next year yet. He's doing an amazing job in the 56 car, and he continues to make me proud."

A female reporter in the back stood. "Speaking of tough times…"

Crap. He'd opened that door, hadn't he?

"…do you feel vindicated from your past troubles?"

He'd eaten a lot of humble pie on that subject. And would no doubt continue to do so. "My past troubles had nothing to do with my driving, but it always feels great to win."

"How are you getting along with your sponsor?" she asked as a follow-up.

"The people at Go! have been wonderful. I appreciate their support, and I'm grateful they took me on."

Thankfully, that ended those questions. They'd all been asked, answered and speculated upon for months, so it was old news now, anyway.

"For Steel, there's a rumor you're working on a comeback. Is that true?"

"No," Bryan answered.

"So the rumor is false?"

"Yes."

"If you guys want Bryan to talk, you're gonna have to speak his language. Ask him about the profit-and-loss statements," Cade said.

Several people laughed, then one guy was brave enough to ask, "How do the P and L's for Garrison Racing look these days?"

"No comment," his typically stoic brother replied.

Cade grinned and shook his head. "Okay. Maybe not."

The NASCAR rep stepped forward. "One last question."

"What do you think about being named NASCAR's most eligible bachelor?"

"Well, I'm really honored—"

"They meant me, Dad."

His father flashed the press the smile Cade had thankfully inherited and used to his advantage endlessly. "Oh, right."

"I'm happy with the title of most eligible bachelor," Cade said. "And interested eligible ladies can contact me at—"

The rep laid her hand over the microphone and shook her head. Then she leaned down and added, "At his fan club address. Thank you all for your attention."

Cade and his father and brother were escorted from the main media room and led to a small room where the drivers' meetings were held. Snacks and drinks were laid out on a table.

Though Roger and Billy were nowhere in sight,

Isabel stood in the doorway with her arms crossed over her chest. "Nice work."

"They acted like I was going to really give out my phone number," Cade said.

She raised her eyebrows. "Weren't you?"

"You need to give it to Isabel," his father said before he bit into a chocolate chip cookie.

"Your licensing department has my number, Mr. Garrison. Any time you want to switch sponsors, you're welcome to call me."

Typically, Isabel had deliberately misunderstood in order to turn the conversation back to a professional subject. She was the most efficient, polished woman he knew. But then companies that sunk millions of dollars into marketing with NASCAR didn't hire the dregs of the business world.

"Please don't call me, Mr. Garrison," his father said, winking. "You'll make me feel old."

"My contract requires me to address all champions that way."

"No kidding?" He jerked his thumb toward Bryan. "You ought to get Bryan to negotiate your next contract. He's tough. Why do you think they call him Steel?"

Cade frowned. "I thought it was his hard head."

"And forget Cade. You need to give *me* your number."

Cade had to clench his jaw to keep it from dropping on the floor. Having a bachelor for a father was just way too weird.

"If you two are through making dates and stuffing your faces, I think we can go," Bryan said, heading toward the door. "Bye, Isabel," he said on his way out. "At least *somebody* still knows how to be a professional."

"What's with him?" Cade asked.

"Who knows?" his father said. "Off to Pocono." He dusted his hands together, flashed Isabel another smile, then followed Bryan out the door.

"Do you get to go home tonight?" Cade asked Isabel as he popped open a soda can.

"No, I'm going to Pocono, too."

He leaned against the wall by the door, close enough to touch her, though he didn't. Wanted to. Thought about it. But didn't. "You wanna lift?"

"No, thanks. I have a flight booked."

"Commercial, I'll bet. The seats on the team jet are as big as a recliner. Leather, too. I may even convince tight-fisted Bryan to open a bottle of champagne. Beats the heck out of stale peanuts and three ounces of soda in a plastic cup."

"I don't think my boss would approve."

"But your boss is your uncle, right?"

"And we all know how forgiving family members as employers can be."

Not wanting her to see the hurt that lingered inside him, Cade dropped his gaze to the floor. "Yeah, we do."

"I'm sorry." She touched his arm, and he jerked his head up. Her eyes were shadowed with regret. "That was completely rude."

His skin tingled where she touched him, but he didn't move for fear she'd pull away. "It's fine. And true."

"I still shouldn't have said anything. Please accept my apology."

He did, but—being a man—he automatically thought of a way he could push his seductive advantage. "Mmm…maybe I should ask for restitution. I think I'd like you being in my debt."

She snatched her hand back.

Undaunted, he leaned toward her. "Not scared, are you?"

She lifted her chin. "Of course not."

"Maybe you should be. I could ask for something pretty valuable."

"I don't see how."

"You're an eligible lady, right?" He smiled, going for mischievous, with just a touch of danger. "I'll give you my private number—not the fan club one—and you give me yours. We could meet for dinner next week."

She sighed. "Aren't you going to miss your flight?"

"Avoiding me? I wouldn't have expected that from you." He slid the tip of his finger beneath her chin. Her eyes darkened, and he felt a spark of triumph surge through him. "I'd even be willing to get rid of the competition."

CHAPTER FOUR

ISABEL BLINKED AT THE intensity in Cade's eyes. Her skin warmed beneath just the touch of his finger on her chin.

Why did the man have to be so insanely sexy? Why did he tempt her?

Her career meant everything, *was* everything. And Cade Garrison was a trip down Career Suicide Lane if she'd ever seen one.

She stepped back. "Competition is best left to the track." She turned away, tossing "have a nice flight" over her shoulder. Confident he wouldn't follow—men like Cade didn't chase women, they were the *chasee*—she concentrated on taking deep and even breaths as she headed back to the media room.

The Cothrens were on their way to Pocono, so her work was done. She just needed to gather her leftover promo items and head to the airport.

Most of the reporters had already left, but a few were still packing their laptops and minirecorders. To avoid thinking of Cade—and get those mesmerizing eyes of his out of her head—she spoke to a couple of reporters.

"Pretty cool to see Cade talking about the future rather than the past," Ricky Jones said when she walked by him to get her box of leftover mini cookies.

So much for getting her mind on another subject. "Yeah. He seems to be headed in the right direction."

Ricky grinned. "As long as he keeps his temper from taking the wheel."

"That would help. You headed to Pocono?"

"Later on. What's going on with the Phillips press conference?"

Ricky was so in touch his fingerprints were permanently enshrined on nearly every breaking story over the last twenty years. "I imagine you've heard what's going on."

"I still want the inside story."

"Your sources are no doubt accurate."

"He's going to Baker?"

"Your sources are no doubt accurate."

He winked. "Buy you a beer back home?"

"Mmm. If I ever get back there."

He hitched his laptop bag on his shoulder. "You will. See ya."

"Sure."

Glancing at her watch, she gathered the few remaining bags of cookies. She needed to get moving to the airport. She thanked Cliff, Sean and Tammy, the speedway staff who'd made everything go so smoothly over the past two days, offered them the last of the cookies, grabbed her overnight bag, then headed out.

The track was nearly deserted. The stands

looked oddly lonely after so much excitement over
the past few days.

As she walked to her rental car, she checked
her BlackBerry for messages. Most were from her
uncle, each e-mail a new update of Bruce Phillips's
press schedule. The announcement would come at
10:00 a.m., just before the driver's meeting. No,
twelve-thirty, live on the air with Racer TV. No, live
on the air with the network. Finally, it was back to
announcing his new team on Racer TV at 11:30
Eastern.

The racing world would soon know he was driving for Baker Racing next year.

How would Cade and his family feel about one
of the veteran leaders of the sport driving for their
biggest rival? Would the hostility extend to a man
Bryan had once said he admired and tried to emulate
in his own career? Would they resent instead of encourage the success Bruce Phillips was likely to
have with such a strong team?

She shook her head. It didn't matter how the Garrisons felt. Her job was the same—keep the press
conferences and communication links between
CATL, NASCAR, their drivers, their teams and the
public running smoothly and professionally. Keep
CATL's brands in the minds of consumers in ever-
increasingly creative ways. Solidify brand loyalty
among NASCAR fans.

Most reps had to worry about only one brand in
the CATL family. As senior rep, she had to keep

tabs on all five. Her uncle's job involved even more juggling. He had to implement the overall marketing plan and meet with executives in other departments. He had to fight for increases in the budget. He had to make speeches and appearances at VIP events.

Her hectic weekend schedule was part of an ongoing test of her viability to be a VP. Sort of like a driver fighting to stay in contention during his first race at Bristol.

She knew it was happening, even though no one said anything besides Susan. At times she was exhilarated by the opportunity. Other times she was terrified.

Was she ready for that much responsibility? Could she really run an entire department? Be a *vice president?*

Given the way her life had begun, she had moments when she was scared out of her wits and felt unworthy of the opportunities available to her. But she also knew she was good at her job, and she'd worked harder than anybody she knew to get it and keep it. She could do it. And well.

Couldn't she?

The last e-mail message was from Susan.

My fortune cookie said, "Don't trust dark-haired, blue-eyed charmers today. You'll meet a bad end." I think it's meant for you. Be careful.

Isabel acknowledged the messages, though her response to Susan—Chinese proverbs suck—would probably earn her a warning phone call later that night.

Half smiling at both the concern and melodramatic tone of her friend's message, she dropped into the driver's seat of her rental car. She needed a hot bath and a good book. A decent night's sleep and a glass of cabernet would be over-the-top fantastic. She wondered if Dr. Rose would mind her dropping by for some spaghetti near midnight on a Saturday.

Most people probably would, but Dr. Rose—and her husband Dr. Joe—Mattioli, who owned beloved triangular track in tiny Long Pond, Pennsylvania, were an integral part of the NASCAR family. They understood the weird schedules and hectic lifestyle of the sport.

Her BlackBerry beeped, so she lifted her head to check the new message.

Dear Ms. Turner,
Flight 2343, Nashville to Allentown has been canceled. You can check with the gate agent for flight reassignment...

"Hell."

After she managed to land in Allentown, she had nearly an hour's drive to Pocono Manor, the historic mountain inn where she was staying for the race weekend. Any delay in flights meant more hours tacked onto an already long day, and she didn't have hours to waste.

She needed to make sure there were plenty of copies of Bruce Phillips's bio and contact information to hand out to the assembled press at the conference tomorrow. She needed to unpack and press her suit jacket. She needed to update the reporters with the new time for the announcement. At least she could do that now—thank God for the BlackBerry. She needed to make sure the VIPs were happy. She needed to check on their banners and signs.

Oh, and she needed to sleep if she was going to put in another sixteen-hour day.

I can count on Blast, CATL'S energy drink, though, can't I?

The Blast reps always sent a couple of cases to the track for the weekend. They'd endeared themselves to many reporters, fans and team members with that ice-cold burst of energy. And this Sunday they'd have even more, since they were launching a new flavor and were giving away tasting samples to the race crowd.

She started the engine and pulled out of the infield parking lot. At least the late hour played in her favor and the traffic had thinned. As she raced onto the interstate toward the airport, a familiar voice echoed in her ears.

The seats on the team jet are as big as a recliner.

"Why won't that man shut up?"

Why couldn't Cade find somebody else's thoughts to haunt? Did they still do exorcisms? She'd have to remember to ask Father Donovan the next time she went to Mass.

But then she was at the track most Sundays, often Saturday night, too. She hadn't been to church in months and doubted even the good Father would be thrilled with her attendance and devotion record.

Exorcisms? Great, now I'm punchy.

She shook her head. Gasoline fumes, scorching temperatures, engine noise and lack of sleep had taken their toll on her concentration.

You could be sipping champagne on a private jet.

With a man she had no business going near. A dangerous man. One she should be giving a wide berth to.

And yet…

Didn't her job require resourcefulness? Didn't she have to constantly adapt to changing circumstances? Wouldn't her uncle be impressed at her ingenuity in getting to Pennsylvania despite the flight cancellation? What if her flight was the last one out before morning?

Her heart raced at the thought. Good grief, maybe the Garrisons' jet was her only hope of getting to the track on time.

She called the airline on her cell phone. Her flight *was* the last one. After investigating other airlines, she realized they, too, had no more flights to Allentown. There were a few to Philadelphia and New York, but that would mean an even longer drive to the hotel.

Cade Garrison was her last hope.

Talk about awkward, showing up at the private hangars and asking him for a favor after she'd blown him off at the track. But she had little choice.

As she rushed along the roads, she pictured the lovely, historic Pocono Manor and its quiet elegance and comfy beds. Even the supposed spirits who made the manor their home wouldn't keep her from resting—if she actually made it out there.

She didn't think about the hot, inviting look in Cade's eyes.

That was a positive sign, right?

When she screeched to a halt between two airplane hangars, she realized she hadn't considered what she'd do with the rental car. Well, she'd just have to figure that out later. She had a plane to catch. Hopefully.

After she scrambled out of the car, she searched the area for Cade. Thankfully, she saw him and a small group of men walking toward a sleek white jet painted with red stripes. Though they had different sponsors, both Garrison Racing NASCAR NEXTEL Cup drivers wore red uniforms.

She recalled the picture of Cade in Victory Lane—dressed in his blue-and-yellow uniform. He was part of the team, yet he wasn't. A subtle separation that had to be anything but subtle to him.

Swallowing her pride and breathing a sigh of relief, she rushed toward the group. "Cade!"

He stopped and turned. As he flashed a grin, he strolled toward her. "Changed your mind about those leather seats?" he asked when he reached her.

"I—" She bit down on a sarcastic response to his charm. "My flight was canceled."

He swept his hand toward the luxurious-looking plane. "Be my guest."

Said the spider to the fly.

She knew her anxiety was ridiculous, yet she couldn't help feeling it. There was something wildly intimidating about the casualness of luxury. If she worked for CATL long enough, would she become used to big corporate dollars, engines that cost upward of a hundred-thousand dollars and money that bought convenience?

She didn't think so. Some part of her would always remember the dirty, desperate trailer where she'd started out her life.

She took a few steps back. "Let me just get my bag from the car."

He grabbed her elbow. "Don't be silly. Bob," he said, turning to the thin, balding man next to him, "do you mind getting the lady's luggage?"

As Bob jogged off, Isabel reached into her purse for her cell phone. "I need to call the rental car company and let them know where I'm leaving the car."

"Don't worry about it," Cade said, putting his arm around her shoulders. "Bob will take care of it."

She spun away from him. "I'm sure he will, but he isn't."

By the time she'd made her call, pulled the car

into a parking space beside the hangar, then boarded the plane, Cade was seated in a taupe leather chair that would have looked at home in any living room.

He patted the identical chair next to him. "Join me?"

Moving down the aisle toward him felt like handing over control. If she did that, would she ever get it back? If she continued to see him in social situations, how would she manage to keep her attraction to him under wraps? She was already holding on to her professionalism by a thread.

She also couldn't help wondering how many women he'd entertained on this plane. Had they been as impressed as she was by the quiet luxury? Had their palms dampened with sweat when he smiled at them? Had they given him their hearts, only to have him move on to the next beauty he spotted?

Very little scared her anymore, but he did. The feelings he roused in her were disconcerting and intimidating.

But even she couldn't hold on to her worries in the midst of the plush and spotless plane. The navy carpet absorbed the impact of her steps, giving her aching feet a break from concrete and asphalt. The overhead lights were reset and soft. Even the air smelled fresh and clean.

There were no tired businesspeople. No cranky kids or harassed parents. No airline attendants moving briskly down the aisles as they checked for oversize luggage or illegal on-board items.

Cade traveled this way all the time. He expected to.

Yet the offhand way he'd asked Bob to do him a favor was something she couldn't ever imagine embracing. Her self-sufficiency was a badge of honor, and asking for help seemed like a weakness, a capitulation that she was incapable of taking care of herself. Probably part of the reason she had a hard time with romantic relationships. Her pride had often been a source of contention between her and her uncle, as well. When they managed to eventually get back on even ground, they laughed and blamed her reactions on her Italian blood.

Even though they both knew her emotions went much deeper.

She returned the brief waves from Mitch and Bryan Garrison, who sat near the back of the plane, then flinched as a champagne cork popped from behind her. Bob had found the bubbly, and apparently Bryan had loosened up long enough to allow a celebration.

She turned to meet Cade's gaze. "Congratulations."

"I'm glad you're here to join the celebration."

"I don't have much of a choice."

"Yes, you do."

The plane's engine roared to life. They'd be moving in mere moments.

She should turn around and leave, no *run* from the plane. But whether it was because she was simply tired, weak or sick of resisting the constant pull between her and Cade, she didn't move.

Until Bob offered her a bubbling glass of champagne.

Then she took the glass and raised it to Cade. "To a winner."

CADE PULLED ISABEL'S luggage from the back of the rented SUV. "I'll walk you to your room."

She reached for her bag. "That's not necessary."

"But I'd like to."

"I'm sure you need to get to the track," she said, giving her bag another tug.

"I'm staying here."

She glanced at the SUV, her eyes widening as Bob lifted his and Cade's bags out of the back. She jerked her hand away from her bag—and Cade's hand. "You're not staying at the track?" she asked, her voice unusually high-pitched.

"My coach is in Nashville, remember?"

"Oh, hel—I mean, oh, *right*." She forced a smile. "How nice."

The blows to his ego were getting sharper and landing with greater efficiency. At this rate, he'd be black and blue for days.

He turned and headed toward the manor's lobby and hoped she followed. The woman always seemed to be trying to escape his company. His mother would have said that Isabel Turner was "prickly." She didn't trust easily and would wound you in a blink if you tried to get too close.

Was it her lack of desire to be around him that intrigued him?

When so many other people clamored for his autograph, to meet him and touch him, her distance certainly made her stand out. But he wasn't a patient man, and he had no intention of pursuing a woman who wasn't interested. That was stupid.

Still…

He glanced over his shoulder. She walked a few feet behind, her luscious lips scowling.

Damn, he liked to watch her walk. She moved with purpose. Efficient. Brisk. But still somehow wildly sexy.

He faced forward. She wasn't interested in any romantic ties. She valued her career and her professionalism. He did, too.

At least, he was trying to.

The fact that his thoughts constantly flew back to the memory of her silken skin, her sighs and the moments of intimacy they'd shared was *his* problem. One he had to deal with on his own somehow. Still… there was nothing wrong with being a gentleman and escorting her to her room.

At the check-in desk, she darted in front of him to speak to the on-duty agent.

Cade shook his head. She did have control issues.

He glanced around the small, darkened, kind of spooky lobby. Built in 1908, the inn had served as a weekend home for quite a few racers over the years. Though it was late, he was surprised he didn't see anybody he knew. Sponsors, NASCAR people and the TV crews all stayed at the manor, as well as other drivers like him who didn't bring their coaches. Maybe he'd wander into the bar after he checked in and see if anybody was hanging out.

Bob approached him. "I'll check us in and store the bags. Wanna meet in the bar in thirty minutes?"

He hesitated. Maybe Isabel would invite him to her room for a drink.

Across the room, she whirled away from the desk and marched toward him.

"Yeah," he said to Bob, realizing from the annoyed look on Isabel's face that no invitation was coming.

He walked her to the elevator without comment. She pushed the fourth-floor button, and when the doors closed, she whispered tightly, "What are we going to say if somebody sees us?"

"That I'm carrying your bags to your room?"

"*Bag.* I have *one* bag. Don't you think that looks suspicious?"

"You're paranoid."

"Why shouldn't I be?" The elevator dinged and the doors swished open. She poked her head out and glanced both ways before inching into the hallway. "I don't want to explain what you're doing walking me to my room."

"I'm being helpful," he said, putting on his best wounded expression. Maybe she went for the meek, vulnerable type. He could do that.

For a good fifteen minutes, anyway.

"People will think we're…together," she said as they walked down the hall toward her room.

"You helped me and my family earlier. I'm just returning the favor."

"I was doing my job."

"And you're not now?"

"No. Yes." She jammed her room key at the electronic reader, but it glowed red. "We're not at the track now." She tried the key again, still with no success. "We need to keep our distance. Go! is a competitor of Blast. Beyond NASCAR's rules of ethics, CATL would not be happy to see us together like this."

"You could tell them you're trying to lure me away," he said, knowing what a joke that was. He was lucky to have one sponsor much less have two fighting over him.

"But I'm not. What if our Blast driver heard we were talking? What if his team thought we were pulling our sponsorship?"

Worry and exhaustion rolled off her in waves. As much as he enjoyed flirting with her, even he could see she'd had enough.

He set her bag down and took the room card from her, their fingers brushing as he did so. Her gaze flew to his, and she jerked her hand away.

He'd never seen her so jumpy. She was always controlled. Was she really concerned about CATL spies jumping out from behind the potted tree in the fourth-floor hallway of the Pocono Manor and yelling "Gotcha"? Did he upset her that much?

Or did he just affect her in a way she didn't like? Did she feel a punch of excitement when he walked into a room, the way he did when he saw her?

Her eyes darkened as she stared at him. Was it possible desire, not worry, had her off balance?

He dropped his gaze to her lips. Sometimes he still dreamed about how she tasted.

Like cherries. Cherries and heat and hunger.

He wanted that sensation again. He wanted to hold her again. He wanted her smiles, not scowls.

His heart raced; sweat rolled down his spine. Leaning forward, half-certain she'd stop him at any moment, he cupped the back of her head and pressed his lips against hers before he could think of all the reasons he shouldn't be touching her. Before she could remind him about her job and his.

Her body molded to his. She sighed against his mouth. When he deepened the kiss, she returned his touch. Her warm, curvy body seemed to melt into his arms.

Memories of the last time he'd touched her swam through his mind. Her skin, if possible, was even softer now. The heat between them sparked to life as if two minutes instead of close to two years had passed.

But when he pressed her back against the door, she turned her head, breaking their connection.

His breath rushed from his lungs. Her cheek was

less than an inch from his mouth. The need to touch
her again surged through him with crazy intensity.

"Step back," she said quietly.

He closed his eyes as he did, then licked his lips.
Cherries.

Oh, damn.

CHAPTER FIVE

CARRYING A CAN OF GO! and boasting a broad smile, Cade strode through the Pocono garage area on Sunday morning.

Though he'd have given anything to have his old ride back, he felt some satisfaction in knowing he'd already posted a win for the weekend, while nearly everybody else at the track was on edge about the outcome of the race due to start in less than an hour.

Crew chiefs, car chiefs, owners and mechanics discussed setups, fuel mileage and their strategy for the afternoon. Drivers attended meetings and sponsors functions, signed autographs and spent a few precious moments with their families before strapping into their three-thousand-plus-pound racing machines for 500 miles.

The atmosphere was hurried and tense. Reporters on a deadline, TV crews with cameras and fans with garage passes added to the frenzied excitement.

Cade preferred qualifying day. The promise of the weekend was bright in everyone's eyes. The drivers were more relaxed. The crews were confident about their hard work and setups. The crowds were lessened.

On race day, everything was heightened.

Though he tried to pretend otherwise, the atmosphere fit his mood.

His senses were still buzzing from his kiss with Isabel the night before. The taste of cherries clung to his lips, despite a couple of showers, a restless night's sleep and the remembrance of the rules they'd broken, the risks they were taking.

He'd kissed many women in his life and wanted to dismiss the moment as casual and impulsive, but he hadn't managed to convince himself. There was something about Isabel he couldn't forget, dismiss or ignore.

At least with her PR duties for the day, they'd probably be able to avoid each other. Though he didn't want to admit it, distance was best. Until he could get a handle on what was happening to him. Until he could figure out how to move forward. Their careers were on the line, as well as the respect of his team and both of their families. They couldn't risk being together.

But that didn't stop him from *wanting* to see her.

He walked past the garages and in front of the NASCAR trailer—given all the trouble he'd been in lately, a spot he generally avoided. As he rounded the corner, Shawn Stayton strolled around the other side.

"Hey, Cade!" Shawn slapped hands with him. "Great win yesterday."

Cade worked up a smile. "Thanks."

He and Shawn had been sort-of friends before this year. But that was when Cade had driven the NASCAR NEXTEL Cup Series car and Shawn had piloted the NASCAR Busch Series car for Garrison Racing. Now their positions were reversed.

The switch made Shawn feel awkward and Cade embarrassed.

Many drivers would be honored to drive in the NASCAR Busch Series, and Cade was, but there was no stopping the realization that he'd sacrificed something precious and rare by losing his ride. It wasn't so much a difference in the series as it was knowing he'd made a mistake that had cost him a position he'd worked his whole life for.

He had no one to blame but himself, and he still couldn't hold back his resentment. Shawn's forced enthusiasm only made him feel more guilty over his self-absorption.

"Good luck today," Cade added.

"Yeah, well…" Shawn's pale face flushed red. "We've got a good car. And, ah, your notes…you know from last year, are really helping."

"Great. I'm glad." He wasn't, but he didn't see how he could say that.

At that moment, for some reason, he remembered his sister forcing him to watch beauty pageants when they were in high school.

He'd been interested as far as the swimsuit competition held on, then Rachel had bribed him with popcorn, homemade cupcakes and soda so he would stick it out to the end. Standing on the stage, the announcement of the winner imminent, the girls held hands, smiled and prayed, then ultimately, somebody cried. He could never understand why the first runner-up didn't grab that sparkly crown and race off stage with it.

Now, suddenly, he did.

"Everybody's really behind you," Cade added lamely to Shawn, just wanting to escape.

Like Miss First Runner-Up on the pageant stage.

"Yeah, well." Shawn shrugged. "I appreciate you including me. I know it's been weird for you."

Guilt suffused him. Not only hadn't he been accommodating, he'd been a jerk. "I'm fine." *Angry and resentful, but fine.* Of course if he kept a list of everyone he felt resentful toward, he'd need to print up a program to keep track. "You kick butt today."

Thrilled to escape the awkward conversation, he started past Shawn, only to have him call out, "Hey, Isabel!"

Cade turned. And had a sudden craving for popcorn. With cherry syrup.

Her BlackBerry held between her hands, Isabel stopped next to them. Since she wore sunglasses, he couldn't tell her expression, but her smile seemed forced.

"Hey, guys."

Her head swiveled between him in jeans and a

T-shirt and Shawn in his red-and-yellow uniform. Did she find the switch as odd as he did?

"Thanks for all your help," Shawn said, all but quivering with excitement.

"With…?" she asked, angling her head.

Shawn frowned briefly. "The press conferences. Remember, you helped me?"

She said nothing for a moment, then smiled and nodded. "Of course. I was glad to." Her BlackBerry beeped. "I'm sorry. This thing is driving me crazy." She pressed a button, then shoved the device into the back pocket of her jeans. "You're doing great with your interviews," she said to Shawn.

"I practiced what I should say in front of the mirror," he said, his face turning red. "Just like you told me. I felt stupid, but…"

"It worked."

I'm not even here, Cade thought. There were times in the past several months where that would have been welcome, but to have Isabel *smiling* at Shawn and *talking* to Shawn and ignoring *him* was beyond lousy.

"Very few people can roll off brilliant, witty comments after a five-hundred-mile race," Isabel continued.

Shawn's gaze darted to Cade. "Yeah."

Cade rolled his shoulders back. He liked to think he was one of those *very few people.*

Isabel pursed her lips. "Mmm, well…your on-track performance is what's most important. The rest will come with experience."

Shawn flushed a deeper red. "I guess so."

Was the guy *that* sensitive to the sun?

Cade cranked his neck back to look up at the sky. Mix of sun and clouds. No, the driver of the 86 car—*his* car—seemed more affected by a certain compassionate brunette than the summer sun.

"Good luck today," she said, pulling her Black-Berry from her back pocket. "I really need to get back to work." She turned toward Cade for a brief moment, then waved and headed off toward the garages.

"Hey, I'll see you later," Cade said to Shawn, though his gaze followed Isabel. "Back to ignoring me?" he said when he caught up to her and grabbed her arm.

She shook off his touch and whirled to face him. "I'm not ignoring you. I'm *busy*. I have a job to do. I know this will come as a big shock, Mr. Superstar, but the world doesn't revolve around you."

"It revolves around Shawn Stayton instead."

She sighed. "Oh, please."

"Take off your sunglasses."

"I have things to do—"

"Please."

"Why?"

"You're a difficult woman to read."

"You're a difficult man."

He smiled. "You're beautiful."

"Oh, good grief." Her shoulders sagged, but she pulled off her sunglasses.

When she raised her gaze to meet his, he saw exhaustion and confusion. A hint of anger. Maybe even a touch of fascination.

Well, at least they were on the same playing field.

He wanted to touch her, to squeeze her hand and remind her she wasn't alone, but conscious of the audience buzzing around them, he didn't. "How did the press conference go?"

She pressed her lips together, then sighed. "I'm sorry for being so difficult. I didn't get much sleep last night. The press conference went fine."

"Phillips is going to Baker Racing."

"Yeah."

He couldn't believe a great champion like Phillips had actually done it. Cade had looked up to him all his life. Now he wasn't sure he could look him in the eye. "Why?"

"You'll have to ask him."

"He's making a mistake. They're scum. You know Chance Baker is dating my brother's ex-wife."

"So I've heard."

"And Phillips is following the money all the way to the cheatin' Baker crowd."

"Oh, come on. They're just a good team. They're not cheating."

"Maybe. Maybe not."

She said nothing.

"Cheating or not, you can admit they're jerks," he said. "You don't have to play the corporate diplomat with me."

"I'm not playing anything. Bruce Phillips has a right to find the best deal—both for his finances and his ability to win races. CATL has invested a lot of time, money and energy in aligning ourselves with Bruce and his fan base, so we're happy when he's happy. And while I appreciate your feelings about the Bakers, they've never been anything but gracious to me, so I have no intention of calling them names like a third-grader."

She had no idea the depths they would sink to, Cade thought. "You've never been on the track with them."

She nodded.

"Some drivers are different on track than they are off."

"*All* drivers are different—for which the general public is grateful. If you flew around on Monday like you do on Sunday, the accident rate in North Carolina would be a lot higher."

He refused to find humor in her comment. "I'm not going to convince you of the Baker family's dirty tactics against my family," he said, realizing she had no appreciation for the humiliation they'd suffered.

She crossed her arms over her chest. "No, you're not."

Astonished, he stared at her. He'd been so wrong. She didn't understand him. Sure, she was beautiful and smart, and he got all hot and crazy whenever she was around. Maybe they'd even shared some amazing moments in the past, but she wasn't the goddess he'd put on a pedestal.

She was way too politically correct. She had thoughts and opinions he didn't agree with. He had people following him around, taking care of his every need, and they all agreed with him. *They* understood the pressure he was under. *She* was unreasonable and difficult. She sided with her company and NASCAR and would never get the driver's side of anything.

"You want to walk with me, or not?" she asked, making him think she'd already asked that question, but he'd been too self-absorbed to notice. "I need to go over to the media center."

"I—" *Unreasonable and difficult.* But then there was that part of her that made him sigh and smile. The way she made his heart leap. "Sure."

They walked around the back side of the garage area, passing dozens of people they knew and waved at along the way. They didn't touch, yet he felt connected to her in a way he neither understood nor necessarily welcomed. When a NASCAR official stopped to talk to her, he wondered if people would assume he was in trouble.

Again.

Just by standing next to her, he opened himself to all kinds of talk and speculation. Was his current sponsor already unhappy with him, and he was begging CATL to help him out? Or, like she'd pointed out, would current CATL drivers wonder if they were soon to be abandoned in favor of him?

Big news stories had been launched with as little

information as seeing two people who normally didn't belong together talking in the garage. Surely he could find a less complicated relationship to explore.

Still, he followed her toward the media center. Since driver introductions were due to start any minute, it was relatively quiet. Cade had been inside a handful of times, the most memorable of which was during a press-conference win two years ago. With its odd triangular shape, three different turns and three different degrees of banking, Pocono was a tough track to master.

He vividly remembered the pride in his father's eyes when his youngest son had rolled into Victory Lane. Bryan's accident the previous January had thrown the family into turmoil, but that Pocono victory had been a shining, hopeful moment when they all realized their racing dreams would go on. GRI could recover and continue to succeed.

How had things gone so wrong since then? His parents had divorced. He'd lost his NASCAR NEXTEL Cup Series ride. His brother had retreated into surly indifference.

Shaking off the memories, both ugly and amazing, Cade followed Isabel into the main conference room. As she worked her way toward the back of the room, she straightened chairs and picked up trash.

"Don't they have people to clean up?" he asked.

"I'm sure they do."

As seemed to be the usual with her lately, he felt like an idiot. "So why are you—"

"Race day is hectic. Everybody's busy. It's mostly paper from my office on the floor. It won't kill me to pick it up."

Before this year, he'd been aware of how many people behind the scenes actually made racing work, but since he now spent most Sundays watching the race from the infield, he'd had time to reflect on their contribution. Officials watched every car roll through inspection and every driver's pit. Motor coach drivers brought all the personal RVs for the drivers and their families to live in for the weekend. Safety specialists kept a close eye on the cars zipping around the track.

Motor Racing Outreach volunteers entertained the drivers' children during the race. His mother still talked about the days when she—and all the other drivers' wives—had wrangled with him, his brother and sister in the infield parking lot, in the family station wagon, listening to the race on the car radio and hoping everybody would take a nap at the same time.

All these people gave up their weekend for thirty-six weeks, just like all the drivers and crew chiefs.

So, he helped Isabel pick up trash, gathered left-over Bruce Phillips bios and press releases about his change of teams.

"Thanks," she said as they headed toward the door. "I'm sure you have more exciting places to be."

"No, I really don't."

She stopped in the doorway and looked up at him. Then she stared at the floor. "Cade, last night…"

"Was amazing."

Her gaze flew to his. "Was a mistake."

From the way she'd jerked away from him and slammed her hotel-room door in his face, he'd guessed that would be her reaction. But a guy can dream, right?

"We need to remember what's at stake here," she continued. "For both of us."

"I'm just too big of a risk."

Her eyes were full of regret. "You're—"

"Hi, sweetie," John Bonamici said as he approached them. He placed his arm around his niece, though his gaze slid to Cade. "And Cade Garrison. How interesting."

"GOOD GRIEF, UNCLE JOHN," Isabel said, ducking out from beneath his arm and glancing around to see if anybody had noticed them. "We're working here. No hugging."

He grinned. "Hugging is part of racing."

"Like bumping and banging, I guess."

"Like family."

Isabel rolled her shoulders back. Even after all the years in her uncle's household, she still squirmed with the touchy-feely family stuff.

"Your serious-businesswoman reputation will survive a hug or two," John said.

"Hopefully."

Her uncle's face grew speculative as he looked at Cade. "Aren't you working with Go!?"

"Yes, sir."

His gaze slid to Isabel, then back to Cade. "You're happy there?"

"Well, yeah, I guess."

Isabel clenched her teeth. *If you look at me, Garrison, you're going to be eating from a tube instead of racing next week.*

"Definitely," Cade added quickly. The sight of him, John and Isabel together might not go over too well with his sponsor. "I'm very satisfied."

Her uncle was a big bear of a man, his dark eyes piercing and serious when he was negotiating a contract, but he was a marshmallow most of the time.

Not that Cade needed to know that.

She needed some distance from him. She needed a barrier between them before she did something stupid and irresponsible.

Again.

"Thanks for the help, Cade," she said, smiling in what she hoped was a professional way—rather than the lusty, embarrassing he's-so-gorgeous-I-could-squeal way that he got from nearly every other woman on the planet.

"Yeah." Cade took a step back. "Ah, I'll just…go."

Isabel had never seen him nervous and uncertain. Maybe he wasn't a cocky playboy *all* the time.

Her stomach tight, she forced a smile. "Bye," she

said as she hooked her arm through her uncle's and headed down the hallway.

After they exited the media center, they wandered back toward the garages.

"Are you okay?" John asked.

"I'm fine." The kiss with Cade flashed through her mind like a guilty pleasure. "Last night was an adventure."

"The Garrisons brought you over."

"It was lucky I saw them at the airport."

He said nothing for a few minutes as they wound themselves through the crowd. "Especially since the airstrip for private planes is completely separate from the regular airport."

She stiffened, then swallowed. She was sure the word *guilty* was tattooed on her forehead.

"There are hundreds of people around us. And thousands in the stands. One of the most exhilarating sports on the planet is about to take place right here. And yet, why am I certain the only thing you're thinking about is Cade Garrison?" He patted her hand. "What's going on?"

"Nothing."

"He's an attractive guy."

"Sure."

"Since when do you drool over attractive guys?"

"I'm not drooling." Isabel squeezed her hand into a fist to prevent herself from checking for evidence.

"Especially a race car driver," John continued as if she hadn't spoken.

"It's just…"

How did she explain what she and Cade were? Especially since she didn't know herself.

She knew he was charming and fascinating. She liked the way she felt around him—even if she spent most of that time worrying about who might see them together. She liked the spark in his eyes when he looked at her. She admired his passion for racing, and the confidence he exuded as easily as most people breathed.

"You like him," her uncle said when she remained silent.

Pretending she didn't was juvenile. And dishonest. "Yeah."

"You shouldn't."

"I know." She closed her eyes and pushed back a spasm of regret. She was talking to her *boss,* not just her uncle. "It's nothing. You don't need to worry. I won't embarrass you."

Her uncle stopped. "I never thought you would."

"I can't be attracted to a driver, I know that."

John brushed her hair back off her face, and she tucked the strands behind her ears. "I really need to find a ponytail holder, but I—"

"You can *be* attracted," her uncle said, laying his hands on her shoulders. "You just can't act on it."

She swallowed again. "I know."

"Hey, John, you got a minute?"

Isabel turned to see a well-known TV producer walking toward them.

"Back to work," her uncle said, squeezing her shoulders, then kissing her forehead.

As she glanced around to see if anybody had noticed, her face heated. "Come on, Uncle John."

As always, he didn't take offense at her reticence. "You'll be happier when I fix spaghetti bolognese tomorrow night."

"I'm sure I will."

She never got her pasta and cabernet the night before. She'd certainly need it even more by tomorrow. Given the tension in her neck and shoulders, she'd probably need a masseuse even more than a chef.

She continued to move through the crowd, and a man waving caught her attention. She smiled broadly as Vincent Dodd, a friend and fellow CATL PR rep, strolled toward her.

"How're you holding up?" he asked, his dark brown eyes focused on her face.

"Didn't sleep. Can't remember when—or what—I ate last. Can't breathe in the middle of all these people. Won't be able to hear in about—" she checked her watch "—fifteen minutes."

He angled his head. "Complaining?"

"Yes."

"Typical race weekend."

"Not the eating part."

"You think about food as often as most people think about sex."

"What do you expect? I'm part Italian."

Vincent extended an unopened can of diet soda.

"This should hold you off until lap twenty. I'll buy you a hot dog then."

She popped the top of the ice-cold can. "You are an amazing man."

"I know."

After she took a bracing sip, she asked, "But a hot dog? Don't you know a suite party we can crash?"

If CATL didn't have a suite at a track, Vincent *always* knew a place to go with good food and fun people. He was sophisticated but mixed easily with the racing crowd. He had tons of friends—mostly female, since he looked like a Greek god. His humor was biting. His sense of style impeccable. His friendship invaluable.

He and Susan were her best buddies, and what she'd do without their loyal, sometimes contrasting opinions, she wasn't sure.

"I'm sure I can work something out for you and your desperately empty stomach," he said, steering her through the mass of people near the driver-introduction stage. "Let's find some shade."

They found a spot in the shadow of the stage, near the line of people leaving the infield for the grandstands. For the rest of the afternoon, only people with hard card IDs or "hot" passes would be allowed in the garage area. As much as both drivers and fans loved the excitement of race day, it was a work day, as well, and NASCAR strictly limited the number of people along pit road to VIPs and people with actual jobs to do.

"You didn't answer your phone last night," Vincent said.

"I was tired."

"Probably because you spent the night writhing around in sweaty frustration over Cade Garrison."

"I did not." Not *all* night.

"And that private plane flight had to be exhausting."

She narrowed her eyes. "How do you know about that?" Not that she didn't plan to tell him, but how did he know *already?*

"I know everything."

He did. She bit her lip. Her reputation—and possibly her job—was on the line. "Who else knows?"

"Everybody who's important. Yours and Cade's names are bouncing around pit road like a couple of runaway tires." He sighed dramatically. "Oh, the winks I've gotten! The breathless questions I've had to answer. Have you ever *heard* the word *discreet?*"

Her heart pounded. "You're kidding."

"Of course I'm kidding. Brother Bryan happened to come by the media center earlier."

"You exchanged gossip with Bryan Garrison?" she asked, hoping her doubt was clear.

"Oh, sure. Stoic Limping Man."

"Vincent, that limp ended his career."

"I'm not being critical."

Of course he wasn't. Was she sensitive because Bryan was Cade's brother, or was she just protective of him because she'd been one of the dozens of people to see Bryan's ex-wife glued to Chance Baker's side a few weeks ago?

"Anyway," Vincent continued, "this guy at the media center asked Bryan if he'd seen you, and he said something typically brief and uninformative like *not since the flight.* But since I knew you were flying commercial, I—"

"Figured out the rest when I gasped like a guppy a few seconds ago."

"You seemed more pissed than surprised." He smiled. "A completely *you* reaction."

"I'm still pissed, you know."

He gave her a quick hug. "Ah, come on, little buddy."

She drained her soda. "You nearly gave me a heart attack."

"You're paranoid." His eyes twinkled. "Feeling guilty maybe? Is there anything you want to tell me?"

CHAPTER SIX

ISABEL DREW A DEEP BREATH and faced her friend. She didn't see any point in pretending she was innocent. "I kissed him."

He gave her a high-five. "'Bout time."

"I shouldn't be kissing him."

"You're a grown woman. Kiss whoever you like."

"As long as he doesn't get me fired."

"Or wind up in the tabloids."

She felt light-headed. Good grief, she hadn't even considered that.

"Personally, I'd have the article framed," Vincent added.

"But you're crazy."

"I'm a risk taker."

"Then *you* kiss him."

He shook his head. "Not my type."

She tossed her empty soda in a trash can. "I don't have to worry about tabloids or my job, because it's not going to happen again."

"Are you trying to convince me or yourself?"

"Both."

"If it's that easy, it must not have been a very good kiss."

It was an *amazing* kiss. Her palms got sweaty as she just thought about the heat they generated, the way he'd completely overwhelmed her senses, luring her into forgetting all the reasons they needed to keep their distance. "Let's just drop—"

Her BlackBerry beeped, and she gratefully pulled the device from her pocket and checked the incoming message. Debating her lip-lock with Cade seemed like a bad idea for her peace of mind.

A text message from Craig, who worked in the licensing department, filled the screen.

Marketing can't find VIP party Blast bottles. Ideas?

She showed the message to Vincent.

"They should be in the storage closet," he said.

"They *should*," she agreed.

She messaged back—several times. But the bottles were nowhere to be found. From the increasingly short, rapid messages, she sensed Craig beginning to panic, as were she and Vincent.

This weekend they'd brought in regional managers from grocery, convenience and specialty stores for a VIP party. One of their cars was painted bright green to promote the new melon flavor. They'd offered samples to the race crowd all day. They'd been planning this event for months.

If they didn't find those bottles, somebody—possibly the entire PR and licensing groups—was in big trouble.

"Who was in charge of bringing the bottles to the track?" Vincent asked as they rushed across the infield, shouting over the cheering crowd to be heard.

Mind racing, Isabel tried to picture the e-mail from earlier in the week. "We had them shipped directly to the track. Phil Barnes was supposed pick up the cases from Receiving and organize the tasting booths. I told him to make sure he left four cases for the VIP party."

He began pushing buttons on his own BlackBerry. "So we need to talk to Phil."

"We'd probably get answers faster in person." She turned around to the side of the media center, where she'd parked her golf cart earlier. "Tell Craig we're on the case. And suggest he introduce the Blast VIPs to the Budweiser VIPs and encourage them to sample their product until we get there."

Vincent grabbed her arm. "Samples. We'll get the cases from the tasting booths," he said as they slid into the front seat of Isabel's golf cart.

"If there are any left." She swung the cart through the tunnel, then to the road around the track where the souvenir trailers and Blast tasting booths had been set up.

But the first booth they came to was deserted.

"What about a little green food coloring in a regular-flavored bottle?" Isabel asked as they bolted toward the next booth.

"You've got green food coloring in your pocket?"

"We could run to the store."

"It's certainly a last-resort plan."

"Maybe if they drink enough beer, they won't want energy drinks."

"Or at least they won't notice that melon-flavored Blast doesn't taste anything like melon—despite the fact that it's artificially colored green."

She pressed the golf cart pedal to the floor—ramping up their speed to a full fifteen miles an hour. By now, the cars had begun their pace laps, the engines rumbling and the fans cheering. Usually the sounds made her smile, instead the tension cramping her stomach intensified.

She excelled under pressure—one of the reasons her uncle and the other department heads saw her moving up the corporate ladder. Would her and Vincent's quick thinking save their promotion? Days like today and yesterday sometimes threatened her confidence. Did she really belong here? Did they let people raised in trailer parks be vice presidents?

Her BlackBerry beeped constantly, so Vincent had taken over answering hers, as well as his. "Craig wants an update."

"It's been ten minutes!"

"Your uncle is now with the Blast people, trying to calm them down."

"Why did *Craig* have to be here today?"

"He always presses the panic button too quickly."

Isabel shook her head in disgust. "And called John."

They reached the next tasting booth and found it empty, as well. They got the same result at the third one, but at the fourth, they saw two guys wearing lime-green polos and stacking boxes on a dolly.

"Oh, please," Isabel said under her breath.

"Aren't you going to promise to do something virtuous like give up chocolate or booze or smoking if they actually have the bottles?"

"*Me?* Why do I have to sacrifice?" She cut her gaze toward her friend. "And I don't smoke."

"Yeah, but I might start after all this."

She slammed the cart to a halt beside the booth, then jumped out and approached the men. "You guys wouldn't happen to have a few spare cases, would you?"

They exchanged a glance. "Yeah. Why?"

Her heart settled back into its proper place in her chest. "I'm really thirsty."

BACK IN HIS OFFICE ON Monday afternoon, Cade hung up the phone after what had to be his fiftieth media interview of the day. Winning was great, but exhausting. He was past ready to meet the boys for a beer.

"Don't forget you have the historical society meeting tonight at seven," his sister called from the other room as if she'd read his mind.

Crap. He *had* forgotten. "Uh-huh."

"They changed their regular Thursday meetings to Mondays to accommodate you, remember?"

"Uh-huh."

"It's a condition of your probation."

"I *know*, Rach."

He wadded up a piece of paper from his desk and tossed it through the basketball hoop hooked on his trash can. The last thing he wanted to do was sit around talking about old stuff with old people all night. Plus, he'd told his dad he was coming by his place to talk about his future.

He wanted back in a NASCAR NEXTEL Cup car, and he was prepared to do everything necessary to make sure that happened.

He called his buddies and told them to meet him at Midtown Sundries—their second-favorite lake-side bar hangout—at ten. Surely the historical society meeting wouldn't take longer than two hours, afterward he'd have an hour to talk to his dad before hooking up with his friends.

After the phone call he headed downstairs to the shop to see how his car for this week was looking. GRI owned a three-story brick office building and race shop in Davidson. All the cars were built, painted and housed in the shop. Each team—two NASCAR NEXTEL Cup Series and one NASCAR Busch Series—had their own sections within the building where they could add their own engineering specifications and setups. Only the engines were made in another facility.

He met with his team and talked about the Kentucky race, then he headed back to his office and signed fan memorabilia for a while. By the time he jumped into his Corvette and started toward Town Hall, the digital clock on the dashboard read 6:52.

He pressed the gas pedal harder, knowing he couldn't be late for the meeting. He was already getting off light for his assault of Parker Huntington. All he needed was for the judge to get the idea that he wasn't taking his assignment/punishment seriously—which he wasn't—and he'd find himself cleaning bathroom stalls with a toothbrush or something equally lousy.

Then he'd have to kill Huntington, and that would create a whole new set of problems.

The guy had made suggestive comments about Cade's sister, so he deserved much worse than a cracked jaw. Not that he'd told anybody but Huntington the reason he'd hit him. He'd told the media Huntington had criticized his driving, which was true, he just hadn't done so at that moment. If the media had gotten hold of the personal aspect of their argument, his sister would have been humiliated.

And though Cade knew his troubles stemmed from not controlling his temper, he wished he could kick creeps like Huntington out of racing. People who thought they were so damn important they could say anything they wanted.

To his credit, Huntington had kept his mouth shut. And stayed away from Rachel. Maybe he wasn't a *complete* idiot.

When blue lights flashed in his rearview mirror, Cade bit back a curse. Great. Stopped by the cops on his way to serve a court-ordered punishment for a previously committed rash and illegal act.

"Cade Garrison?" the cop asked as he leaned down to the window.

He vaguely recognized the about-his-age guy from local autograph sessions where the promoter hired extra security. "Yeah?"

"You goin' to the historical society meeting, too?"

"You're on the committee?"

The cop smiled. "Sure." He shook Cade's hand. "Matt Bonner. The mayor likes the force to have a rep on the committee. I'm the youngest, so I got the honor." He grinned as if the honor was more like a burden.

Cade returned his smile. He'd pictured little old lady librarian types with hard eyes and pinched smiles as fellow committee members. Maybe this wouldn't be too bad after all. Maybe he and Matt could bring some new ideas to historical preservation. Was it really necessary to save every falling-down pile of lumber that was built before 1900?

Plus, with his record, it couldn't hurt to have a friend on the police force.

"I'll give you an escort," Matt said.

Legalized speeding had to be the coolest thing about being a cop. The Corvette took the tight turns with ease, and Cade's anxiety slipped away. Maybe he didn't know a thing about old stuff, maybe he'd be bored out of his mind, but he'd at least make a decent impression by being on time.

They arrived at Town Hall quickly, and Matt helped him negotiate the maze of corridors to find the conference room where the meeting was being held.

Introductions were made by Matt, and the rest of the committee were closer to expectations—three elderly ladies, who all narrowed their eyes suspiciously at him, and one older man dressed in white pants, a navy blazer and a small billed cap. He looked like he'd stepped off a yacht. In 1923.

"Now," Mrs. Millie Fitzgerald began as they all sat at a round conference table, "as chairperson of this committee, I call the meeting to order. I'd like to welcome—" She stopped and nudged the woman next to her, who'd fallen asleep. "Margaret, you're supposed to be taking minutes."

She snored.

Cade bit his tongue to keep from laughing.

"Margaret!" Mrs. Fitzgerald said loudly in her fellow committee member's ear.

Margaret jerked awake. "Are we having pie yet?"

"We've just gotten started, dear," the woman on Margaret's other side—whose name Cade couldn't recall—said, patting her hand. "Do you need me to take the minutes tonight?"

Margaret huffed. "*I'm* the secretary, Minnie."

Right. Minnie. Minnie, Margaret and Millie. Surely he could remember that.

"Proceed," Margaret said, her pen poised above a pad of paper.

Still looking annoyed, Millie Fitzgerald began

again. "I welcome our newest member, Mr. Garrison."

Cade smiled, toning down his supercharmer grin. No need to overwhelm the ladies the first night. "You can call me Cade." Mr. Garrison was his father. Actually, his *grand*father.

Mrs. Fitzgerald glared at him. "This is a *formal* meeting, Mr. Garrison. Ladies and gentlemen address one another properly. As I was saying, Mr. Garrison is taking the place of our beloved Petunia Swaggart."

"God rest her soul," everybody said in unison.

Mrs. Fitzgerald looked expectantly at Cade.

"Ah…amen?" he said.

Mrs. Fitzgerald frowned, but the other two ladies smiled at him. Though Margaret could have just been thinking about her pie.

"The first topic on our agenda today is the fundraiser to save the Cotton House. For Mr. Garrison's information, I'll explain again that this house has been involved in a legal dispute between the descendants of Mr. Cotton for more than a decade, which is why it has fallen into disrepair. The city now owns the property and has agreed to hold it until we have a buyer who will agree to repair the house, not tear it down.

"The house is of the utmost historical significance. Built in 1849, it survived the War Between the States and a community fire in 1924. The president of Davidson College even lived there for a short time while his residence was being constructed. Plus, it's located in a primary location in town."

"Are you talking about that gray house—" and Cade used the word *house* loosely "—on Griffith Street?"

"Yes, Mr. Garrison," Mrs. Fitzgerald said. "You have a suggestion on how we can save it?"

Why would you *want* to save it? he thought, but obviously didn't say so. He'd always wondered why somebody didn't tear down the crumbling eyesore.

"I still think it would make a nice museum," Minnie said.

The guy who looked like a yacht captain patted her hand. "We can't afford to bring it up to code, much less decorate and stock it with a staff."

"What if we offered it for sale to businesses?" Cade suggested.

"It has always been a primary residence," Mrs. Fitzgerald said. "The area around it is zoned for residential."

"But nobody's lived there for fifteen years," he said.

"He's got a point, Millie," Margaret said. "A business might be able to afford to fix it up."

"*That's* why we're doing the fund-raiser," Mrs. Fitzgerald said firmly.

The rest of the meeting was devoted to what kind of fund-raiser they would have. They could sell barbecue, have a carnival or a formal ball. They could hold an auction of donated items. Cade even offered to get NASCAR-driver-autographed merchandise for the auction. Mrs. Fitzgerald responded by glaring at him.

Okay, so maybe he'd been forced upon the committee, and he really didn't see the benefit in saving a falling-down house when it was much easier and cheaper to just build a new one, but he was making an effort to be helpful at least. Mrs. Fitzgerald could cut him a break.

Annoyed, he kept quiet the rest of the meeting and entertained himself by going over what he planned to say to his dad. He'd come a long way the past year. He'd matured, he'd worked on controlling his emotions and maintaining his professionalism. He'd come to appreciate the opportunities he'd had in his life. He'd learned his lesson. He wouldn't cross the line again.

All that sounded great, though he knew his heart wasn't in it. For one, he wasn't really interested in maturing. Not too much, anyway. He liked hanging out with his buddies, taking off for the beach at a moment's notice, having fun with the ladies. Was he supposed to turn into Mr. Serious and Boring like Bryan?

And while he *did* appreciate the opportunities in his life, he thought his father's punishment was excessive. Sure, he'd lost his sponsor, and the one GRI had gotten as a replacement hadn't wanted him as the driver, but Bryan and his dad could have stood up for him more. They could have found another sponsor if they'd really wanted to.

Instead, they'd told him he was lucky Go! was willing to stay and allow him to drive the NASCAR Busch Series car.

He shook his head.

"You don't approve of the black-tie dinner, Mr. Garrison?"

Mrs. Fitzgerald's question brought him abruptly back to the present. "Ah, no. I mean, yeah, it's fine."

"So, it's decided, then. Minnie, you check with the college to see when the Visual Arts Center is available. Margaret, work on catering."

"And I'll handle ticket sales and publicity," the captain said.

Everyone looked at Cade. "I'll help with publicity." He was in front of a TV camera nearly every week. How hard could a little PR be?

Plus, he knew just the person he could ask for advice if he needed it.

Since it was apple rather than cherry—the only fruit he was interested in these days—he declined the offer of post-meeting pie and coffee and headed toward his dad's condo. During the drive, he considered the last promise he planned to make—not crossing the line again. Maybe he ought to rethink that one, since his greatest noncareer ambition was hooking up with a NASCAR sponsor PR rep.

Isabel haunted his dreams at night and dominated his thoughts during the day. He'd replayed their kiss over and over in his mind, searching for flaws and improvements. Flaws, zero. Improvements, maybe the length—it could have been longer—and a few less clothes could be interesting.

Staying out of trouble and away from her didn't seem likely. Even if she thought he was too much trouble. In fact, the more he thought about her, the advantages and consequences of seeing her, the more he realized he had no intention of forgetting about her.

His private life was his own. As was hers. Cumberland Atlantic didn't have a right to dictate who she could see and who she couldn't. It was archaic—and a bit control-freakish.

But maybe he could accomplish both—staying out of trouble and seeing Isabel. They didn't have to take out an ad in the newspaper, after all. They could, well, not *sneak around* exactly, just be *discreet.*

He pulled into the parking lot near Turn One at the speedway in Charlotte, then walked toward the main entrance and up the elevator to the condos. His dad had moved into the family's condo after his parents' divorce, and every time Cade visited he grew more concerned. His father was turning the place from a professionally decorated, classy retreat for family, team members and sponsors to a tacky, seventies-era bachelor pad. The living/dining area now contained black leather sofas with leopard-print pillows; red, fuzzy fabric-covered bar stools; lots of gilded mirrors; a disco ball for a light fixture; and a bearskin rug. Cade had never ventured into the bedroom, afraid he'd find a velvet-draped, heart-shaped bed.

He'd learned a few months ago that his dad had, in fact, hired a decorator, whom he was dating. Along with what seemed to be every woman under thirty in the Mooresville-Concord-Davidson area.

It was cmbarrassing.

Cade could hardly believe his parents' once-idyllic marriage had come to this. He knew the pain of Bryan's accident and the strain of running a multi-car racing team was intense, but he didn't understand how things could go wrong so quickly.

Why didn't his mother understand that racing was their lives, as well as their livelihood? Why couldn't his father see that his wife needed atten-tion and given at least an equal footing with the latest engine diagnostics?

Simple. Relationships were complicated.

And here he was contemplating one. Though he and Isabel had shared a one-night stand, he'd sensed she wasn't a woman who did so normally. She was classy, confident and had a great deal of respect for herself. A man who pursued her would have to be prepared to get involved in more than sex.

Scary, but then so was roaring into Turn Three at Talladega.

He tried to put Isabel out of his mind as he knocked on the door of his dad's condo. Loud, base-pulsing rock music greeted him in a blast of sound before he saw his dad.

"Hey, son!" He clapped his hand on Cade's

shoulder and pulled him inside. "I've got company coming over. Can we make this quick?"

"Ah…" Cade glanced around at the dozens of lit candles, the filled ice bucket on the bar and the flickering flames in the fireplace—though it was June. He closed his eyes. His father as a big-time player was beyond uncomfortable.

Let he who is without sin, cast the first stone….

Okay, so maybe he'd paid attention in Sunday School occasionally. And maybe he'd even set the same scene a few times.

He opened his eyes long enough to look at his dad. He wore a black shirt, unbuttoned almost to his navel, tight jeans and his hair was slicked back with something oily.

Hell.

His father was supposed to be the parent. Settled and steady. Experienced and wise. A source of comfort and advice. Cade was the kid. *He* was supposed to be wild, irresponsible and lure hot women into his lair. His father was *old.* Well, maybe fifty-six wasn't old. But old*er.*

How had the world's axis turned on its side?

"You okay?" his dad asked.

"I…I need a drink."

"Got it right here." He crossed to the bar and started tossing ice in a glass. "Whiskey, vodka, beer?"

All three. Okay, maybe not.

He and his friends flipped for the designated driver when they went out. Or, if they all wanted a beer or two, they hired a driver. Even if NASCAR didn't drill safety and responsibility constantly into them, he knew he had accountability to himself and his community.

"Water is good," he said.

His dad shrugged but poured the drink. "Did you want to talk to me about something?" he asked as he handed over the glass.

"Yeah." Taking a gulp of water, Cade sank onto the sofa. "I want back in a Cup car."

His dad glanced at him over his shoulder. "You do?"

"I've come a long way this season."

"The season is barely halfway over."

"We've won two in a row. We're fifth in points, and we'll win more before November. I've matured. I'm more professional."

His dad sat next to him. "Memories are long in this business, son."

His stomach tightened. "I deserve another chance."

He was silent for a long time, sipping his drink. He finally rose and crossed the room, looking out the window to the view of the darkened track below. "You represent the family now, Cade. You alone."

"That's not true. You and Bryan—"

"Are retired. We aren't racers anymore."

Inside they were. Yes, retired, but that desire for speed and excitement never went away.

For him, anyway, he couldn't imagine the feeling subsiding. Wouldn't he be angry, even bitter, if he was forced to give up doing what he loved? At least his father had had a choice about retiring. Bryan had been forced. His body couldn't perform the way it once had. How devastating would that be not just to accept, but to live with every day?

Cade felt guilty suddenly for even coming. He'd only changed series, and he'd been singing the *why me?* blues for six months.

"We're *executives,*" his dad continued, shaking his head. "We're owners and businessmen." He turned to face him. "You represent the family on the track, where it counts."

At the determination and authority in his father's voice, Cade raised his head. "I won't let you down. I won't—"

He swallowed the rest of his promise—the one about not crossing the line. Sneaking around with Isabel would be crossing the line. Not even he could bring himself to promise something he had no intention of doing. He shook his dad's hand. "You can count on me."

"So, you're driving in the Cup race at Chicago," Cade's buddy, Dean, said.

Sitting with his friends at their favorite lakeside patio table at Midtown Sundries, Cade set down his half-full frosty beer mug. He was still having a hard time accepting his good fortune. "A sponsor would be nice."

"But even without one, you're in," Jay said, dragging his gaze away from a pair of hot blondes strolling by the table.

"Yeah," Cade said, "but I don't want to ride around the track on my dad's dime like some kind of charity case."

"Who're you going to get as a sponsor?" Dean asked.

Cade stared into his mug. "I have no idea. I'm going to put Rachel on it."

"So you'll use your sister, but not your dad?" Jay asked.

"I *pay* my sister," Cade said.

"And your dad pays you," Jay said, "so, isn't that the same as—"

"No." Cade glared at his friend. It sounded the same, maybe, but it wasn't. "Dad would be impressed if I found a sponsor. It would show him that a Cup-worthy company will work with me."

Dean clapped him on the shoulder. "We're behind ya, buddy, but one race is a long way from an entire season."

"It's a start," Cade said.

"Can we talk about something besides racing?" Jay asked, turning in his chair. "Unless those two blondes are fans, and Cade can get them over here with the promise of autographs and pictures."

Dean shook his head. "Can't you add, man? Two of them, three of us."

Jay waved at the women, who smiled. "Maybe they've got a friend."

Cade took a gulp of beer. "You guys go ahead. I'm not fit for women tonight."

Jay whipped his head around. "You're not?"

"I'm going to make a list of companies for Rachel to contact." He held up his hand to signal their waitress, hoping she had a piece of paper and a pen. If his brother could become an *executive*—he shuddered at the thought—he could put his mind on business every once in a while to help. Especially to help himself.

"You're joking," Dean said.

"No."

"Don't you have people at GRI to do that?" Dean asked.

"The licensing department, but I want to do it on my own."

"But…" Jay leaned forward, looking at Cade as if he didn't recognize him. "They're *blond*."

And why was that even less appealing? Why did he suddenly have a thing for brunettes? One in particular? "Yeah, I know."

While Dean and Jay argued over who got which blonde—never once considering one or both women might be taken, or refuse their attention—Cade got a pen and paper from the waitress and started his list. He started with random companies, then narrowed them down to the ones he thought he might actually have a prayer of connecting with.

He looked up several times, staring out at the darkened sky that disappeared seamlessly into the lake. Floodlights lit up the sandy shore just beyond the patio, where volleyball nets were set up for the bar-sponsored Tuesday-night leagues. His team was, naturally, undefeated.

As he crossed off a company that was a competitor of the company that made Go!, a movement out of the corner of his eye caught his attention.

Looking up, he saw Susan and Isabel walk onto the patio.

He froze, like the first time Tiffany Meadows had walked across the lunchroom in sixth grade and mesmerized him with her swaying hips.

Of course, he didn't get a smile and a blush from Isabel, the way he had from Tiffany. No way. Susan waved, but Isabel, after noticing him and doing a double take, shoved one hand in the back pocket of her jeans, grabbed Susan's arm and strode to the farthest table away from him.

Another ten feet, and they'd be in the lake.

Jay nudged his arm. "Hey, don't those two chicks work at the track?"

"Yeah…" Dean said slowly, as if searching his memory to place them. "Susan and…Annabelle."

"Isabel," Cade said.

"Oh, yeah." Jay smiled. "The one who made the shots at Rusty's a few weeks back. She's foxy—in an intense, kick-your-ass kind of way. You're friends with her, right, Cade?"

He'd never shared the details of his and Isabel's night together with his closest buddies. Not that he bragged on a regular basis, but they usually told one another when one of them scored. Why hadn't he said anything? "Ah, sort of."

"So, she's free?" Jay asked.

"Well…" Now the image of Jay and Isabel together raced through his mind. And he was raving jealous. He blinked, trying to shake it away.

This was ridiculous. He had a list to finish.

Yet his fingers tingled with the urge to slam his pen on the table, run across the patio and grab Isabel before his friend did.

Jay polished off the rest of his beer and started to rise from the table. "*Now* there's enough women."

Dean shoved Jay's shoulder. "Dude, now we're three against four."

"I'll take two," Jay said.

"I'm finishing my list," Cade said, pointing at his paper.

Sighing, Dean rose. "We're circulating. Then we're gonna find a thermometer. You've *got* to be sick."

"I'm being mature."

Openmouthed, his friends stared at him.

After they finally walked away, Cade tried to get his mind back on racing business. This was a test, he decided. If he could resist the deep, clawing urge to go over to Isabel's table and flirt with her, to lure her in the shadows of the sandy volleyball court and kiss her until neither of them could breathe, he could finally get her out of his head. If he couldn't, he'd know he had to go after her.

Haven't you already decided to do that?

Not if he was being mature and responsible.

Damn, is that what he'd decided to be? In addition to arguing with himself, he'd *grown up* in the past hour? No way. He shook his head. Not possible.

He was the baby of his family. The fun one. The charming one who got away with everything. He had a duty to fulfill that role.

He dropped his pen and shoved back his chair. He started toward Isabel's table, but stopped when she rose from her chair and headed toward him. "Hey, Is—"

She glanced over, then swung around him as she headed toward the door into the restaurant.

Ignoring him again, huh?

He followed her, catching up as she headed across the lobby toward the bathrooms. "I guess you didn't see me on the patio."

Not looking at him, she kept walking. "I saw you. I thought you hung out at the Rusty Rutter."

"I do—sometimes. Sometimes I come here." He grabbed her arm and turned her toward him. "This is becoming a thing with us."

She angled her head, annoyance in her brown eyes. "What thing?"

"You trying to ignore me."

Pulling away from him, she crossed her arms over her chest. "Guess I'll just have to try harder."

"Or you could give me a break."

"You could stop trying to follow me into the bathroom."

"We'd have some privacy in there." He grinned. "No telling what we could do."

The door swung open, and two women walking out, giggling and talking. They saw him and stopped. "Aren't you Cade Garrison?"

"Ah, yeah."

They giggled again. "Could we have your autograph?"

"You bet."

After a moment or two, autograph in hand, they wandered away, and Cade turned back to Isabel. "Where were—"

"There is no privacy for you," she said, an odd look of disappointment on her face.

He sighed. "I know."

She turned to the bathroom door again.

"Do you like me?" Oh, he hadn't seriously just asked that. "I mean—"

He swallowed. Was he prepared to beg for her attention? There had to be a place between maturity and kindergarten.

If so, he hadn't found it. He grabbed her wrist, turning her to face him.

"Are you kidding me?" she asked, meeting his gaze.

"No."

"We're not in the fourth grade."

Don't I know it. It was *sixth* grade. Though it had been a lot easier to get Tiffany Meadows to kiss his cheek in the hall after Social Studies than it was to get Isabel to just talk to him. "It's a simple, direct question. Do you like me?"

She sighed, then she leaned back against the hallway wall and stared at the floor. He remembered her telling her uncle not to hug her. She was the least mushy woman he knew. Most of them talked endlessly about their feelings and wanted to have ongoing discussions about other people's.

Isabel did not.

Asking her to answer a question about her feelings—even a simple, direct one—was a challenge he wasn't sure she was willing to take on.

So, she surprised him by speaking. "After the fight with your sponsor last year, I picked up the phone to call you a hundred times. As competitive as you are, I knew something really serious must have pushed you to hit him. I wanted to know what, I wanted to ask you why." She pressed her lips together briefly. "But then I remembered the last time I'd talked to you, after our...night together. We didn't know what to say, or how to deal with what happened."

He remembered that awkward phone call, where they'd agreed they'd been impulsive by sleeping together and that their careers meant everything to them. They'd been intimate before they knew each other more than to just wave or say hi.

"So I reminded myself that we never had a chance, anyway," she continued. "But then you flirt with me in a bar, and you keep looking at me and talking to me and kissing me, then looking at me again." She glanced up, met his gaze, then closed her eyes. "Like now, just like you're doing now."

"What am I—"

"That *look*—the, I don't know, the attraction look or *longing,* or maybe you're just picturing me naked or something."

He was, but it wasn't just that. He stepped closer, but she laid her palm against his chest to stop him.

"Then we have this other problem—namely, you driving more than 180 miles an hour with forty-two other professional lunatics driving that same speed on a weekly basis. As a fan, I can appreciate your talent and love to watch you sail around the track, and at the same time, I know the kind of person who does that is just a bit crazy." Her breath and words were coming in bursts, as if it had all rushed to the surface in one eruption. "I don't do that kind of drama. I have control over my life. I have stuff to do, goals to meet.

"Then I have this other issue with you. You're not *just* a crazy, run-of-the-mill race car driver. I read these online blogs and find out—"

"You read my blogs?"

"I find out you always participate in the motor-cycle charity drive and volunteer at the camp for chronically ill children. I learn you like cats, mint chocolate chip ice cream and Cary Grant movies. You're on the historical society board."

"My probation—"

"Right. I know. Your court-mandated community service. But I live in a historical house in Davidson and Mrs. Fitzgerald is my landlady."

Mrs. Fitzgerald was her landlady?

She hates me.

"So, there's all that. Plus, you have this vulnerability in your eyes. And you dealt with your switch to the Busch car with such…dignity. You kept going and striving. You didn't blame anybody but yourself. You respected your sport and your family—even though they might have given you a bad deal. There's something to be said for moving on, for putting one foot in front of the other." She paused and smiled even though she didn't look happy.

"Or pressing on a gas pedal. You moved forward. You accepted responsibility." She slid her hand down his chest, a brief caress that made his pulse thrum and his mouth go dry. "Responsibility is a rare thing." Turning away, she sighed. "So, yes, Cade, I like you." Then she shoved open the bathroom door. "And I'm pissed as hell about it."

CHAPTER SEVEN

BREATHING HARD, ISABEL leaned over the sink, bracing her hands on the bathroom counter.

Responsibility is a rare thing?

Dear heaven, she'd become a simp. Sometime in the past few minutes, outside the ladies' bathroom of Cade Garrison's second-favorite bar hangout on Lake Norman, she'd lost her edge and started uttering endearing things. She'd let her emotions take over, delve into her rocky past and allow it to humiliate her.

She closed her eyes, not wanting to see herself in the mirror over the sink. *Responsibility is a rare thing.*

Old mistakes. Old problems.

It wasn't her mistakes, but her parents' choices that had pushed that confession out of her. Why did Cade affect her that way? Why did he touch her so deeply? Why couldn't she take their one-night stand for what it was—a one-night stand? Why hadn't she been able to move on past her impulsive mistake? Why was she suddenly wondering if it might have been a beginning instead of an ending?

And why did that scare her even more?

The door burst open and Cade strode inside. "We can keep it a secret."

Isabel jumped. Whipping her head in his direction, she rushed around him and leaned against the door to close it. "This is the woman's bathroom!"

He braced his arm above her head and hovered over her. "We can keep it a secret."

"Keep what a secret?"

He stroked her cheek with the back of his hand. "Us."

Heart hammering—out of fear they'd get caught and his proximity—she put her weight against the door. "Somebody's going to come in here any minute."

"Maybe. You better give me your answer quick."

Outside, she heard voices. *Somebody was coming.* "You didn't ask a question," she whispered, pressing her ear to the door. The murmur of voices faded, but given the beer-flowing atmosphere, it had to be only a matter of moments before somebody's bladder called. Then she'd be caught in the bathroom with a man she shouldn't be looking at too closely, much less touching and having a significant, personal conversation with.

"Have dinner with me," he said, pressing his lips to her jaw.

"No."

"No?"

"I can't deal with you and my uncle's job at the same time."

Cade pulled back. His gaze slid to hers. "CATL offered you his job?"

"No." But the possibility of that power and validation hovered before her like a lure for a hungry trout. "Not yet."

"If they do, won't that mean you'll be in an office more than at the track?"

"Yes."

"That's certainly a way to avoid me."

She shoved her hands in the back pockets of her jeans, but that moved her closer to him, so she yanked them out and settled for fisting them at her sides. "I'm not trying to avoid you, Cade."

He raised his eyebrows. And looked really cute and nearly irresistible doing it.

"Okay, so maybe I am. But not because I don't, well...like you."

His gaze dropped to her lips. "So you said."

"Stop it. You're looking at me again."

"I'm looking at your lips. They're very tempting."

She turned and yanked the door handle, then marched through the opening. He followed, the lunatic. The Most Eligible Driver in NASCAR was literally at her heels. How out-of-body insane was that?

"The point is I'm avoiding you because it's safer," she said, desperately wishing she hadn't volunteered to be the designated driver. She could really use a beer about now. "I can't deal with you and my uncle so—"

"Yes, you can."

She halted in the doorway to the patio. Her gaze

swept the tables outside, noting all the racing-related faces. She saw mechanics, officials and engineers. Despite the vast popularity of the sport, they had a small community. One she'd always wanted to be a part of, one that had given her focus and direction.

Cade might think a secret relationship would solve everything, but he was an optimist. At the speeds he drove every weekend, she supposed he had to be. But she was a realist. There was no way they could work.

No way at all.

From their table at the back of the patio, her friend Susan waved. She would *dis*courage her. Thinking of her conversation with Vincent, she knew he'd *en*courage her. In the middle, she had no idea what to do. "Okay. Fine." She faced Cade. The intimate look in his eyes forced her to swallow before she could speak. "I'll think about it. Dinner, I mean."

"I want an answer now."

"Then the answer is no."

"No?"

"Read my lips. No."

He leaned close. "I'd rather taste your lips."

"I am *not* here."

"Then let's go somewhere else. My place works for me."

"I am going to turn around now. I'm going back to hang out with *my* friends. You are going to go back to hanging out with *your* friends."

"And you'll think about dinner."

"You said you wanted an answer now."

"But you didn't give me the answer I wanted."

Determination—another race car driver requirement. But he'd give up eventually, right? He had women who *literally* chased him. She'd seen him and his manager trying to outrun groups of them in his souped-up golf cart more than once. She'd seen fans *cry* when they met him. She couldn't compete with that.

If she put him off a few days, he'd drop this crazy idea of them together, and she could concentrate on her career. She'd go back to remembering their night together with distant fondness and feeling only a mild tingling when she saw him at the track.

In other words, she'd go back to suppressing her feelings and lying to herself.

"Good night, Cade," she said sharply, then turned and started toward her friend.

"'Night, Izzy."

She stopped. How did he manage to make even that simple statement sound illicit?

Forcing her feet to move again, she strode back across the patio without commenting—or looking back. He'd forget this crazy idea, and everything would be back to normal.

THREE WEEKS LATER, nothing was normal except the usual, undying resentment of her coworkers. In the middle of a crisis, you'd think they'd pull together, but they were holding firm in their bitterness of her success and nepotism.

"Isabel! Line two!" Somebody called out as she rushed down the hall, clutching her fifth cup of coffee for the day.

Another reporter, no doubt. Between her, Susan and Vincent, they'd talked to what had to be every motorsports writer in the country. The rest of the office was happy to field calls from anxious and concerned team members and be all *oh, you poor thing, we understand,* but nobody wanted to be quoted in the newspaper or online. Nobody wanted to risk saying the wrong thing and have the CATL brass breathing down their neck.

That they left to her.

Ms. Related-To-The-Boss.

Thank God for her two friends, or she'd have run screaming into the hills by now. As for the scowling crowd in her office, she simply resented them right back. More than half of them had gotten their jobs because their dad, uncle, brother or whoever knew somebody who knew somebody, so they hardly had much of a high horse to climb onto.

"Isabel Turner," she said into the phone.

"Hey, Isabel. Frank Bonder, *Tampa Tribune.* What's up with this weak-ass punishment for cheaters?"

After taking a bracing sip of coffee, she drew a deep breath and launched into her practiced spiel.

At the New Hampshire race two days ago, a rules

violation had been discovered on their NASCAR Busch Series car during the post-race inspection. Since the car had finished second, several drivers, owners and crew chiefs were screaming for the driver and owner to lose championship points. CATL, the driver and the rest of the team contended that a mechanic had simply miscalculated, that they weren't cheaters, that they'd simply made a mistake.

NASCAR had handed down its ruling this morning—a $10,000 fine and probation until the end of the season for the crew chief.

The media went nuts. Teams seethed. Everybody wanted points deducted. Some even called for the crew chief to be suspended. NASCAR argued that the violation was relatively minor, and the team had a pristine record, but that all seemed to get lost in the furor.

Personally, she'd give anything for a good old driver-versus-driver fight. Not a physical one, she amended, thinking of Cade and all he'd gone through, but couldn't somebody compare somebody else to a little old lady driver? Or could somebody say something bad about somebody else's wife or girlfriend? Anything juicy and distracting would do.

She hung up the phone and laid her head on her desk. "I should've stayed in school."

"You did," Susan said as she walked into her office and sank into one of the chairs in front of her desk. "You've got a degree from one of the most prestigious liberal arts colleges in the country. Back up from the ledge, for heaven's sake."

"We have Daytona Saturday night—a super prestigious race coming on the heels of the uplifting July Fourth holiday, where the whole country pulls together and remembers all they have to be thankful for."

"Sappy?" Susan leaned close, angling her head and staring at her in disbelief. "You're sappy *and* depressed? Do you have a fever?"

"How are we supposed to spin angry hordes of fans, teams and reporters into sparkly fireworks?"

"You need a break, girl. Let's go to Midtown Sundries tonight."

"No. Oh, no." She lifted her head and got busy shuffling papers around on her desk. "No way."

"Why did you say no three times?"

"I just can't go. I'm busy. Busy, busy."

"That's three times for busy." She squinted suspiciously. "What's going on?"

Isabel pictured Cade hovering over her in the women's restroom. His broad shoulders filled out his T-shirt. His wicked smile made her heart race. His blue eyes stared straight into her weak, needy, vulnerable soul.

Oh, man, she *was* sappy.

"The ledge isn't such a bad place to be," Isabel muttered, straightening a stack of press releases.

Susan jumped to her feet. "I'm calling in reinforcements."

"That's not—"

"Vincent!" she yelled out the door. Turning,

Susan crossed her arms over her chest and tapped her foot, looking like an annoyed—and red-haired—Tinkerbell. "He'll talk some sense into you."

By the time Vincent strolled into the office, Susan had begun to pace. "It's been a sucky day," he said, sinking into a chair. "How 'bout late-night volley-ball at Midtown Sundries?"

"I'm busy," Isabel said, though she was nearly positive nobody was listening to her.

Susan wrinkled her nose. "Won't we get all sandy and sweaty? I was thinking more along the lines of a cosmo and a cool breeze off the lake."

"It's July," he said. "You're gonna get sweaty just breathing. And we're not *playing* the game, we're watching."

Susan pursed her lips. "So, we're watching guys get sweaty and sandy while we relax on the deck with our alcoholic beverage of choice?"

"That's the plan."

Despite her efforts to ignore them and pretend to be too busy to leave the office before midnight, Isabel stared skeptically at Vincent. "What's in this for you?"

"Who do you think comes to watch sweaty guys play beach volleyball?"

"Us," Susan said on a breathy sigh, collapsing into the chair next to him.

"Exactly." He grinned. "Hot chicks. While my gender mates are playing, I'm working the curvy crowd."

Susan glared at him. "That's disgusting."

Isabel thought it was pretty smart. Maybe a bit devious, but then this was Vincent they were talking about. Given Susan's indignation, she said nothing.

Vincent leaned back in his chair, linking his fingers over his stomach. "You're having a *Top Gun* fantasy, and *I'm* disgusting?"

"Are you interested in ever finding a meaningful relationship, or are you going to be a gigolo all your life?"

Watching the familiar bickering between her buddies, Isabel fought a sigh. She wanted to be miserable by herself. Why did she have to have friends?

"A *gigolo?*" Vincent asked, sounding amused. "Are you serious?"

"That's what you are. Own up to it," Susan said.

"I'm twenty-something and single."

"And loving it way too much."

"Since you're getting paid for being the judge and the jury, you buy the drinks tonight."

"We're supposed to be supporting Isabel, not tending to our own—" Susan curled her lip "—*needs.*"

"Isabel just needs to get laid and she'll be fine."

Susan rose, then marched toward the door in a huff. "I'll call for a taxi, since it seems like we could all use a drink tonight."

"Or maybe you do," Vincent muttered, staring after Susan into the tension-filled silence.

"Get laid or have a drink?" Isabel asked, curious despite her morose mood.

"Both." He rested his forearms against her desk. "You don't want to go to Sundries because Garrison might be there, right?"

"Right."

"His volleyball team is first in the league."

"Naturally."

"You can't avoid him forever."

Though she loved Susan and her emotional outbursts, there was something to be said for Vincent's dispassionate directness. "It's working for me so far."

He raised his eyebrows. "Is it?"

"Go away, Vincent. I have work to do."

Shrugging, he rose. "Until seven. Then we go to dinner and onto the volleyball games."

On top of the past few miserable days all she needed was to have to face Cade and the dinner date he wouldn't let go. Every Monday he called and left a message on her cell phone, calmly asking her to go out with him. Every Monday she ignored him.

Every Monday night, in the privacy of her apartment, she cried like a baby.

It was ridiculous. A humiliation between her and her conscience. And possibly Mrs. Fitzgerald, who'd delivered hot tea last night after seeing Isabel, who—in her words—had trudged through the door looking like she'd tried to stand in front of Sherman just before he'd marched through Georgia.

But then Mrs. Fitzgerald was a bit too overly involved in historical reenactments.

Isabel couldn't go on like this. She had to find her backbone and make a decision. "Fine," she said to Vincent. "Whatever."

"I've never seen you avoid a confrontation so desperately," he said quietly from the doorway. "He must really mean a lot to you."

Embarrassingly close to tears, she balled up a piece of paper and tossed it at him. "Go away, Vincent."

"I'M HERE UNDER protest," Isabel said, stumbling through the door of Midtown Sundries courtesy of Susan's bony finger poking into her back. "I could be watching *American Justice*."

"What?" Susan asked.

"That true-crime show on A&E," Vincent said.

"You'd trade skanky criminals for *Top Gun* volleyball?" Susan asked in disbelief.

"Well—"

"Just keep moving toward the bar," Vincent said.

Isabel ground to a halt as they reached the vast, packed-with-partiers main dining room. "We should rent movies and gorge on ice cream."

"We should keep moving toward the bar," Vincent said.

Knowing when she was beat, Isabel forced herself to take the remaining steps to the bar across the room, where they ordered drinks. Vincent went for whiskey, Susan got her cosmo, which she insisted on also ordering for Isabel. The first sip was intense, but the second and third weren't so bad. By the time they'd claimed a table on the patio with a prime view of the volleyball court, and Isabel had sipped her way close to the bottom of her V-shaped glass, she'd decided cosmos, hot, sweaty guys and sand were a pretty good combination.

They'd arrived halfway into a game, so Susan and Vincent joined in with the rest of the crowd in encouragement and good-natured jeering.

Isabel struggled to put her lousy day behind her. She should be used to professional jealousy, the accusations of family favoritism. She recognized that, from the outside, her life seemed privileged. A degree from Davidson College, an uncle with an important position in a successful company, a quick rise up the corporate ladder.

She wasn't about to sing a sad song on her behalf, so that image would just have to stick. Isolation and resentment were fair trades to keep her pride. And her past private.

The upcoming week in Daytona Beach wouldn't be a picnic, either. Daytona was where NASCAR began racing on the beach in the late 1940s. The fans loved and lived for those two races where they all went back to the beginning, where the speeds pushed close to 200 mph, and even the infield banks of Lake Lloyd rippled with excitement.

Because of that, the media followed in increasingly record numbers. The PR teams from both NASCAR and all the sponsors would work long hours, manage endless press conferences and TV, radio or print interviews, handle dozens of VIPs and manage at least three serious crises. That was the average, anyway.

She needed to put her troubles at work behind her and try to get some sleep while she still could. But lately Cade had been visiting her in her dreams, and she inevitably woke up in a cold sweat in the middle of the night.

When Mr. Irresistible finally arrived, dressed in a form-fitting gray T-shirt and faded jeans, Isabel paused with her second cosmo-filled glass next to her lips. A flush that had nothing to do with alcohol surged to her face. Embarrassed, she glanced around, noting that every female was staring at him. As he was flanked by his buddies—the almost-as-sexy Dean and Jay—who could blame them?

"So maybe dinner isn't such a bad idea," Susan whispered, leaning toward Isabel, though her gaze remained locked on Cade.

"Yesterday you told me if I accepted his dinner offer, the county would be overrun with hail and locusts."

"But he's really hot."

Isabel bit back a smile. Clearly, the stress and long hours were getting to somebody besides her. "Unfortunately, yes."

Susan turned her head and laid her hand over Isabel's. "You're doing what's best for your career."

Why did that sound cold and pathetic rather than smart? "Yeah."

"Hey, Cade!" Vincent said, rising to high-five the driver as he passed their table. "Good luck tonight."

"Thanks." Cade's gaze flicked over Isabel and Susan. "Ladies," he said, then he turned and headed toward the patio steps leading to the sandy volleyball court.

Used to his flirting, his calls and charming messages, Isabel was shocked by his casual dismissal. She stared after him. Disappointment shot through her body.

"Ignoring him *does* seem to be working," Vincent commented.

"Of course it is." Isabel rolled her shoulders. "I wanted him to stop calling and now he will. Mission accomplished."

"But you'll be miserable," Vincent said with a sigh. "And if you're miserable, *I'll* be miserable."

Susan glared at him. "She'll be fine."

"Does she look fine to you?" Vincent countered in an angry whisper.

Isabel stood. "I'm going to the bathroom."

Susan also rose. "No way. You'll try to escape."

Isabel gaped at her friend. "Escape? Are you serious?"

Susan returned to her seat. "I guess not."

"I'll be back," Isabel said.

A trio of blondes had caught Vincent's attention, so she didn't think he was listening. Susan's expression reflected her skepticism.

Isabel fled to the ladies' room to gather her thoughts.

We can keep it a secret, Cade had said. What if they could? If that was possible, would her feelings toward him change? What if she could keep her job safe and see Cade?

The idea was tempting. Risky, but tempting.

Could she really ignore the practical voices in her head—one of which sounded a lot like Susan—and take a chance on something wild, even reckless?

As she walked through the lobby, she nearly ran into Cade. "We've got to stop meeting like this," she said lightly, trying to ignore the excited pounding of her heart.

His gaze was cold as it passed over her face. "Fine by me." He turned away.

Isabel grabbed his arm. "Don't." She licked her lips. What was she doing? What had she *done?* "Don't go."

He stared at her over his shoulder. "I've had enough of this. You don't want to go out with me? Fine. I've got better things to do." He pulled away from her and walked off.

Isabel dragged her hand down her face. She should be happy.

But she wasn't.

She sensed something wonderful and rare was slipping through her fingers. She'd always passed off her attraction to Cade as just a physical thing, but the sinking in her stomach told her differently.

Now? I have to realize this now, *as he's walking away from me?*

She couldn't have figured this out weeks ago, when he was on her heels every time she turned around? Or maybe while she was listening to one of the weekly messages he left, or—hello—*yesterday* when he again left a message and renewed his dinner invitation?

What an idiot she was.

She rushed through the restaurant to the patio, hoping to catch him before the game started. But just as she stepped outside, the ball sailed through the air.

"You came back," Susan said.

Isabel kept her gaze on Cade, tipping the ball over the net. "Yeah."

Before tonight, that man, that gorgeous, successful, exciting man, had been *chasing* her. How often did that happen in a woman's life? Especially a woman with a serious focus on her career?

Idiotic didn't even begin to cover her mistakes.

She sank into her chair and sipped her cosmo, hoping the hollowness would pass. After watching the sweaty, well-built guys on the court for a few minutes, it did. Hot guys pulled a girl away from pitiful desperation every time.

Though, admittedly, it had been a while since she'd paid attention to hot guys. Other than Cade, anyway. In college, she was surrounded by nerdy guys with wire-rimmed glasses rather than hot, confident ones. And for the past five years, even surrounded by both the NFL's and NASCAR's best, brightest and hottest stars, she'd managed to keep her eye on the professional prize.

Other than Cade, anyway.

She crossed her arms on the table and pillowed her head on top.

Susan nudged her. "Stop. You're missing the best part."

Isabel glanced over just as a darkly tanned member of Cade's team spiked the ball into the sand on the other side of the net. "Nice moves."

"*Who is he?*" Susan asked in a breathy whisper.

Isabel squinted. "I'm not sure. Not a NASCAR guy. Probably somebody who works at Garrison Racing." She straightened, angling her head. "He's cute."

"He's *beautiful.*"

Clearly, there was something in the air. Normal, sensible, professional women were falling like teens at a pop star concert.

Around race car drivers, Isabel was used to craziness and even sighing, screaming and fainting women. Most of the time she was embarrassed for her gender. In the case of an overly excited fan, she was either sympathetic or impatient, depending on just *how* excited he or she was.

But since she herself had been afflicted with a recent case of Driver Obsessionitis, she was withholding judgment on everybody.

She watched Cade and Jay slap hands, and her mind drifted to the past, when the slaps between her parents wouldn't stop, when she dreamed that Prince Charming would arrive at the ratty trailer door and take her away from the pain and uncertainty.

She'd envisioned a flawlessly handsome man with dark hair, bright blue eyes and a kind smile, a man who would pull her into his arms and make sure she never suffered again.

Eventually, her Prince Charming *had* come. Only he'd been a relative, a man with warm *brown* eyes who usually smelled like garlicky marinara sauce, but who had the all-important comforting embrace.

Her uncle John had saved her, but with his appearance, part of her romantic, little-girl dreams had disappeared. He'd taught her to rely on herself—her brains, her ambition and her drive to make her life a success—not wait for a prince to come along and give them to her. It was a lesson she'd learned well.

Maybe too well.

As Cade smiled and sweated against the backdrop of the night sky and the dark, rippling lake, some of those dreams rekindled. She didn't have to be alone to be independent. And while she trusted few people, somehow she'd added Cade to that list in the past few months.

He never pretended to be anybody but himself. His motives and goals were stated, and he worked hard to make them come to fruition. He went after what he wanted—which, lately, had been her. He treated everyone with dignity and respect.

Yet, she sensed other layers in him. She was curious about his family dynamic. She wondered how it felt to try to live up to not just one family legend, but three. She wondered if his charming smile sometimes hid private pain.

And she wanted to peel back those layers.

We're talking about one date, Isabel. Get a grip.

When the match was over and Cade's team had won, the patio crowd moved to the sandy court. Most of the audience members were friends or family members of the players, but because of Cade—plus two NASCAR Craftsman Truck Series drivers on the opposing team—fans were mixed in. They stood out by their stunned stares or shyly held-out autograph books.

Cade was, naturally, surrounded by women. And though Isabel's blood heated, she refused to acknowledge her reaction as jealousy.

"I'll be back," she said to Susan as she rose.

"What're you doing?"

"Something I should have done a long time ago."

She headed toward Cade, hanging back while the Flirt Squad did their thing. When he finally realized she was there, their gazes caught over the sea of women. She gave him a self-conscious wave as a few of the women turned to glare at her. He looked away and—she thought—kicked his flirting into high gear. At this rate, the only way she was going to talk to him was if she followed him and whichever woman he chose to their illicit motel room.

You had his attention, and you blew him off.

Her conscience certainly wasn't helping her efforts to be patient, but she had other strengths—

namely, inventiveness. As she'd stepped onto the court, she'd noticed several players digging into a cooler filled with water, ice and towels. Cade's dark, wavy hair was plastered to his forehead, and his shirt was soaked in sweat. One of those icy towels would feel pretty darn great about now.

Humming to herself, she strolled back to the cooler, then bravely plunged her hand into the frigid water and pulled a towel from the depths. After wringing it out, she walked back toward Cade.

He noticed her—or at least the towel—immediately, making her think he'd been watching her the entire time. *Maybe he's not as indifferent as he seems.*

She continued smiling and holding the dripping towel—the precious drops of refreshingly cold water plopping uselessly into the sand—while Cade made an obvious effort to extract himself from his Flirt Squad. The ladies wandered off only after getting his promise that he'd share a beer with them.

Saying nothing, Isabel stepped forward and handed him the towel.

"You couldn't have tossed it?" he shot back. Closing his eyes, he pressed the towel against his flushed face and made even that simple move sensual.

She crossed her arms over her chest. "You can't handle a little heat?"

She hadn't meant the question to come out with multiple meanings, but it did. When Cade wanted to act on their chemistry, *she'd* retreated, not him.

"Seems to me, you're the one who melts," he said.

In more ways than one. Her knees were weak just standing within touching distance of him. "I guess I do."

"What do I owe for this?" he asked, his blue-eyed gaze still distant as he flipped the towel across the back of his neck.

"Nothing."

He held on to the ends of the towel and studied her face. "You're talking to me in public, there must be a reason."

Okay, so she deserved that dig. "I wanted to apologize for ignoring you, for not responding to your messages."

His eyes finally showed signs of interest. "Why didn't you?"

"I was scared. Stupid."

"And you're not anymore?"

"Oh, I still am." She tried out a small smile. "I'm just admitting instead of denying."

"Yeah." He glanced out at the lake. "I've been there."

The humidity-laden air was thick, but surely the tension between them was even thicker. She swallowed. The last time she remembered feeling this awkward she was wearing a frilly pink dress at the ninth-grade Valentine's Day dance. She'd tolerated her classmates' derision because her aunt and uncle had bought her the beautiful—if silly—outfit, hoping she'd feel special.

She searched deep into her soul for a hint of her

normal spine and wound up asking "You still want to go out or not?" with a bit more aggression than she'd planned.

"I don't think so."

Well, what had she expected?

She turned away, but he moved in close behind her, not touching her, but she could feel the heat of his body and his breath stirring the strands of her hair tucked behind her ear. "Don't go."

Her heart leapt, and she recalled asking him the same thing a couple of hours ago. Hesitant to say anything more, but knowing she had to, she pressed her lips together. "Were you serious about—" she lowered her voice "—keeping it secret?"

"Keeping what a secret?"

"Us."

"There's an us?"

She closed her eyes. "There is."

"Then I guess we'll have to keep it a secret." He paused. "Unless you want to quit your job."

Over a guy? she almost said in disbelief. But she kept silent—one, because he was the guy in question, and two, because she wasn't swearing against anything she might do concerning him. Last season, safely tucked away from him and trekking around to NFL games, she never would have believed she'd be behaving as dishonestly and unethically as she was now. A few weeks ago, firm in her belief that her career was everything, she was running from him as fast as she could.

Tonight, she wanted him like never before.

"No, I don't want to quit," she said finally, turning to face him.

He smiled, and she realized everything was going to be all right.

At least until somebody at NASCAR or CATL found out she was going out with a driver, and they called Security just before they fired her and tossed her out of her office and into the business world with nothing but her smart mouth, her pride and her diploma.

"So, I'll pick you up at your house…."

She shook off her paranoid thoughts. "Monday night."

"That's a week away."

"I'm leaving for Daytona in the morning."

"I'll be in Daytona tomorrow night."

"But I'll be working. *You'll* be working."

"I'll see you, though, right?"

"Maybe." She knew he was used to women hanging around for hours just for the opportunity to catch a *glimpse* of him, much less spend exclusive time with him, but she had a job to do. "There's a lot going on."

His eyes flashed—maybe with irritation?—but he nodded. "So Monday."

She fought back the deep, dark-dwelling fear that this attraction to him would be the end of her, and nodded. "Monday."

CHAPTER EIGHT

"MOM'S ON THE PHONE!" Rachel yelled from the outer office.

Cade darted to the doorway. He shook his head violently. "I can't talk to her now," he whispered.

Rachel didn't even bother to turn away from her computer screen and look at him. "You don't have to whisper. She's on hold."

He breathed a sigh of relief. "Great. So tell her—"

"I'm not telling her anything, brother dear. It's your turn."

"But she wants to talk about a new silverware pattern for Thanksgiving dinner. I've been avoiding her for two days."

"She decided on Le Pois from Williams-Sonoma."

"So what does she need me for?"

"She's trying to decide on china."

"*China?* As in the country or the plates?"

"As in plates."

He tugged on the ends of his hair. "She's obsessed with Thanksgiving!"

Rachel continued typing. "Look at it this way, she

could be obsessed with St. Patrick's Day and spend all day singing songs about death and drinking green beer."

That didn't cheer him up very much. "It's July. Don't you think it's a little early for Thanksgiving?"

"She's a planner. She always has been."

"It's worse since the divorce."

"Which is why she needs our support."

"I don't know anything about china," he said desperately.

"Don't worry. She'll do all the talking."

"I can't—"

"Go, Cade," Rachel said, glaring at him over her shoulder. "She's your mother."

Sagging, he banged the back of his head against the door frame.

"*Now,* Cade."

"I'm going, I'm going." He trudged across his office, then picked up the phone. "I was just on my way over to the shop, Mom."

"The shop can get by without you for a few minutes, Cade Michael."

Oh, boy. The middle name. "Yes, ma'am."

"Thanksgiving is a time for family."

"Yes, ma'am."

"Not that your father ever remembered that. There was always another race, or test or sponsor event."

Since that was Cade's mind-set, too, commenting didn't seem smart.

"*This* year will be different."

He swallowed. How did mothers manage to be stern and sympathetic at the same time? "Yes, ma'am."

"I decided on the Le Pois. Did your sister tell you?"

"Yes, ma'am."

"But I just can't narrow down the china patterns. How do you feel about bluebells?"

Cade closed his eyes. *Please don't let anybody I know hear this conversation.* He'd been through a lot of weird stuff with his parents—his dad's bearskin rug came to mind—but he had to draw the line somewhere. "Mom, I'm not really—"

"You're right. Bluebells are too…precious. How about daffodils?"

"Are we eating these daffodils?"

"No, sweetie. They're part of the pattern. Haven't you ever walked through Macy's china department?"

The only time a man went into the china department was when he was dragged there by his fiancée, and Cade had no plans to walk down the aisle anytime soon. "Mom, I don't really—"

"We could always go with the plain silver or gold band." She paused, and he prayed she'd made her decision. "But then that's *too* plain, isn't it?"

He slumped in his chair.

"So we're back to daffodils. They're yellow and cheerful, but really more of a spring flower."

"And Thanksgiving is in the…fall, right?" Cade said hesitantly.

"That's exactly right, sweetie," his mother said as

if he'd just rattled off his times tables correctly—the way he had in fourth grade. "They really need to come out with a mum-pattered series."

Cade's gaze jumped around the room. Was that window wired to the security system? Could he survive a jump from the third floor? "Sure they do."

"Or maybe fall leaves. They have dozens of Christmas patterns now. Why not Thanksgiving?"

"I have no idea."

Was there any liquor in his office? A six-pack maybe?

He rose from his chair and stretched toward the bookcase, while still keeping the phone next to his ear as his mother continued to make the argument for Thanksgiving plates.

The grocery store had plenty of plates. He saw them on the charcoal/dishwashing soap/toothpick aisle when he bought supplies for his annual Last Game of the College Football Season party. They were paper plates, but did anybody care?

No. At least not the wings-'n'-beer crowd he hosted. And he wasn't much interested in anybody beyond that.

She's your mother, his conscience reminded him.

Plus, this wasn't about plates.

"There *is* a lovely pattern with swirls and dots," his mother said, obviously talking about china, not paper.

Unable to find any booze and deciding the ground

was too far away to jump from the window, Cade
sank into his desk chair.

The break-room fridge had plenty of Go!, but
that would energize him, not dull the pain. Rachel
was always advocating herbal tea. Maybe she'd be
willing to share.

"How do you feel about swirls and dots,
sweetie?"

"I—" His head pounded. His mind reeled. "I... love
swirls and dots. I think swirls and dots are *perfect!*"

"But I haven't even told you what colors they
come in."

"Swirls and dots, ah...transcend color."

His mother was silent for several long moments—during which Cade prayed she'd agree. He
was pretty sure his brain was going to explode if he
had to talk about plates, swirls and dots and daffodils for one more insane second.

"You're right, dear," she said finally. "It *is* perfect.
And I have plenty of time to decide the color later."

Cade sighed in relief. "Yes, you do."

And thought of his brother.

Specifically, he recalled their conversation earlier
that morning, when he'd asked Bryan if he'd make
some phone calls to potential sponsors. Cade had a
money-pit car under construction courtesy of his
family's business, plus a reputation and career to
rebuild, but no one's name or logo to put on the
outside of his race car.

His brother, grumpy as usual, had groused and

scowled before agreeing to help. Grudging help was better than no help at all. Still…

"Why don't you ask Bryan about the color?" Cade suggested to his mother.

"I don't know, sweetie. He's so temperamental these days."

"Not to you. You're his mother."

"Well, yes, I am." She cleared her throat. "Thank you, dear."

"Glad to help. Bye."

Cade dropped the phone in its cradle and smiled as he leaned back in his chair.

"That was cold," Rachel said as she walked into his office.

"If I have to talk about plates, so does he."

Rachel sat in the chair in front of his desk. "And he has a payback coming because he's not doing more to get you a sponsor for Chicago."

"I'm not driving a blank car."

"We'll find somebody. We're supposed to hear back from Grant Tools today."

Cade rolled a pen across his desk. His cheerfulness at messing with his brother faded. "Some mistakes you never stop paying for."

"Give it more time."

"Yeah. Sure."

"Why don't you talk to Isabel Turner at CATL?"

Cade fumbled the pen, which rolled off the desk.

"You guys are friends, aren't you?" Rachel continued.

"Ah, no. We, ah, know each other, but I'm not sure we're, ah, friends exactly."

"Well, *ah,* I think you should use every contact you've got."

"Sure. Okay." Sweat broke out on his forehead. If Rachel caught wind of anything going on between him and Isabel, she'd lose it.

His sister had stood by him all his life. She continued to support him while he fought against his now-volatile reputation. She'd calmed down Bryan and Dad when they'd wanted him pushing a broom around the shop rather than driving a race car for them. She kept him on schedule, ran his fan club and made sure his bills were paid.

If he got them involved in another scandal, when he was trying to change his image, when he was trying to attract a NASCAR NEXTEL Cup sponsor, when he wanted to build the one-race deal into a full season, well, he wouldn't need NASCAR's reprimand.

His sister would kill him.

"Though I guess CATL's Blast energy drink is a competitor of Go!," Rachel said. "So you can't use them."

"Right." Cade grabbed onto the excuse as if it were a lifeline. "That definitely wouldn't be good."

"In fact," Rachel said, leaning forward, "you probably shouldn't even be talking to her."

"Oh, come on, Rach. That's kind of extreme. Talking to her isn't going to violate my contract with

Go!. Besides, she's at the track all the time. I'm supposed to ignore her when she walks by?"

Rachel's eyes gleamed, and he realized he'd given away too much. "She's at the track all the time, huh?"

"CATL sponsors twenty drivers," he said.

"Five, actually."

He'd known that, of course, but he said nothing. The look in his sister's eyes was unnerving. It was time to cut his losses and get moving before he blew everything. "No kidding?" He rose. "I'm—"

"You're not doing anything stupid, are you?"

"What would I be doing?" he asked, going for shocked and hurt—and pretty sure he was pulling it off.

"Isabel is a smart, beautiful woman."

He angled his head. "Is she?"

Rachel slapped her hand on the desk. "Now I *know* you're doing something stupid."

"I'm not."

"You're lying. There's no way that a woman who looks like her has escaped your wandering eye."

She's not just pretty, Cade wanted to say. *She's kind and has the sharpest wit. She's—*

He cut himself off. So he had a thing for her. Big deal. That was as far as their relationship went. And as long as they flew under the NASCAR, CATL and Rachel radar, that's all it would ever be.

"I've seen you and your buddies sitting on the pit wall, commenting on the hot chicks who walk by," Rachel said.

Because of this thing with Isabel, he hadn't done that in weeks. He hadn't wanted to. Hadn't even considered it. Maybe keeping his and Isabel's relationship—and their secret—wasn't going to be as simple as he'd thought.

"I think I'll go over to the shop," he said as he headed toward the door.

"Don't even *think* about avoiding me," Rachel said, following him into the hall. "We need to talk."

"I've got to check on my car for the race Friday night." He darted down the hall. "We'll talk later," he called over his shoulder.

"Your car for Friday night is in Daytona Beach, you idiot!"

CADE PUSHED HIS WORRIES about his sister aside as he rode the elevator down to the bottom floor.

He didn't want to face her, or the mistake he might be making in his pursuit of Isabel.

Though from the outside GRI seemed to be housed in an ordinary three-story brick office building, inside most of the space was devoted to a manufacturing plant. Only one wing was devoted to office space, and only on the second and third floors. The first floor contained the company racing museum, which was open to the public.

On a Wednesday, just before noon, the museum was deserted, so he strolled through, sliding his hand across the hood of a mangled car his father had wrecked and walked away from at Talladega many years ago. He smiled in the direction of his Busch championship car from '03. His gaze shifted to Bryan's car from his 2004 win in Atlanta.

His *last* win.

He turned away from those memories and rounded the corner where the floor-to-ceiling, octagonal-shaped trophy case stood. Inside were his father's and grandfather's championship trophies—two for Dad, one for Grandad. On the shelf under them was Bryan's inaugural NASCAR NEXTEL Cup trophy.

A bit farther down sat both his and Bryan's NASCAR Busch Series trophies. The guitar he'd won at Nashville last month took up most of the bottom shelf on one side. Three trophies from the season opener in Daytona were scattered through the case—one for his grandfather, two for Bryan.

Like his father, Cade had never had the honor. Though at least he had a chance to still get the win. His father, thanks to that scumbag Joe Baker, had never gotten his.

Mixed among the trophies were pictures. Group pictures of teams after winning at Bristol, North Wilkesboro, Texas, Atlanta and dozens of others. Pictures of his father during his racing years at Hester/McCray Motorsports, where he'd won both his championships, and before GRI had even existed. Pictures of his family at the awards banquet in the Waldorf-Astoria ballroom in New York. Pictures of victories, pit stops, burnouts and wrecks that spanned more than fifty years.

The clothing styles, uniforms and equipment had changed quite a bit. Not so long ago, the drivers had worn open-faced helmets, and pit crew hadn't even worn helmets at all. The race cars had once looked like they'd been driven directly off the highway and onto the track. As the sport grew, the tracks had added luxury skyboxes, bigger and better stands, more conveniences and attractions. The fans had changed from mostly rural Southern men to people of all genders, locations, races and economic levels.

As he walked through the museum and toward the restricted access door to the shop, he passed two Martinsville clocks—one each for Bryan and Dad. His father actually had another one. It had always sat in the basement rec room at their house. He wondered if it was still there.

Pausing, he stared at the clocks.

How did you separate thirty-two years of combined assets? Was it still *their* house? Their family house? Or was it now only Mom's place?

Who did the plates and silverware belong to? Who got the photo albums and lamps?

His mother had a great sense of style and favored traditional antiques. Clearly, given the state of the track condo, his father hadn't taken any of the furniture. Had he wanted to buy new stuff, or had there been a bitter argument over the chairs, candlesticks and monogrammed towels?

"Hey, Cade, when do ya leave for Daytona?"

Cade turned toward GRI's best—and only—security man, Barnie. "Plane leaves at three."

Barnie, his dark hair slicked meticulously to one side—probably with some ancient oil product—hooked his thumbs through the belt loops on his pressed khaki pants and eyed Cade shrewdly. "You gonna get me a win?"

Cade smiled. So maybe his fan club membership was down, and he didn't have a sponsor for Chicago, and his sister might find out he was breaking some serious rules and dump his rebel backside in the street, but he had Barnie. "I'll certainly try."

Barnie rocked back on his heels. "Gotta do better than try. Everybody wants to win at Daytona."

"We've got a hell of a car."

"That's what I like to hear." He lowered his voice. "But I won't tell anybody."

"I'd appreciate that. We don't want to show our hand too early."

"I'm used to keeping secrets, ya know. You can count on me."

"I know."

Barney had served on his grandfather's pit crew toward the end of his career. Back in the day, when, *ahem*...skimming the rules had been just a part of smart competition, Barney had been a fuel-mileage expert. He'd gotten extra miles out of tanks that the rest of the field could only dream about.

"Tuck behind somebody," Barney said. "Draft

and save that fuel." He winked. "Ya never know when ya might need it."

"I'll do it." Cade swung open the shop door. "Thanks."

As he walked through the bright, spotlessly clean shop, he waved at the guys working on cars in various forms of preparation.

All the cars at GRI started out the same way—molding and fabricating, building the frames and adding the shell of the car to conform to NASCAR's template specifications, so that the measurements were identical to every other Chevrolet in the field, either NASCAR NEXTEL Cup Series or NASCAR Busch Series. Then, once they had the car built, the individual teams' engineers took over to add their own setups. The cars then all slid down to the next section, where the paint and decals were applied. Eventually, they were loaded into the haulers and transported to a race.

Just beyond the fabrication section of the warehouse, he walked past NASCAR NEXTEL Cup drivers Shawn and Kevin's engineering sections, where the technical people were checking balance and studying wind tunnel data, always trying to find a little more power to gain that extra edge. After that, he reached his team's prep area. True to Rachel's astute understanding of the manufacturing schedule, his Daytona car was long gone. At the moment, they were working on his car for Gateway, the St. Louis-area track.

He talked to the team engineers for a while about

the handling, and their strategy for changes, depending on how the car ran in practices. His record in St. Louis was good, so he was pretty confident about how the car would run.

When his cell phone rang, and his office number appeared on the screen, he excused himself and walked over to the corner. If it was his mother, needing his advice about tablecloths, he was tossing the phone out the window.

"Hello?"

"Are you sitting down?" Rachel asked.

"No. I'm in the shop." Was he supposed to sit while the guys fought and sweated to weld, mold and balance *his* cars? Why couldn't she— He stopped as he considered the quiet tone of her words. Something was wrong. "Should I be sitting down?"

"Yes."

His heart dropped to his shoes. "Is Mom okay? Dad? What—"

"Oh, good grief. It's not anything like that. Parker Huntington just called."

"Huntington? As in the Huntington I slugged to end my Cup career?"

"Your Cup career isn't over, and do you know somebody else with a pretentious name like that?"

"What did he want?"

"Are you sure you don't want to sit down?"

"No."

"He wants to talk to you about a sponsorship for Chicago," Rachel said quietly.

Several emotions rolled through Cade—excitement, disappointment, then guilt over both reactions. He ended up at suspicion. What was behind this generous offer? It certainly wasn't to make up with him.

Or was it? Was it possible the Huntingtons realized he was a benefit instead of a liability? They hadn't signed on with another team. Had their business suffered?

He'd always been a great spokesperson for Huntington Hotels. He'd been happy there—at least until Sumner Huntington, Parker's father, had promoted his son to president, grooming him to take over complete control of the company. Then that slick, Harvard Business School graduate Parker had started putting more pressure on the team. He'd given Cade and his crew chief advice and he'd demanded more time from Cade's schedule for promotion and personal appearances. He'd questioned expense reports. He'd criticized Cade's driving. He'd been overbearing and annoying. The final straw had been his interest in Rachel.

Cade had snapped and thrown the fateful punch in August of last year, just after the Michigan race.

"Are you okay?"

"I guess."

"What do you want to do?"

He sighed. Why did he feel like he was being offered a deal for a cooling retreat to the mountains from the Devil himself? "I guess I have to talk to him."

"I think we should."

"I'm not sure it's a good idea if you're there."

"Why?"

"He has a thing for you."

"Maybe he'll offer us more money if I'm there to distract him."

Cade clenched his jaw. "That's not funny."

"I'm kidding," she said with a sigh. "He doesn't have a *thing* for me. He tries to smooth-talk everybody. And even if he was attracted to me, I don't like him."

"I must be desperate to even consider working with him again."

"You're desperate, all right. And it won't hurt to listen to what he has to say. I've already set up a meeting for Friday morning at the track."

Did he have a choice? Cade couldn't imagine the humiliation if he showed up in Chicago with an unsponsored car. He wished he could talk to Isabel and ask her advice. Once he got to his motorcoach tonight, maybe he could find a moment alone to call her. Maybe Go! wouldn't object to one of CATL's other brands sponsoring him. But then that would push his and Isabel's personal relationship even farther into forbidden territory. She wasn't supposed to get involved with *any* of the drivers, but if he asked her to make a special deal for him, and he became one of CATL's drivers— even temporarily—they would be crossing all the way over the line, not just putting a toe over on the other side.

No. He couldn't ask her. Her business ethics were

an important part of who she was, and he'd already asked her to risk a great deal for him. It looked like he was stuck with Huntington.

"Cade?"

"Yeah, okay. Meeting, Friday."

"It was a nice punch, by the way."

"Thanks."

"Just not one you want to repeat."

He managed a weak laugh. "No kidding."

"Especially during lunch and definitely not before he gives us a check."

"I'll try to restrain myself," he said. "Bye, Rach," then he flipped the phone closed.

CHAPTER NINE

"TRAVEL PACK OF WIPES?" Isabel asked.

Susan, sitting cross-legged on the floor of the media center conference room, inspected a box next to her. "Check."

"Mini pack of Fudge Stars."

"Check."

"Travel sunscreen."

Susan turned to the box behind her. "Check. This is going to take all night, you know."

Isabel checked off sunscreen on her list. "Not if we're organized. Credential holder?"

Susan crawled to another grouping of boxes a few feet away. "Check. Maybe we could get some cute guys to help?"

"All the cute guys went to the beach bars."

"Where *we* should be," Susan whined. "Come on, Isabel, let's have some fun. We could do this in the morning."

"If you go to a bar tonight, you won't feel like doing this in the morning, either."

"You don't have to drink, you know. It's a social

thing. You remember that, don't you? Interaction with other humans?"

"You're interacting with me."

"You're not human," Susan muttered.

"I heard that. CATL logo backpack?"

"That's what's in those huge boxes against the wall." When Isabel glanced up to stare at her, she added, "I saw them earlier. Twenty-something females do not come to the beach and spend every waking moment locked up in a conference room, stuffing VIP gift bags."

"They do if they want to keep their job."

"All work and no play…"

"We just went out on Tuesday."

"That was for you. This is for me."

Isabel sighed. "You're pouting."

Obviously sensing when to push her advantage, Susan rose and poked her lip even farther out. "Wasn't I a true and supportive friend on Tuesday? Didn't I pull you out of your funk? Didn't I tell you I would back your decision to go out with Cade Garrison—even though I still think you're making a mistake?"

Isabel felt the first stirrings of guilt. Though watching Cade play shirtless volleyball had had more of an impact on lifting her mood than anything else, she would have missed the whole thing if Susan and Vincent hadn't dragged her out in the first place. "I want half the stuff in the bags tonight."

Susan yanked her into a hug.

"And we start again at 8:00 a.m. tomorrow."

"*Eight?* But—"

"We still have a meet and greet before the Busch race tomorrow, then two on Saturday."

Susan leaned back, her blue eyes pleading, but she obviously saw that Isabel wasn't giving any more leeway than she had. "Deal."

"Let's get moving."

They worked for two hours, laying the 125 VIP bags in rows and placing the gift items inside one by one. The Race Day Survival Pack was a big hit with the customers they brought to the races throughout the year. They included practical, as well as fun items and tried to make their track experience special and memorable, which would hopefully translate to more sales and loyal customers for CATL. Her uncle received more compliments about this initiative than any other program, and Isabel was proud of the changes she'd contributed.

"That's the last of the disposable cameras," Susan said, walking to Isabel's side to help her distribute the sunscreen packets left in her box.

Once that was accomplished, Isabel kept her promise and set aside her clipboard. She followed Susan out of the conference room, and they headed to the parking lot.

They rode to a favored beach bar called the Ocean Deck in Isabel's rental car with the windows rolled down and the rushing Atlantic Ocean breeze pushing away all their job-related stress. Susan told her she'd found out the bronzed volleyball player she'd seen earlier in the week worked for a racing team. He was Derek Foster's jack man.

"The jack alone weighs thirty-five pounds, did you know that?" Susan said dreamily, staring out the window at the nearly darkened summer sky.

Somehow that useless bit of trivia had escaped Isabel's notice. "No kidding?"

"That doesn't even count the power it takes to hike up a 3,400-pound race car."

"I imagine not."

"And yet he's so sweet. And gentle. He has the softest voice."

"Does Mr. Jack Man frequent the Ocean Deck by any chance?" Isabel asked as she wound her way through the bar's parking lot.

Susan's smile was dazzling. "Now that you mention it…"

Given that Isabel had her own gorgeous man to obsess about, who was she to judge anybody else with the same affliction?

The club's music was louder than she liked and was packed with lots of barely clothed, partying beach-goers, but after convincing Susan to sit on the deck, Isabel happily sipped soda and enjoyed the ocean breeze and tangy salt in the air. Okay, so maybe getting away from the track had been a good idea. Race weekend was always hectic and stressful. Daytona was even more so than others.

Mr. Jack Man—whose name was actually Rex— found Susan and joined them after a while. Being protective of her sometimes too-trusting friend, Isabel was prepared to be skeptical, but she, too, found him sweet and gentle.

With Susan and Rex cooing over each other, and the romantic rise and swell of the ocean just yards away, Isabel's thoughts drifted to Cade. She wondered where he was. Partying at a similar club with his buddies? Attending a team dinner or strategy meeting? Entertaining fans at a sponsor function?

She knew he'd flown in yesterday and had hoped he might call, but she hadn't heard from him. The irony that she'd gone from avoiding his phone calls to wildly anticipating them in a matter of days wasn't lost on her.

"I think we're boring Isabel," Rex said.

Isabel turned her head away from the white-capped waves. "No. I'm just tired. And thinking."

"She's planning more work for herself." Susan gave her a teasing smile. "And probably me."

Isabel raised her eyebrows. "We *do* have an early day tomorrow."

Rex rose. "Me, too. We've got pit stop drills to run at seven." He pulled Susan to her feet, then moved back Isabel's chair. "Come on, ladies, I'll follow you back to your hotel."

"I'll be fine," Isabel said. "You take Susan."

"Susan, you can ride with me if you want, but I'm going to follow Isabel either way."

Susan hooked her arm through Rex's and gazed up at him adoringly. "Such a gentleman."

"Thanks," Isabel said to Rex, somehow holding back her smile.

They wound their way through the rowdy club and to their cars, with Susan and Rex following Isabel. On the drive back to the hotel, she wondered if she was as obvious about her attraction to Cade as Susan was with Rex.

Surely not.

She was pretty good with poker faces, and she was pretty positive *adoring* wasn't an emotion in her repertoire. Maybe someday she'd feel that open with a man. For now, she needed to keep her emotions in check, or their big, fat secret date was going to blow up in their faces real quick.

Susan and Rex decided to sit in the hotel's bar for a while, but Isabel excused herself and headed to the elevators. If she and Cade made it through their first date without getting caught, and then made it through a second or even a third, to the point they could be considering "dating," their public moments would be extremely limited.

She wasn't interested in flaunting her private relationships. She didn't like Cade because he was a famous race car driver. In fact, their relationship would be a whole lot simpler if he wasn't. But would never being seen in public together wear thin? Could she really lie to everyone but her closest friends about their relationship? What if some flirty blonde tried to crawl all over Cade and Isabel couldn't even slug her?

Shaking her head at her crazy speculations, she slid her room card into the door lock. She'd worry about all that if it became a problem. For now, she was dealing with things day by day.

Just as she closed the door, her cell phone rang.

She sighed. If this was some problem at the track… Glancing at the ID screen, though, she saw Cade's number. "Hey."

"Hey, Izzy."

A rush of happiness flooded her at the sound of his voice. The nickname that usually annoyed her was suddenly endearing. Smiling, she flopped backward onto her bed without turning on the lights. "What's up?"

"I wanted to call you last night, but by the time I was alone it was after eleven. I didn't want to wake you."

The sound of his quiet, deep voice in the darkened hotel room made the casual conversation seem much more intimate. She wished she could see him, touch him. "I was still at the track."

"That late?"

"We have a lot of VIPs coming in tomorrow."

"Where are you now?"

"At the hotel."

"Where at the hotel?"

"Lying on the bed. Where are you?"

"Lying on the sofa in my coach." He paused, then his voice deepened further. "You wanna lie together?"

She laughed. "I like the way you think, Garrison."

"I could be there in ten minutes."

Wow, the man was a temptation. Swallowing hard, she reminded herself that not only did she need sleep to prepare for the long day tomorrow, his day was bound to be even more grueling—with driver meetings, sponsor functions and driving a 400-mile race. "Too bad you have to rest up for tomorrow night."

"I'm pretty resilient."

"I'm exhausted."

"I bet I can wake you up."

Her heart kicked at her chest. Remembering his skills in that area, she waved her hand in front of her flushed face. "I'm sure you could."

"I'll be right there."

"Cade," she said quietly, with genuine regret, "if you come over here now, we're going to take a step we're not ready for. Look what happened the last time we jumped ahead without thinking."

"We had a really good time."

They had. And while she didn't have a problem with good times, she wanted to see if there was more. "Is that what you want with me—a really good time?"

"No. Yes."

He sighed, and she understood his frustration. Their attraction was electric, and their one night together wasn't something easily forgotten.

"Let's have our date and see what happens," she said.

He sighed. "I'm gonna have some pretty detailed suggestions then."

"I can't wait to hear them."

"Are you planning to wear a dress?"

"I hadn't thought about it. Why?"

"I've never seen you in a dress."

He'd seen *everything*. What difference did a dress make? "So you want me to wear one?"

"Yeah, if you—"

Knock, knock, knock.

"Hang on, somebody's here." She rolled off the bed, then peeked through the hole in the door. Susan was standing in the hall, grinning like a fool.

Though Susan knew about her and Cade, Isabel was self-conscious about talking to him in front of her friend. If the positions were reversed, she wondered if she'd be as understanding about Susan breaking the rules. Would she judge her friend as unprofessional? Even reckless?

"This is the price you pay for keeping secrets," she whispered to herself.

"What?" Cade asked.

"Nothing. Susan's here." She opened the door and waved her friend in, watching her sway and twirl toward the large window overlooking the ocean.

Oh, good grief, she's in love.

Again.

"I need to go," she said to Cade, leaning back against the door briefly before heading to the desk so she could fill a glass with ice and water for her high-on-love friend.

"I'll see you tomorrow?"

"Maybe. Hopefully," she added. "It'll be a crazy day."

"I want a good-luck kiss before I race."

Isabel literally stopped in her tracks. "How the devil are we supposed to manage that?"

"I don't know, but we will. Keep your Black-Berry on."

It was *always* on. Usually it signaled a problem, urgent summons or question. It *never* signaled a kiss.

As if he sensed her hesitation, he added, "I need to see you."

She closed her eyes and absorbed the emotion behind those words. "Me, too. We'll manage." She disconnected the call, sighing with equal parts anti-cipation and dread.

When had her life gotten so complicated? Work was hectic and multifaceted, but not complex. Her personal life was…well, hanging with Vincent and Susan, hoping Vincent could remember which in-credibly beautiful woman he was dating and hoping Susan didn't lose her heart—again—to another guy who didn't deserve her devotion.

All predictable. Relatively simple. Mostly fulfilling.

Sure, there was a lot missing. Nobody to go home to. Nobody to really share everything with. Nobody to hold her when she was exhausted and unmotivated.

But did she have to go from 20 mph to 180? Did she have to go from steady to wildly exciting and dangerous in one step?

From life as she'd known it to Cade Garrison?

"Who were you talking to?" Susan asked dreamily as she flopped back on the bed.

"Nobody."

"I'll bet it was Cade." Smiling, she waved her hand in the air, distinctly drawing the shape of a heart. "He's so cute."

"Are you drunk?"

"No." She heaved a sigh. "I'm in love."

To keep from laughing—or saying *I told you so*—Isabel pressed her lips together, then extended the glass of ice water to her friend. "No kidding."

ON FRIDAY MORNING—race morning for him—Cade walked through the infield toward his team's hauler. Since the race wasn't until that night, he was still dressed in jeans and a T-shirt. Maybe he should have fixed up more for his meeting with Parker Huntington.

But he hadn't.

He still carried a giant chip on his shoulder for Huntington. One he couldn't completely explain. Huntington was the supposedly injured party, after all. After Cade had slugged him, Huntington had simply glared at him. He'd barely flinched. He hadn't rubbed his rapidly bruising jaw. He'd said nothing. In fact, they hadn't exchanged a word since that moment. Their lawyers had done all the talking since that fateful day.

After he'd calmed down and realized the full extent of his rash swing, Cade had done some research on his nemesis. He'd always dismissed Huntington's critiques and advice on racing. He'd always taken the comments as a personal attack rather than genuine concern for improvement. What did a rich, pretty boy know about racing, anyway?

Apparently, a lot.

Parker Huntington had raced motocross for five years. He'd done so under an assumed name, won some significant titles and broken some bones. Cade wasn't sure what had driven him to give up the handlebars for the boardroom, but he was interested in finding out.

As for his sister…

Rachel could date anyone she wanted—though he didn't like to think about what went on *during* those dates. But it was his brotherly duty to look after her, and Parker Huntington somehow brought out the protective worst in him. There was a look in that guy's eye he just didn't like, didn't want to acknowledge.

Still, it wasn't just Rachel that made him clench his fists as Cade walked through the hauler doors. He realized the pressure to live up to his family name had gotten to him way before Huntington had. He'd just been a handy target.

Moving through the hauler, toward the office/locker room in the back, the quarters were tight, so he turned sideways as he passed a couple of crew members arguing over how best to heat the popcorn bag in the microwave. They barely acknowledged him. He could only hope they'd be more attentive to their crew chief later tonight.

He opened the door and found Sam Benefield, his crew chief, sitting at the small desk and cursing at the computer screen.

"I hope that's not our engine specs," Cade said as he reached into the minifridge for a can of Go!

"Do you have any idea what it costs to have packages shipped these days?" Sam asked, still glaring at the screen.

Cade collapsed onto the curved black leather sofa fitted into the corner of the room. "Too much?"

"Hell, yes." Sam clicked through a few screens. "I'm trying to send my niece a birthday present. You'd think I was trying to go three-wide into a turn at Bristol."

"At least you're not sitting through the meeting from hell."

"You and Huntington together again, huh?"

"How do you—"

"Son, you can't sneeze in the garage without somebody reporting it to me. Well, hell, yeah, I want to pay an additional four dollars and ninety-five cents for gift wrapping. You think I'm some kind of cheapskate?"

Sam was talking to a computer that couldn't talk back, but Cade had no intention of pointing that out. He was through alienating team members. And sponsors. If Rich Boy Huntington wanted to give him some money to put his family's hotel empire on his car, then Cade was swallowing his pride and pretending to be grateful.

Well, maybe he'd be genuinely grateful, but the whole out-of-the-blue nature of this meeting still had him on edge.

"Oh, good, you're here," Rachel said when she walked through the door. "Hey, Sam."

"You have any idea what it costs to ship a damn doll these days?"

As Rachel leaned over Sam to commiserate with him about unfair shipping costs, Cade tried to relax. He glanced out the window at the people wandering by the hauler. NASCAR officials and team members in their uniforms, track workers, TV crews and fans all buzzed about. Most people were already red-faced and sweating. July in central Florida was an endurance race meant for only the strongest of humankind. In fact, without air-conditioning, he'd bet only alligators had flourished.

Isabel is out there somewhere.

She was doing her job, talking to people, solving problems. He wanted to see her. He wanted to watch a reluctant smile break over her face. He wanted to see her scowl at him when he suggested something rule-bending. Or breaking.

He wanted that kiss.

"So, are we ready, little brother?" Rachel asked as she turned away from Sam to face him.

Cade shrugged, trying not to betray how much he wanted and needed this meeting to go well. "Sure."

"We're going to keep the past in the past and move forward?"

"Sure."

"We're going to be nice?"

"This isn't kindergarten."

She stared down at him and crossed her arms over her chest. "Isn't it?"

Okay, so maybe it was long past time for a face-to-face apology with Huntington. But if he gave his sister that look...

"Yes, thank you," said a familiar voice from just outside the room. "Coffee would be very much appreciated."

Cade clamped down on the urge to roll his eyes at the bowing and scraping from the crew member who answered Huntington. NASCAR wouldn't exist without big-money sponsors like Huntington Hotels. Unlike stick-and-ball sports, racing was far too expensive to support itself without help from the corporate world.

"Be nice," Rachel said quietly as she sat beside him, just seconds before Parker Huntington appeared in the doorway.

He was a tall, athletic-looking guy most women would go for without any prompting. He had a sculpted face and jet-black hair that was so perfect Cade just knew it had to be colored. His eyes were a piercing bright green, which had no doubt intimidated many men and seduced many women.

Cade wasn't intimidated, and he wouldn't let his sister be seduced.

"Good morning, Cade, Rachel." Huntington

walked forward with his hand outstretched in that too-smooth way he had of moving and talking. "It's good to see you both."

They both rose and shook his hand briefly. Personally, Cade thought Huntington's gaze and hand lingered too long on Rachel, but he was willing to *be nice.*

Provided the guy had a big, fat check in his pocket.

After exchanging a few words with Sam, who then left the room, and accepting a foam coffee cup from a crew member, Huntington settled at the opposite end of the sofa from Cade and Rachel. "So, I hear your season is going well," he said, then smiled at Cade.

Huntington's teeth were also too white. And they stood out even starker against his tanned face. He'd bet his race car's engine the guy got his rays in a tanning bed, not sweating in the sun.

Cade held Huntington's gaze. What the hell was he doing? Was he really desperate enough to accept help from this guy? "Look, I—"

Rachel kicked him. "The season is great. We're fifth in the championship standings."

"Sam is an excellent crew chief." Again, Huntington smiled. "And we all know what a talented driver Cade is."

Talented, but abandoned by his sponsor. Did Huntington have any idea how humiliating that had been? And he sure hadn't bothered to tell him about talent. He'd been too busy giving driving advice. "I'm not so—"

"He's got those Garrison genes," Rachel said tightly. "And he's matured a lot over the past year."

Cade was fed up with being talked about as if he wasn't there. "Look, I was mature before—"

Rachel ignored him and continued. "The Busch series has been wonderful for his career in the past, but we all know he belongs in a car on Sunday."

"Does he?" Huntington asked, looking amused.

"You know he does, Parker," Rachel said, leaning back and giving him her *this is my meeting* look. "And you called us, remember?"

Huntington sipped his coffee, but his gaze lingered on Rachel's face. "I did."

Did he even need to be here? Cade's gaze shifted to his sister. Rachel looked nice, but she always did. Was Huntington overwhelmed by her beauty, her brains or her steely glare? He didn't seem flustered. But there was that look in his eyes—one he was obviously trying to control, though he didn't quite pull it off. One thing was certain as far as Cade was concerned.

Parker Huntington wanted to see his sister naked.

"I agree Cade should be racing on Sunday if that's where he wants to be," Huntington said.

"I want what I had," Cade said, holding on to his temper by a thread.

Huntington finally shifted his gaze to Cade. "I'm sure you do."

As if she sensed his anger, Rachel leaned forward

to gain Huntington's attention. "Cade's talent is a valuable commodity."

"But not so talented or so valuable to keep you from dumping me last year," Cade added.

Huntington looked amused. "You hit me."

"You deserved it."

Huntington rubbed his jaw—maybe unconsciously or maybe to remind Cade of what he'd lost. "Perhaps I did."

Cade still got the sense that Huntington had another agenda. Was he really admitting he'd made a mistake? Somehow, he didn't think so. Clenching his fists, Cade rose. "What do you want?"

"I thought it was time to put the past behind us."

Cade continued to stare down at him.

Finally, Huntington sighed. He held his coffee cup between his hands and stared at the floor. "My father is retiring. Next year, *I* will be president *and* CEO of Huntington Hotels. Our association with NASCAR has been a family tradition. One I'd like to continue. And I want to continue it with a proven winner."

"Me."

Huntington looked up. "Whatever's happened between us, Cade, you were good for my company. You're a competitor, the fans like you and you don't give up. That's the kind of man I need."

"So…"

"So, I'm offering a sponsorship for Indy, Charlotte and Homestead. If your performance is up to par—"

"We'll need specifics there," Rachel interrupted. "Do you want him to just qualify and finish? Or are you expecting something more?"

"As he's so eloquently pointed out, Cade knows what he's doing. He's no nervous rookie. I want top-ten finishes, and anything below twenty is unacceptable."

"That's a pretty demanding requirement," Rachel said.

"I'm a pretty demanding guy." Huntington stood, his height and breadth equal to Cade's. "And remember," he continued, "if the performance is there, I'd like to continue our association into next year with a full NASCAR NEXTEL Cup Series sponsorship."

Cade went rigid. "A full season?"

"Contract money, TV and print ads, the works. You'll be our spokesman, and we'll expect your loyalty, appearances and performance on the track. In return, we'll give you the money to afford premier equipment and salaries for your team. I want to win races. I want you in the Chase. I want a championship. Are you ready to meet that challenge?"

What he wanted was within his grasp. He wasn't intimidated by the performance pressure. In fact, he'd missed it.

There was Isabel. There was the line he was crossing.

But he could manage that.

"I'm ready," he said to Huntington.

"I figured you were." Huntington shifted his grip on his coffee cup. He seemed to be searching for words, which was weird since he always managed to find the right thing to say. "I reacted emotionally by dropping you when I should have made a business decision." He shook his head. "Actually, it was my father who made the decision. I just went along with it."

"But now you're in charge," Rachel said.

"I will be. In two months."

The door opened, and Bryan appeared in the opening. His gaze swept the room and settled on the man who was just about to offer them a full NASCAR NEXTEL Cup sponsorship, worth—conservatively—fifteen million dollars. "Surely you're not attempting to negotiate with my employees without me present, Huntington?"

"We're *fine,*" Rachel said as her eyes sparked and she rose slowly to her feet.

She was pissed, as was Cade. They were handling the negotiations. Certainly better than Bryan and Dad had dealt with the situation before.

"I've got it, Bryan," Rachel said, advancing toward him.

"You can't sign a contract without me."

"I'm not signing anything. I'm getting an offer." She grasped the edge of the door. "We'll present it to you at the staff meeting on Tuesday. Goodbye."

She shut the door and leaned back against it.

"Working with family sucks, huh?" Huntington asked.

Cade exchanged a look with his sister. He wasn't sure what was more surprising—bonding with their former, and maybe future, sponsor, or Huntington's loss of his proper, ten-dollar words.

"Yeah, mostly it does."

CHAPTER TEN

ISABEL HOVERED AT THE back of the stage where Roger Cothren was hosting a question-and-answer luncheon with his fan club. This morning she'd already assisted their NASCAR Busch Series driver through his Q & A, and he drove for Encore Toilet Paper. It was always a challenge to keep your dignity when fielding questions with a personal-hygiene product stitched across the chest of your uniform.

But, hey, ya gotta have TP, right?

She should be focused on Roger's event—and some part of her was—but mostly she was tuned in to the barest glimpse of a dark-haired, blue-eyed charmer through the sea of people in the infield.

The NASCAR Busch Series race was due to start in a few hours, and she hadn't seen or heard from Cade. The silence made her edgy.

Surely he'd given up the risky, impractical idea of them kissing before the race. He had a hectic schedule of his own to manage, and they'd agreed to keeping their relationship a secret.

Still, she wouldn't mind seeing him before he

strapped himself in for 300 miles of intense concentration and stifling heat. She could at least give him an encouraging smile and wave.

As Roger answered a question about whether or not he had a retirement schedule, her BlackBerry beeped. A message filled the screen.

Where R U?

It was from Cade, but sent from somebody named Bob Miller's BlackBerry, whom Cade had apparently brought into the conspiracy in the past two days without her being aware.

So much for discretion.

Stepping back farther behind the stage, she called Cade's cell phone.

"Oh, hi, Isabel," said an unfamiliar voice. Bob?

She ignored the irrational burst of joy in her stomach at the idea that she was programmed into Cade's cell phone, allowing this stranger to know her name. "Hi. Is Cade around?"

"Yeah. Hang on."

"Hi, Izzy," Cade said a moment later.

"Why is there some strange guy answering your phone?"

"Bob's not strange. He's my manager. You met him in Pocono, remember?"

"Yeah, I guess." She did remember meeting him, and he seemed nice, but then her issue wasn't with Bob. "I thought your sister was your manager."

"She is, but she doesn't travel to all the races. Bob's her assistant."

"You told him about us?"

"No. I told him I needed to send a message on his BlackBerry. I didn't know where you were or if you'd be able to talk. Where are you?"

"And he answers your phone."

"Sure."

"Even when you're right next to him."

"Usually," he said, clearly oblivious to the problem. "Where are you?"

I'm in Bizarro World. Did she really date guys who had people answering their personal cell phone for them? "I'm working," she said finally, rubbing her temple. "Q & A for Roger Cothren."

"Can you get to the driver's compound in the next hour?"

"For…?"

He cleared his throat. "Hang on." After a minute or two, he said, "I'm back in my bedroom now."

"Cade, I can't—"

"I want my kiss."

"Oh, I *really* can't do that."

"Why not?"

"You want a list?"

He said nothing for a minute, then said, "No. No, I really don't."

Too abrupt. Too unapproachable. Too *me.*

She glanced over her shoulder, then cupped her

hand around the phone. "I'm not trying to put you off."

"Yes, you are."

Hadn't she decided she wanted to see him? Hadn't she decided to move their relationship forward? Was she backing out? Was she that big of a chicken?

Oh, no way.

So what was it? Why couldn't she let her reservations go? Why couldn't she take a chance?

She always thought there were absolutes in life. When faced with moral dilemmas, a random crisis or two, a forbidden guy, she thought she knew how she'd react. Even considering what-ifs and might-have-beens, she would be responsible. And though she might not admit her weakness to anyone else, she'd still do the right thing. Deep inside she knew what she'd do.

And that was just a bunch of crap.

There were times to do the irrational thing. The irresponsible thing. The crazy thing.

"I'll be there within an hour," she whispered.

The crowd applauded, and she quickly signed off. How she would manage to get to the driver's compound, by herself, without getting noticed, she had no idea. But she'd done a lot of pulling away in this attraction to Cade, and it was time she showed she was really in this—fears, reservations and all.

"Hey, Isabel," Roger Cothren said as he approached. "I heard you saved the Blast promo at Pocono."

She smiled. "Hey, R.C., that rhymes."

"I appreciate your quick thinking."

"That's my job."

"Well, later, when you're not doing your job, and after the Busch race, I'm having a late cookout at my motor coach. Just my family, some of the guys from the team. My driver neighbors will probably smell the steak and drop by."

"I couldn't."

"My wife is even making her famous cheese dip." He grinned, and Isabel was reminded why he was one of the most popular drivers in NASCAR. "I know you're busy, but everybody needs some downtime."

"Thanks, Roger. I'll try to come."

After making sure he was tucked into his golf cart and off to his motor coach, Isabel sent the other reps off on minor errands while she slid into her own cart and headed for the driver's compound.

She had a ready excuse—a Double Fudge Star's gift bag. Which, for no apparent reason at all, she was handing out to drivers on CATL's behalf. Hopefully, nobody would look too closely in her cart, since she had a grand total of one bag. *This* was her grand plan.

The CIA certainly wasn't going to call to try to lure her into the espionage game anytime soon.

Trying to forget Cade lived in a multimillion-dollar condo on wheels—and that was only on the weekends—she grabbed the bag and knocked on the coach door.

Naturally, Bob answered the door. "Hi, Isabel. Come on in."

"I, ah, brought this for Cade," she said as she stepped inside.

"A beautiful woman bearing gifts," Cade said, walking toward her. "Who needs trophies?"

She refused to be nervous. Her hands were just shaking from the cool blast of air-conditioning. As she handed him the bag, their fingers brushed. She jerked back.

"I'm going to get lunch," Bob said from the doorway. "You want anything, Isabel?"

"I, ah, no. I'm not, ah, staying." She rocked back on her heels. "I just came to give Cade the bag."

Oh, real smooth, Turner.

Bob smiled, and she wasn't sure whether he did because that was his job, or because he knew what a complete moron she was. "Okay. See ya."

As he pulled the door closed, it occurred to her that she was alone with Cade. *Oh, boy.* Not good. She'd sort of envisioned this kiss being a quick, stolen-in-the-hallway kind of thing while his agents, PR people and trusty Bob all fluttered around in various part of the coach.

But, no, they were *alone.*

Swallowing, she turned toward him. "So, I—"

He yanked her against him, and his mouth captured hers. Her brain froze, but her body knew instinctively what to do, molding against him, absorbing his heat and hunger while her head spun and she tingled all the way to the tips of her toes.

When they separated, she blinked him into focus. "You know, there are just cookies in that bag."

His gaze drifted over her face, his amazing blue eyes bright with desire. "I like cookies."

Embarrassed and pleased to still find herself breathless, she nodded. "No kidding?"

"How do you feel about china?"

She frowned in confusion. "The country or the plates?"

He kissed her again. And while she knew she should probably question him further, she simply handed herself over to his expert knack for distraction.

"I've got to stop," he said after a few minutes. He dropped his arms from around her. "Or I won't." Smiling, he peeked in the bag she'd given him. "Why did you bring me cookies? Not that I'm complaining."

"It's my decoy," she said as he pulled out the pack of Double Fudge Stars and tore it open. "Are you eating cookies before lunch?"

He settled onto the sofa and patted the spot next to him. "I'll share."

"You're just a born rule-breaker, aren't you?"

"Yes." He held out his hand. "Come on, you'll like it."

She took his hand and dropped onto the sofa next to him. She also took a cookie.

"Decoy?" he asked.

She swallowed her cookie. "I didn't realize you'd be alone, well, except for Bob."

"I wouldn't do anything to risk your job."

"I know."

"But you don't trust me, either."

"I do as much as I can to trust anybody."

"Why do I think that's not very much?"

She glanced at the floor, then back to him. Her face heated. "I have issues."

"Don't we all."

As long as she'd cracked the door to the past, she supposed she'd better open it all the way. Cade came from a respectable, wealthy family—though, like any racer, his father had struggled during his early career. He deserved to know who he was getting involved with. "My father's in jail. This is his fourth time."

"Okay."

"I don't even know where my mother is. She *used* to be in jail."

He pulled her against his chest and kissed the top of her head, the way her uncle John did sometimes. "I'm sorry."

"It's okay." Well, it really wasn't, but hearing his heart beat against her cheek helped. She felt surprisingly good for sharing her ugly beginning. He didn't push her away, or look at her in disgust, as if her genes made her undesirable. She hadn't expected that kind of reaction from Cade. But, as he'd pointed out, her trust level wasn't very high.

She glanced around the room, taking in the glass, chrome and marble, the plasma TV, the general opulence of the coach. The comparison to her first home had her blinking back tears. "I spent the first fifteen years of my life in a run-down trailer park, getting smacked around by my drug-addled parents."

He blew out a breath and tightened his hold on her. "Where was your uncle?"

"He didn't know about me until my parents were arrested and Social Services tracked him down."

Cade was quiet for a while. "I want to hurt them for hurting you," he said finally. "I guess that's part of being a rule-breaker, too."

Warmth spread through her, kicking back the tears. She lifted her head to look at him. "I happen to like rule-breakers."

He raised his eyebrows. "Since when?"

"It's a recent thing."

"No kidding?" He gave her a quick kiss, one of casual affection, but one that meant more to her than any passion they'd shared. "What are you doing after the race?"

"Sleeping." Then she remembered Roger's invitation. "After I drop by Roger's coach for a few minutes. He asked me to come to a cookout."

"Can you come by here after that?"

"I don't know." She squeezed his hand and straightened. "I want to. But keeping something secret at the track is completely different from laying low at home."

"Yeah, I know."

"We have our date on Monday to look forward to."

"Do we really need an official date to make it sink in to you that there's something between us?"

"No, but don't you think we need to separate *us* from the track?"

"Good luck with that"

"Yeah." Closing her eyes, she leaned her head back against the sofa cushion. "It's complicated."

"But not between us."

She turned her head to look at him.

"All this craziness goes on out there." He pointed toward the door. "Between you and me, it's simple. We want to be together."

She swallowed. Wasn't this a casual affair for him? After a month or two, wouldn't this whole, crazy attraction peter out?

Wouldn't it?

"I like you," she said finally.

"I got that, you know, weeks ago."

"Right. Of course you did." She stood, sliding her hands down her jeans. "I should probably go."

He rose and grabbed her arm. "Running again?"

"No, I just have to get back to work."

"It seems like you're running."

"The only one running is you. A race." She glanced at her watch. "In just a few hours. I'm in the way."

"You belong—"

Rap, rap.

"I'm sure that's Bob with your lunch." She leaned over and kissed him briefly. "Good luck today."

He slid his grip to her hand. "Thanks for coming."

Warmth and understanding, the likes of which she hadn't felt since Uncle John and Aunt Emma first came into her life, washed over her. She squeezed his hand. "I'll see you."

DRESSED IN HIS fire-retardant uniform, Cade hoisted himself through the window of his race car. Alan, one of his crew members, handed him his gloves, which he slid on.

Though the sun was waning, the leftover afternoon heat from the track wafted upward, permeating the air and the car like the electricity of the roaring crowd. The grandstands held more than 160,000, and the infield campgrounds many thousands more. The sheer size of the Daytona track was jaw-dropping. The history humbling. The excitement inspiring. The pit-road tension mounting.

Alan handed him his helmet. "Belt secure?"

He yanked on the five-point safety harness. "All set."

"Pedal down, buddy. Stay cool and sharp."

Cade nodded, inserting his earphones before putting on his helmet. The pep talk, while seemingly obvious to a lot of people, reminded him of what he needed to focus on. It helped him put aside the potential sponsorship with Huntington, the trouble with his parents and even his alternating joy and worry about his relationship with Isabel.

Maybe they were being foolish, maybe they were risking too much, but he couldn't turn away.

His job was all about making split-second decisions. This was one he could actually think about, turn over in his mind and consider all the options, advantages and consequences. A year ago, he wouldn't have paused long enough to think about any of that, but his parents' divorce and his dustup with Huntington had changed him, and maybe for the better.

Good grief, he *wasn't* maturing. Was he?

"Watch your mirrors. Be smart. We're fifth in the championship. We could win it all."

Gentlemen, start your engines....

Cade flipped the switch to fire his engine along with the rest of the field, and the grandstand crowd flew into a frenzy, yelling and snapping pictures. As he smiled, his heart gave him a swift kick, then he grew calm. After all the sponsor meetings, fan events and practices, he was finally where he belonged. Racing.

Alan gave him a thumbs-up, then fastened the safety net over the window. As Cade glanced out his windshield, he saw crew members and family of other drivers step back from his competitors' cars. With one last pat on the hood from Alan, Cade followed the other drivers down pit road, following the pace car onto the track.

As they rolled around the brightly lit track, Cade clutched his glove-covered palms around the steering wheel. It was just another race, but no matter how many times you reminded yourself or anybody else reminded you, it was *Daytona*.

The place everybody wanted to win. Whether you were a twenty-year veteran or a wide-eyed rookie, you wanted to roll into this Victory Lane more than any other. NASCAR NEXTEL Cup or NASCAR Busch Series, Cade had never won at all at the hallowed track. He wanted his name in the history books. He wanted to be part of that winners club, the best of the best. He wanted to prove that he hadn't just fallen into a good deal because of his family.

Was tonight the night?

After the excruciatingly slow warm-up laps, Cade's heart pounded like crazy when the pace car peeled off and headed down pit road. The start-finish line was in sight. When the green flag waved, the roars of the forty-three-car chain and the pumped-up crowd merged into one long stream of noise and excitement.

Since he'd qualified third, he watched his rearview mirror just as much as he looked out the front windshield. Almost immediately, the cars behind him jockeyed for position, going three wide as they neared Turn One. Cade stayed tucked behind the two cars in front of him, letting the draft pull him along and hoping he avoided the craziness and the trouble.

They weren't even up to full speed yet.

As he drove through the three-story, thirty-one-degree banked turns, it seemed the cars would slide all the way down to the apron. In fact, in a wreck, they did, which was why the track was called "self-cleaning." But at race speed the cars all miraculously stuck to the track, and the pack was on the back-stretch seemingly before he could blink.

Behind him, the cars settled down a bit, into two long lines. They made it around the track several times with everybody playing it cool and sticking together. The front four cars pulled away a bit, with the rest of the field lined up two by two behind them. The outside line would push forward, then the inside line would come roaring back. A few cars danced around a bit, shifting lanes or trying to move up.

Cade held his position. This wasn't his first time around the giant granddaddy track, and he knew he had a strong car. He wasn't about to blow his chance at a win by being too aggressive, too early. Would his past—and maybe future—sponsor be impressed with his restraint and planning?

For his part, Cade knew he should be thanking Huntington. He should be giddy with relief over the possibility of getting back into the NASCAR NEXTEL Cup Series. But he was suspicious of the smiling hotel owner's motives, and he hoped he and Rachel could find another option, at least for next year. For now, they'd likely sign the contract for the three races he offered, as long as Bryan approved. Beyond that, Cade really wasn't sure he wanted anything more. The whole thing seemed almost too easy.

"Lookin' good, buddy," his crew chief, Sam, said into his ear. "Hang in there."

Cade pushed all thoughts of the next race, next year or even the next hour out of his mind. Keeping focus on the moment was critical. He concentrated on keeping the nose of his car in the air pocket formed by the car in front of him. The engine rumbled, vibrating through his body as the car ate up the asphalt. He had ultimate control over this powerful, fickle machine. Dozens of team members had spent weeks building the sleek body. The engine department—which he personally thought rivaled even the legendary Cothren engines—had given him the power he needed. Engineers had tested and studied the diagnostics. His crew and car chiefs had studied the notes from the February race at Daytona and made adjustments. His race-day crew had checked every nut, bolt and hose; they'd readied the tires; they'd set up the pit box.

Now it was up to him, Sam and the pit crew to make everyone else's efforts turn into the winner's purse and a trophy.

On lap 12, a movement in his rearview mirror caught his attention. One car had jumped out of line. A blue car with a yellow stripe on his bumper.

Not a good idea, rookie.

Sure enough, nobody followed him. Hung out of line without the draft to pull him along, the rookie flew backward so quickly he looked like he'd hit the brakes. Unfortunately, he also got tipped in the rear by another car, who'd started to make a move on the car in front of him.

Both cars went around, slid down the track and collected a few more cars on the way. The caution flag flew, the field slowed behind the pace car, and the safety crews jumped into action.

"How's the car?" Sam asked over the radio.

"Good."

"Not too tight?"

"No."

"Okay. No chances, then. Let's think big picture here. We could gain some serious points today."

"Yeah?"

"Calhoun was in that wreck. He's just ahead of you in points."

He was? Cade had been focused so completely on getting back into a NASCAR NEXTEL Cup car, he hadn't paid much attention to the series he was actually driving in. Could another NASCAR Busch Series championship be within his grasp?

"Pit road open this time around," Sam said.

Cade followed the two cars ahead of him off the track and onto pit road. Numbered signs were displayed in a long row. Ready to spring into action, the pit crews held tires, jacks and gas cans and hovered on the other side of the wall.

"No adjustments. Four tires," Sam said as Cade rolled toward his pit box.

The guys leapt over the wall and went to work servicing the car. Cade took the fresh bottle of Gatorade that one crew member handed him and sipped greedily, since he only had about ten to twelve seconds to take down all he could. Then he tossed the bottle onto the sweltering asphalt for one of his crew to gather up after the pit stop was complete.

As the temperature in the car soared, he had to replenish the valuable fluids he was losing or risk losing his concentration or, even worse, passing out. The team completed their mission in 13.9 seconds, and he pulled out of the pits in second place. "Great job, guys!" he yelled over the radio.

Pumped by the fast stop and his position as the race restarted, Cade made deals with guys behind him. Unlike the rookie's earlier move, when Cade pulled out from behind the leader ten laps later, he had friends. The outside line of cars surged forward, and he took the lead.

He kept it through another wreck, a set of pit stops and the setting sun. But as the tires wore down later in the race, he began to fade while other cars maintained and some moved forward. On lap 83, twenty laps from the race finish, he was passed and slid back to twelfth. A late race caution saved him, and with fresh tires he fought back to fourth as the checkered flag flew.

Still no Daytona win.

He swallowed his disappointment and thanked his team as he rolled onto pit road. Everyone had worked hard, and they'd done well. Not the best, which was hard for an intense competitor to take, but he knew how important—now, more than ever—it was to put on a smile for the guys and the media. Nobody wanted to feel like they'd let down the team.

He climbed out of the car in his pit stall and noticed nonteam members rushing toward him from two sides. On one side was a TV crew, and on the other was Bob, heading his way and holding out a cell phone.

Bob got to him first. "It's your mother. She says it's important."

Something was wrong at home. His grandparents? Had somebody gotten sick? He grabbed the phone. "Mom?"

"Hi, dear."

She didn't sound panicked at all. "Is something wrong?"

"Oh, no. Everything's perfect."

Cade eyed the TV crew, who'd now reached him. He and the pit reporter had known each other for years, and he clearly didn't get why Cade was blowing them off in favor of a phone call. "I'm a little busy here."

Now her tone rose. "Too busy for your mother?"

The camera operator shifted his feet. That thing had to weigh sixty pounds. "I'm about to be interviewed."

"Oh."

"You did know there was a race tonight, didn't you?"

"Was there *really?*"

He closed his eyes. When he opened them again, he forced a smile at the TV crew. "My mom, calling to congratulate me."

"Honey, if I didn't even know there was a race tonight, then clearly I wasn't calling you to congratulate you. Did you just lie to somebody?"

He turned away from the reporters and cupped his hand over the phone. "Mom, I—"

"There are other things going on in the world besides racing."

"I'm sure there are, but—"

"I was calling to tell you I finally decided on the swirls-and-dots color for the Thanksgiving plates."

He glanced over his shoulder and noted that two print reporters with minirecorders had now joined the TV media. She *had* to be kidding.

"Aren't you going to ask me what I decided on?" she asked.

She *wasn't* kidding. The only way out of this was to fall in line. "What color did you decide on?"

"Orange," she said dramatically. "I've chosen orange."

"Sounds perfect. I can't wait to see them. Gotta go now, Mom. I'll talk to you later."

He flipped the phone closed before she could respond, knowing he was destined for a serious speech about respect for his mother, but not seeing how he could continue to put off the interviews.

"Does your mother always call you after a race?" the print reporter asked.

He put on his most sincere smile. "Only the most important ones."

CHAPTER ELEVEN

BY THE TIME CADE HEADED to Roger Cothren's cook-out, he was calmer and he'd let go of most of his frustrations about his mother's Thanksgiving obsession and not winning the race. He had new concerns now.

At the top was figuring out how Isabel would feel about him showing up at the party.

He could honestly tell her he'd been invited. He wasn't crashing—though he *had* told Roger he didn't have anything to do, and hey, did he want to get together for a beer?—to get that invitation. So he was cheating a bit, and she wouldn't like that.

On the other hand, she was fully aware he was a rule breaker, so she should sort of expect him to show up, right?

Either way, the woman he wanted to be with was just a few motor coach rows over, so he didn't see any reason not to go be with her.

Especially since there was grilled steak involved.

When he rounded the corner to Roger's row, he saw a couple dozen people milling around Roger's coach, as well as the ones on either side of him. It was still hot, but there was a slight breeze, and somebody had lit tiki torches to keep the bugs away. Smoke billowed up from three giant grills. Several coolers were lined up beside long tables loaded down with bowls of chips, hot wings and other snacks. Kids waved sparklers. Adults held plastic cups and beer bottles.

The cookout had obviously turned into a no-holds-barred block party.

When he walked up, Roger's wife immediately spotted him as she was carrying a tray of foil-wrapped potatoes. After she set the tray on the table, she pressed a cold beer into his hand. She looked a little frantic. "Cade, go check on the guys by the grill, would you? I think they're burning something."

"Sure." He headed that way, but by the aromas he detected, he became much more interested in sampling the menu than directing the grill master. "What's up, guys?"

"Nice run tonight, Cade," Roger said, lifting his beer bottle into the air.

"Thanks." He spoke to the other drivers and team members standing around, and Roger introduced him to the people he didn't know, who were buddies of Roger's from his early days in sprint car racing.

They talked about his race, the feel and condition of the track, then discussed tomorrow night's race and speculated on drivers changing teams. Normally,

Cade would have been intensely involved, but tonight he was distracted, looking around for Isabel.

If she didn't come, he was going to feel like an idiot, as well as disappointed.

While he liked Roger and his family, he'd come for Isabel. He hadn't chased a woman in a long, long time, and yet here he was, literally throwing himself in her path.

At least he had a thick, juicy steak to distract him.

When Roger passed out plates of food, he settled at the table and dug in with everybody else. After the long day of appearances, meetings and the grueling race, he was starving. "You know your way around a grill like you do the track," Cade said to Roger.

"Tell that to Patsy. She always thinks I'm going to burn something."

In the process of buttering her potato, Patsy stuck out her tongue.

"There *was* that time at Richmond…" one of the guys said.

"Once," Roger said. "I burn something once, and ya'll can't let it go."

"Didn't you say it was a bad gas control valve on the grill?" somebody asked.

"It couldn't have been all those beers you guys drank," Patsy said drily.

"Hey, Isabel," Roger said.

Cade glanced over his shoulder. Isabel stood a few feet away. As his pulse pounded, she carefully avoided looking at him.

"Grab a plate and join us," Roger continued.

"I can't stay," she said.

"Oh, nonsense," Patty said, rising to drag Isabel over to the table. "You sit right here while I fix you a plate."

"I'll get it," Cade said, wiping his mouth with a napkin as he stood.

Patsy nudged her husband. "Finally, a gentleman."

"Hey, I'm a gentleman," Roger said.

"Only when I swat you first."

Cade had reached the grill, where Roger had piled the leftover meat on a plate. "You want steak or a burger?" he asked Isabel.

"What are you doing here?"

"I don't think we have that particular variety of cow. We have rib eyes, sirloins and burgers."

She said nothing, and he didn't turn, knowing she was scowling at him and had crossed her arms over her chest.

"You sound like you could use some serious protein. It's a proven cure for orneriness, you know."

"Orneriness?"

"The state of being ornery. Irritated. Annoyed." He finally glanced at her, disappointed to see his prediction about her scowling and arm-crossing was accurate. He handed her a plate with a thick rib eye on it. "You know what I mean."

She didn't even glance at the steak. "You shouldn't be here."

"I was invited. Are you suggesting I should be rude?"

"You're being sneaky."

"Just for a change of pace, it wouldn't hurt my feelings if, for once, when you saw me, you threw your arms around me and laid a big one right on my lips."

She cast a look over her shoulder. "Shh."

"If I'm sneaky, you're paranoid."

"Somebody has to be."

He sighed. "I'm going to eat."

As he started to walk away, she said, "The reason I'm late is because I went by your coach first."

Smiling, he stopped. The woman was certainly unpredictable. Another interesting trait he'd like to explore. "Yeah?"

She returned his smile. "Yeah."

His pulse leapt. She'd wanted to see him. She'd tried to see him. But she hadn't exactly looked thrilled a few seconds ago. "So what's with the orneriness?"

"Me coming to see you was private. This is public."

"Do you need help finding a steak, Cade?" Roger called out.

"Ah, no. We got it."

As they walked back to the table, Isabel whispered, "See what I mean?"

He returned to his spot at the table, several seats away from her, and had to silently admit she had a point. If he'd stayed in his coach, he might have gotten a whole different greeting.

Despite what she thought, he wasn't used to being sneaky. In his teens, he'd snuck beer out of the house and snuck in after curfew many times, but these days he was pretty much used to doing what he wanted, when he wanted, with whom he wanted.

Maybe this was like having a crappy day on the track, but telling the media the team worked hard for everything they got.

Or maybe this was like driving loose into Turn Two. You just knew it was only a matter of time before there was gonna be a crash.

ISABEL KEPT A CAREFUL distance from Cade as she ate her steak. Not that it was too hard to do. The men had gathered at the other end of the table from the women and were talking about yet another *unforgettable* race.

"How can they possibly remember every turn of a race that took place five years ago?" Patsy Cothren asked.

"I can barely remember last *month's* races," Angie Holloway said. "Except that Bobby Jr. got sick at one of them. Pocono, I think."

"When I look back at the scoring data, I can remember some details, I guess," Patsy said, angling her head. "But unless Roger won, why would I want to?"

"Good point," Angie said. "When Bobby and I

first got married, I used to write his important stats on my hand. I was always paranoid some reporter would ask me a question I didn't know the answer to, and Bobby wouldn't speak to me if I embarrassed him."

"At least you didn't fall over the shrubbery in Victory Lane and expose your panties to the entire racing world."

Angie grinned. "That'll teach you to wear a skirt."

"I'd been hosting a party in the suite. What was I supposed to wear?"

Isabel sipped iced tea to hide her smile. Though she only knew Patsy professionally, she seemed so savvy and smart. Picturing her red-faced and picking leaves off her backside didn't compute.

But then the whole party was surreal.

Angie's husband Bobby was a three-time NASCAR NEXTEL Cup champion, and Angie was a former Miss North Carolina, who now ran one of the most successful, high-profile foundations in racing. Roger had been racing for more than twenty years, and Patsy had been his scorer and business manager for almost that long. There wasn't a race that went by that she wasn't sitting atop her husband's pit box, except when their kids were born. Patsy's father and uncle had raced NASCAR in the early years. Their whole family, like the Garrisons, were icons of the sport.

Isabel felt privileged just sitting at the same table with them, much less being privy to their private conversations.

Was this what happened when you dated a driver? Were you enfolded in this world, this family and traveling circus that was professional racing? Did you exchange random comments with other wives and girlfriends, complaining about the everyday relationship irritations like *who's turn is it to do the dishes?* And *are you ever going to fix the garage door opener?*

At the track, did you borrow a cup of sugar from your neighbor, even if your neighbor was so famous he couldn't walk through the garage area without being mobbed? Did you worry about the regular stuff—the time balance between family and career? Did you wonder how your husband would respond to a flirty coworker if you weren't around?

Were you nervous when TV crews followed you around? Did you fear or hope your children would also catch the racing bug?

But you're not married to a driver. You're not even really dating. You're having a double-secret something-or-other.

Okay, maybe triple secret.

Listening to Patsy and Angie, Isabel decided their lives were different, yet the same as "regular" people's. Over the years, she'd learned that about the drivers, but until now she hadn't considered their partners. These women, even amid their lighthearted complaining, were the foundation and the strength behind the success of their husbands. There was no way the drivers could keep their dream of racing alive if they didn't have amazing, selfless support beside them.

"Do you think they remember we're here?" Angie asked, glancing at the men.

"Sure they do. We're hot," Patsy said. "Well, you're hot, Isabel. Angie and I look good for moms over forty."

Isabel nearly choked on her tea. "What are you talking about? You guys look great—for *any* age."

"We can certainly compete with asphalt," Patsy said.

"Or concrete," Angie added.

The guys roared with laughter, then they all sipped from their beer bottles.

"Or hops," Isabel said.

Patsy and Angie stared at her, and Isabel was sure she'd made some kind of serious faux pas, but then the other women smiled.

"I have a bottle of wine around here somewhere," Patsy said.

"Get it," Angie said, slumping forward onto the table.

Once the corking and pouring was complete— though Isabel would have preferred beer—they made a toast to themselves, the strongest of the species. While the guys continued to rehash races, they talked about work, kids and the men. A couple of times Isabel caught Cade's gaze out of the corner of her eye, and while it was nice to know she was more appealing than asphalt, concrete or hops, she resolutely avoided looking in his direction.

All she needed was for the relationship talk to get around to her love life.

"So you're single, right, Isabel?" Patsy asked.

It's just my luck lately.

Isabel was suddenly regretting she'd insisted on only half a glass of wine. "Yep."

"Got any plans to change that?" Angie asked.

"Not at the moment."

"Smart girl," Patsy said, toasting her with her glass. "You're only young once."

"Bobby Jr., stop running with that sparkler!" Angie yelled in the direction of the boys. She turned back toward them. "I love my boys more than anything, but there are times I miss being selfish." She met Isabel's gaze. "I don't mean you are."

"I know." Isabel had seen how devoted parents could be, and though she loved her aunt, uncle and cousins, she had no concept of loving a life you created. Someday, maybe. Someday, maybe her career wouldn't be the primary focus in her life.

"Who are you?" a boy of about ten asked, jutting out his chin as he stopped next to her.

"I'm Isabel."

"Are you a fan of my daddy's?" he asked, almost like a challenge.

"Bobby Jr.!" Angie said with a glare in her son's direction.

Actually, Isabel was more comfortable with the

kids than anybody. They were unfailingly honest. And living in Bobby Holloway's shadow must be pretty intense—at and away from the track. She had some experience with the pressure to be better. "I think your daddy is an amazing racer, but I work for the company that sponsors Roger Cothren."

Nate, one of Roger's boys, punched Bobby Jr. in the shoulder. "Be cool, dude. She always has Double Fudge Stars."

Bobby Jr.'s aggressive expression softened. "No kidding?"

"No kidding." Isabel reached under the table for her bag. *Oh, yeah, this wasn't her first time making kids happy with chocolate.* "Okay, Moms?" she asked Patsy and Angie, thinking of the challenges of parenthood. Once they nodded, she said "Here ya go" to the boys and handed out small bags of cookies, making sure she gave them extra to share with their friends.

"Nice move," Angie said when the kids walked away smiling.

"They've saved me quite a few times." Isabel nodded toward the guys. "They work with the grown boys, too."

"They're not grown," Patsy said. "They're just bigger."

Isabel rose. "I might as well go out on a high note."

"Stay," Patsy said. "Have another glass of wine. We never get to really chat."

"I'd like to, but I can't," Isabel said. "I have to be back here early in the morning. It was nice to meet you, Angie."

"You, too."

Patsy followed Isabel as she headed toward the guys to say good-night. "Roger, take Isabel to her car. Where are you parked, honey?"

Isabel shook her head. "I'm just over by the hospitality tents. I can walk."

"No way." Roger rose. "Thousands of people are camping around in the lots all around here. It's not safe."

"They'll mob you, not me," Isabel said.

"You need to follow her to her hotel, too."

"Ah, Patsy, I've had a couple of beers. I can't drive anything faster than a golf cart."

"I'll follow her," Cade said. "I started on a beer earlier, but I was so set on eating Roger's steak, I never finished it. I was about to head out, anyway."

Patsy patted Cade on the back, and Isabel didn't trust herself to look at either of them. None of this was in any way discreet, much less triple-secret.

Nobody else, however, seemed to think anything about Cade's offer, so within minutes they were bundled into Roger's golf cart, which they used to get to Cade's coach and pick up a rented SUV.

After thanking Roger again for the meal, Isabel climbed into the seat next to Cade. In the close quarters, the night seemed to press in on them.

Laying his arm across the back of the seat, Cade

angled his body toward her. "You wanna charm me the way you did those kids?"

She raised her eyebrows. "I already gave you cookies."

"I want more."

Sighing, she opened her bag. *Men.* They were always thinking with their stomachs. "I've got more—"

He grabbed her wrist. "I don't want more cookies."

What *did* he want?

Flicking her gaze to his and studying the smoky look in his eyes, she didn't have to spend a lot of time guessing. A ripple of echoing desire rolled through her body. As complicated as their relationship might be or get, there was one thing that never seemed to waver—the heat between them.

She swallowed and prayed for strength. "I, uh, shouldn't we, uh, get going?"

He leaned closer and cupped her chin with his fingers. "Do I make you nervous, Izzy?"

"Oh, yeah," she admitted without thinking.

He smiled, his teeth stark white in the dimly lit parking lot. "Good."

As he leaned back and started the car, she flushed. Thankfully, *hopefully,* he couldn't see her flaming face. Where was her attitude? Her coolness?

Gone, apparently. Long gone in the wake of the intense, sigh-like-a-googly-eyed-goofy-girl effect of Cade Garrison.

Hoping desperately her dignity would find her again, she clenched the door handle as he pulled away from his coach and drove slowly through the lot.

Even though she'd spent little time with Cade, she'd enjoyed the party. Getting to know the drivers and their families personally instead of just professionally was a neat kick that she'd resisted over the years. She'd never wanted to be considered unprofessional or *too* friendly.

Maybe she'd attended out of obligation to CATL, but she felt like she'd made friends, not just business connections.

She glanced at Cade as he pulled out on the infield road and headed toward the hospitality village. The barrier of their secrecy was both a sacrifice and a measure of protection. It kept them from being together when they wanted, but it also prevented her from getting too close, too quickly for her comfort level.

Was that why she couldn't relax and have fun? She should be enjoying the excitement and intrigue, not having an angst attack like a teenager with the hots for the wrong kind of boy. Why couldn't she live in the moment and to hell with the consequences?

Because she might find the sacrifice of secrecy more than she could handle. Or, worse, she might find she needed to be with him *too* much. What if she let him all the way in? What if he broke through that wall of protection she'd built over her heart?

"Which one is yours?" Cade asked as they pulled into the lot by the hospitality tents.

"It's a white Tahoe." She leaned forward to get a better view. "There," she said, pointing at the one near the end of the row. When he pulled alongside, she opened the door. "You really don't have to follow me. I'll be fine."

He leaned over and kissed her, softly, casually, as if he did it every day. "Maybe I'm hoping you'll invite me up to your room once we get there."

Her heartbeat started a serious gallop, but she smiled vaguely at him, then made a quick retreat to her rental car.

Invite him to her room? she thought as she drove through the infield tunnel. Oh, no pressure there. She wasn't really a *why don't you come up and see me sometime* kind of woman. She was a bit more reserved. But then she didn't have a string of successful relationships to brag about, either.

She'd had a couple of empty, short-term, mostly physical connections. And she could look back at her love life and call two guys *boyfriends*. Mostly, she'd worked. And if there was more to life, she hadn't found it so far.

She glanced in her rearview mirror at Cade's SUV behind her.

No, not so far.

When they reached her beachside hotel, she drove to the front and handed her Tahoe over to the valet. Behind her, Cade did the same thing. Clearly, neither of them had thought this through. They couldn't exactly have a drink together in the lobby of the Hilton.

He'd get mobbed. They'd get recognized. Her uncle's room was only two floors below hers.

You should be enjoying the excitement and intrigue.

She should have her head examined.

"Room 2123," she said quietly to Cade, then she headed through the revolving doors as if she didn't have a care in the world.

Her heart pounded as she rode up in the elevator. She'd just invited a man to her hotel room when she was supposed to be working. She had an insanely long day to face tomorrow. She had a date to face when she got home. She had a protective, supremely professional uncle *two floors below*.

But there was excitement and intrigue.

As the elevator dinged on the twenty-first floor, she closed her eyes briefly, then stepped out into the hall. If she saw somebody she knew at this point, she was going to melt into a pitiful puddle on the floor.

She held her breath as she strode to her room, slipped the key into the lock, then leaned back against the closed door.

Oh, boy.

Why did the hungry look in Cade's eyes not just grab her hormones, but her heart? She wasn't *going* to melt into a puddle, she already *had*. Being with him, standing next to him, feeling his touch and watching him smile had become an addiction.

When had that happened? When had lust become personal?

She tossed her bag into the bathroom to her right, then dragged her hand down her face. "I bet I look lovely."

After taking two slow breaths, she stepped into the bathroom and flipped on the light. She winced. "*Lovely* doesn't even begin to describe that face."

She grabbed her makeup brush and frantically buffed on powder, then swirled blush on her cheeks and spread gloss across her lips. After reapplying deodorant, she pawed through her measly overnight bag for perfume. In the bottom of a side pocket she found a sample that still smelled relatively fresh, so she dabbed it on her pulse points.

Knock, knock.

She pressed her lips together, flipped off the bathroom light, then rounded the corner and peeped through the hole in the door.

Cade stood on the other side.

Of course it's Cade. Were you expecting somebody else?

She still had the right to be nervous, though, didn't she? She liked to think that this flushed-faced, heart-pounding state was how Aunt Emma would have felt if Elvis had ever appeared at her hotel room door.

Isabel let Cade in, and they stood in the foyer by the closet, staring at each other for a good minute. "I figured it would be best if we talked privately," she said finally, staring randomly at the carpeted floor. "You know, in case fans or whoever was in the bar downstairs. I wouldn't want to have your family talking about us, and you know my uncle is staying here in the hotel. Plus, I think I saw the film crew from Racer TV, so we should be, well, cautious."

"You're still nervous."

She glared at him. "I'm just cautious."

"It's cute."

"Cute?" She took a step toward him. "Look here, Mr. Hotshot Driver, I'm a professional business-woman. I handle twenty problems before ten o'clock in the morning, before you even *think* about getting out of bed. I do professional stuff every day." She poked him in the chest. "You smile, sign autographs and press a gas pedal for a living. I have *serious* respon-sibilities."

He brushed her hair off her face. "I have a serious crush on you."

She licked her lips, knowing she was going down fast. "Did I mention I'm a professional?"

Leaning in, he cupped her cheek. "Twice, I think," he said before he laid his lips over hers.

She wrapped her arms about his neck and nestled close to his body. The warmth and connection she felt with him was like none other in her life. She wanted to resist him, but she either wasn't strong enough or she'd already spent all her energy.

"I'm sorry about the gas-pedal-for-a-living thing," she said against his cheek.

"Kiss me again and I'll forgive you."

As she did, her breath hitched in her throat and her stomach pitched sideways. He exhilarated and overwhelmed her. He challenged her. He made her smile. She wanted to be with him, to explore the feelings bubbling deep inside, the ones she didn't even want to admit she had. She couldn't voice them. But she could show him how much he meant to her.

Their kisses deepened. He pressed her against the wall, and she felt every line and muscle of his body molded next to hers.

He stepped back suddenly. "We have to stop. *I* have to stop." His burning blue gaze met hers. "Before I can't."

Smiling, she wrapped her hand around the back of his neck and tugged him against her. "Don't stop."

CHAPTER TWELVE

HEARING THE DISTINCTIVE, annoying ring of her cell phone, Isabel fumbled blindly in the direction of the bedside table. The moment she wrapped her hand around the phone and held it in the general vicinity of her ear, she sank back into her pillow. "Yeah?"

"Hey, Isabel, Ricky Jones, NASCAR.com."

"Mornin'," she said, her eyes still closed. *Was* it morning? It couldn't be. Not already.

"The dawn-rising rep is sleeping in on race day?"

"The race isn't till tonight," she said, confused and slightly annoyed that Ricky had woken her up. She'd been having this great dream about Cade.

"Right," Ricky said. "Well, I need to talk—"

"Who's 'at?" Cade asked, pulling her against him.

"And clearly you're not alone," Ricky continued, obviously surprised. "O-*kay*. Well, when—"

"I'm alone." Isabel's eyes flew open as she pushed Cade's hands away. She was suddenly wide awake. On race morning. And *the press was on the phone.* "I'm definitely alone. I'm just—" She leapt out of the bed and yanked the bedspread with her, wrapping it around her body. Realizing in a flurry of panic and consciousness that her dream about Cade wasn't a dream, she pushed her tangled hair out of her eyes and didn't dare look back at the bed.

Oh, man, what have I done?

Again.

"You caught me off guard," she said to Ricky, scrambling to locate a few coherent brain cells and a wide-awake-sounding tone of voice. "I was, ah, working late last night. Must have overslept. What's up?"

"I was hoping you could comment on behalf of Cumberland Atlantic for a story I'm doing about Bruce Phillips."

The shortness in his tone stiffened her shoulders. Bruce changing teams was old news. Ricky couldn't be calling at dawn to rehash that story.

Ricky was one of the best reporters out there, but Isabel had learned from experience to let the reporters ask the questions, otherwise, you wound up giving more information than they might know in the first place. She worked for CATL, and her job was to protect and promote them over any other agenda. Even friendship. "Ask away," she said, though her heartbeat picked up speed.

"Bruce isn't happy," Ricky said.

Isabel closed her eyes, trying to block out a surge of dread.

"He told me that he and his crew chief rarely talk. His equipment is substandard, and since he announced his departure to Baker Racing, he's not allowed in team meetings. He's had enough."

Isabel swallowed. She'd heard tremors of tension, but nothing this bad. When a driver announced he was changing teams midstream, things sometimes went south, but there was a lot of money on the line, and the team members were generally professional.

But they were also human. Emotions always came into play. Working around motorsports for so long, she understood the drive to succeed and the frustration when that success was elusive. Still, it was her job to let the drivers do their job while she did hers, presenting the most positive image for her company.

"Bruce told you this?" she asked, trying to clarify what was happening.

"He poured out the story last night in his coach."

Her mind raced with the implications. While she was eating steak and laughing it up with the Cothren family, Bruce Phillips was spilling his woes to the media, probably just a few feet away. Had she missed something? Had her preoccupation with Cade distracted her in some way?

She rubbed her eyes and tried to focus.

With Phillips's team problems going public, the tension would escalate. What if Phillips left midseason? CATL's contract was with his current team, TR Motorsports. They couldn't switch their sponsorship over to Baker and Phillips's new team until next year. Instead of an entire season of Phillips speaking for them, they'd have only half. TV ads, print ads and who knows what else would have to be pulled.

In other words, a giant, messy disaster for her to wade through.

Bruce, you crazy hothead, why couldn't you hang on for a few more months?

"Izzy?" Cade asked, his voice thick with sleep. "What's going on?"

She glanced at him over her shoulder, his broad, bare chest exposed above the sheet as he sat up.

Dear heaven, he was beautiful.

And the fact that *he* was foremost in her mind, and not her job, not the monumental disaster she was potentially facing, and the reality that nationwide media exposure was literally at an arm's length, told her just how far she'd fallen. She wasn't *that* girl, the one who risked everything for a guy, for a whim, for a good time.

What have I done?

Again.

"Isabel Turner has no comment?" Ricky asked, his curiosity and surprise obvious.

She turned away from Cade and cleared her throat. "Isabel Turner, senior PR rep for Cumberland Atlantic, says CATL is proud to have Bruce Phillips as their driver in the NASCAR NEXTEL Cup Series. CATL will continue to support him in all his endeavors."

"You didn't know things had gotten this serious?" Ricky asked after a long pause.

"I can't comment any further."

"It's a mess."

She said nothing.

Ricky sighed. "I'm sorry. I have to write the story."

"I know."

"See ya later?"

"Yeah."

Closing her eyes, she snapped the phone closed.

"What's wrong?" Cade asked.

She clutched the phone between her hands. "It's work. Bruce Phillips has gone public with his team's problems. I have to go."

"Now?"

Preparing herself before she turned, she managed to do so without sighing at the amazing sight of him. "Yes."

He slid his hand through his hair, mussing it even more. "But we—"

"Last night is over, Cade."

His head jerked up; his gaze locked with hers. "Don't you dare say we made a mistake."

"We rushed into something we're not ready for. Just like before."

"Is that why you lied on the phone? Why you said you were alone?"

"That wasn't a friend or a fan or even room service, Cade. It was a *reporter.* Should I have told him we were in bed together?"

He dropped his head. "No."

"We're risking a lot."

"Too much, right?"

She wanted to agree. She wanted to argue. She wanted the freedom to touch him, to turn to him when her world was crashing.

What she did was back away. "I've got to get into the shower."

He grabbed her wrist. "But I'll see you later, right?"

"Maybe. I don't know."

He said nothing, his gaze locked on hers.

Was he mad? Disappointed? Relieved? She tugged her hand. "I've got to get to the track."

He didn't let go and yanked her into his lap. "Not before I get a kiss goodbye."

"Cade, I—"

He laid his mouth over hers, scattering her thoughts and heating her blood. When he pulled back, she was out of breath, and she could see he wasn't mad, disappointed or relieved.

He was determined.

"You're not going to push me aside," he said.

"I'm not. I just—"

He raised his eyebrows.

"Last night is over," she said weakly.

"You said that already, and it doesn't matter, since my plans are for today."

"We tried this before, and it didn't work."

"No, we didn't try. I told myself we'd made a mistake. I let you convince me we'd jumped over too many steps to make a relationship work. But we're ready now." He paused, his gaze dropping briefly before connecting with hers again. "At least I am."

She knew she was back-pedaling. She knew she was a big, fat chicken. But the need to wrap her arms around him and hold on for dear life scared her. She shouldn't want him that much. She *couldn't*.

"I want to see you tonight," he said. "And tomorrow. Am I going to have to beg?"

Her eyes widened. He *had* to be kidding. He didn't want her that much. This was about the competition, the fun. Chasing. Winning.

Wasn't it?

"Silence. That's great." He sighed. "Are you trying to think of a way to let me down gently? Are you trying to figure out how to get out of our date on Monday?"

She wriggled off his lap. "Speaking of that…"

"Oh, hell."

"Where are we supposed to go on this date? We can't go out anywhere in Davidson or Mooresville. Are we going to Charlotte?" She angled her head. "Oh, can't do that, either. Everybody knows who you are there, too. Maybe Atlanta?" She pursed her lips, considering the idea. "No. Everybody knows you there, too. How about Tasmania? How's your fan base in Tasmania?"

"We'll find a way. You could always cook dinner for me at my place."

"I don't cook. I reheat."

"Oh, well. Maybe I'll call Mom. She can send something over."

"This is never going to work. We'll never keep this a secret." Isabel sat on the edge of the bed, though she was careful to keep her distance from those mind-fuzzing lips. "We have to be practical."

"Why?" Cade asked with maddeningly calm reason.

"Because we just do!"

"Practical is overrated and zero fun."

She hung her head. "You're the most irritating man I've ever met."

"But you're crazy about me anyway."

"But I don't want to be."

He winced. "Ouch." He rose from the bed, and she squeezed her eyes shut. She was finally getting through to him. She couldn't get distracted by his body now.

But he messed that all up by picking her up off the bed and pulling her into his arms. He'd put on his jeans, but left his chest bare, so the warmth of his skin seeped into hers. "I'm not asking you for your undying love or a lifelong commitment," he said. "Don't take everything so seriously. We're just having fun. Didn't you have fun last night?"

Last night was intense. Crazy. Rash. But Cade was no doubt used to that kind of casual enjoyment. She wasn't. Clearly, she'd panicked and overreacted. Of course they were just having fun. Cade Garrison didn't have serious relationships.

Calmer, she nodded.

"See, I'm not such a bad guy."

She leaned back. "I never said—"

He laid his finger over her lips. "If I don't hear from you by the time the race starts, I'll call you."

"Okay."

"I'm sorry your day is going to be crappy."

Good grief. Bruce Phillips and his media tantrum. She'd nearly forgotten about him. She kissed Cade quickly, then, holding the bedspread tightly around her, backed toward the bathroom. "Me, too. But it started out pretty good."

He flashed her a grin, and she knew everything was going to be okay.

And fun.

She was going to have fun.

AFTER A QUICK SHOWER in his motor coach, Cade headed toward the Cup garage area. Since the race wasn't until that night, there weren't too many fans around. He passed crew members drinking coffee, NASCAR officials talking in small groups and track security setting up their barricades. Normally, he wouldn't even be out of bed at this hour, but seeing Isabel on a regular basis might just change that habit.

Would his brother be impressed? After Rachel had thrown Bryan out of their meeting yesterday, Cade had convinced her to let him talk to Bryan today instead of waiting until Tuesday. The sooner they jumped on this sponsorship, the sooner they could start building and painting race cars.

He and Bryan had agreed to sleep on Parker Huntington's offer and talk this morning, but he'd bet his brother wasn't expecting him quite this early.

He had another problem with the meeting, though—he hadn't gotten much sleep. He hadn't given Huntington's offer more than five minutes of thought. He'd been too consumed with Isabel.

He'd lied to her. Big-time lied.

He wasn't just having fun. He was very, very serious.

The panic that had crawled over him when she'd been about to toss him out of her room and out of her life was a real wake-up call for how serious he was taking their relationship.

If any other woman had said "Hey, it was great, but last night's over," he would have shrugged and gone on his way. In fact, he would have been relieved there wouldn't be any morning-after conversation about how he felt or what their hookup meant.

How ironic that now *he* was the one who wanted answers to those questions.

"You already know the answers, you just don't like them," he muttered.

"Talkin' to yourself, Cade?" a member of Roger Cothren's crew asked as he walked by. "Not a good sign."

"I just need coffee."

He nodded toward one of NASCAR's equipment haulers. "They've got a whole breakfast set-up back there."

"Thanks, man." Cade headed that way, trying again to push Isabel from his thoughts.

Bryan wouldn't appreciate him being distracted, and he was pretty sure his brother would be one of those people he and Isabel would have to lay super-low around. His brother kept both a mental and physical list of rule infractions Cade committed.

After grabbing coffee and a doughnut, Cade headed to Kevin Reiner's hauler for the meeting. Isabel wouldn't stay in the back of his mind, though.

Typical. She was a stubborn woman.

He'd done the right thing by treating last night as casual. She'd calmed down and sort of agreed to keep moving forward. Knowing that her lousy childhood, not just her professionalism, stood between them, added a whole new level of understanding and challenge. But he was determined to overcome their obstacles.

Everybody had stuff in their past to deal with. Everybody remembered bad relationships. Those experiences didn't have to dominate the future.

Wondering about her feelings had also led him to admit—at least to himself—some things about his own. Being with Isabel wasn't about the thrill of the chase or the adventure of breaking the rules. Not anymore. It wasn't just a physical attraction, though last night had proved he hadn't exaggerated the memory of the first time he'd touched her. It wasn't just curiosity about what might have been. It wasn't just loneliness or the need to find someone he could trust.

The connection with Isabel went much deeper than all that. She'd wrapped herself around his heart, and he wasn't sure if she'd ever let go.

But if he shared any of those thoughts with her, she'd run the other direction so fast she'd leave skid marks all over him.

"Mornin'," his father said as Cade approached the hauler.

Cade sat beside his father in one of the empty chairs that were lined up on either side of the back door. "Where's Bryan?"

His father sipped from a coffee mug. "He'll be along."

"Leg bothering him?"

"A bit."

Cade glanced at his father briefly. "That seems to be happening a lot lately. I thought it would get better."

"It would if he'd go to therapy more."

Classic Bryan. Work was all he ever had time for. "We should hire a trainer to come to the office," Cade said.

"Tried that. He yelled at her and she quit."

Cade shook his head. It was heartbreaking. The brother he'd always known and looked up to had been a powerful man, a fantastic racer, a babe magnet, who eventually became a loyal husband and a family leader. Now he was shouting at people whose only job was to make him feel better.

"I don't think it's the leg so much," his father went on. "He's still having a hard time with the divorce."

"Yours or his?"

"His. He understands about your mother and me."

About to sip his coffee, Cade paused. "I'm glad somebody does."

"She wanted me to retire," his father said with a distinct edge in his tone.

"Would that have been so bad?"

"Yes."

"Maybe she just wanted you to spend more time with her. You could have done that."

"You've been talking to Rachel."

"No." He'd been *listening* to Rachel. When she got on a roll there was no room for anybody else. Still, she'd made sense. "You couldn't compromise?"

His father rose. "I'm not going through this again, son. Marriage is complicated. One day you'll see." He headed into the hauler.

Cade slumped in his chair. *That went well.* What kind of arrogant idiot was he? What right did he have questioning his father about his relationships? He certainly had no experience maintaining anything long-lasting.

Bryan walked—or, more accurately, limped—up a few moments later. "You're up early."

"Not by choice."

"Where'd you get the coffee?"

Cade stood. "You go on inside. I'll get you some when I get a refill." He headed in the direction of the break station before Bryan had a chance to question his generosity. His stubborn brother would crawl to the coffeepot if he realized Cade was volunteering to save him and his leg the pain of getting there on his own.

Bryan might even be as stubborn as Isabel. Hey, maybe his brother could give him some insight into figuring out this woman he couldn't get out of his head.

Carrying the two coffees, Cade headed to the hauler. He stepped inside, then skirted a few crew members as he walked down the narrow passageway toward the office in the back. Once inside, he handed Bryan his cup, then sat next to him on the sofa.

"Is Kevin cool with us meeting in here?" Cade asked after the first sip. "We could have gone to my hauler."

"I'm meeting with Kevin's sponsor after this. It seemed simpler to already be here."

"Anything wrong?"

"No, just a bit of smiling and VIP attention."

Glancing at his brother's face, at the obvious annoyance and dread, Cade added "team president" to his list of careers he'd rather avoid. "Sounds fun."

Bryan shrugged.

"So, what do you think about this deal with Huntington?"

"It's a good offer. The contracts are in order. The money is excellent. You get the three-race deal for this year, then the week after Homestead we sit down and go over the contract for next year. You'll be back in the Cup Series." Bryan looked over at him. "Isn't that what you want?"

"Yes." Maybe too much. He couldn't get perspective on the best decision. He needed to talk to Rachel. And Isabel. "His requirements for finishes are a little tough."

"He expects a lot from you. We all do."

So much for family unity. "I don't trust him."

"I think we'll find that Parker Huntington will run the company much differently than his father."

"How's that?"

"With business sense instead of emotion. His father was the one who pushed the police to file charges against you last summer." Bryan shook his head. "Hotheaded fool."

Cade gripped his coffee cup. "How do you know that?"

"It's my job to ask around and find out who we're doing business with. Offering you this contract is Huntington's way of trying to make amends."

Cade leaned his head back and stared at the ceiling. He'd hated the guy, and now he finds out his father, not him, was behind the arrest? Had Cade misjudged him? Had he been caught up in the emotion of the situation and been a hotheaded fool, just like Parker's father? Was Huntington now trying to *apologize?*

Cade lifted his head. "Hang on. Huntington was a complete jerk to me. He ragged my driving every chance he got."

"And he knows a thing or two about driving. You were out of focus last year. It showed."

"So you agreed with him?"

"Yes, I did."

Cade narrowed his eyes. "Don't hold back, my dear, supportive brother. Just tell me how you feel."

"Hell, Cade, if you can't take criticism, you're in the wrong business."

"I can take it. From my competitors, from the fans, from the media. Call me crazy, but I'd like some support from my sponsors and my family."

Bryan said nothing for a long moment. "You have my support. Always."

The fire taken out of his argument, Cade slumped. "You could say so once in a while."

"I just did."

"After I dragged it out of you."

"I'm the stoic one. If you want a hug, I suggest you find Rachel."

And what about Rachel? Huntington had a thing for her. Cade didn't doubt it for a second. Should he tell Bryan about that? If his brother had really asked around, how had he not uncovered that flashing neon sign?

"I'm still not sure I trust Huntington," Cade said.

"Why not?"

"Just a feeling."

"Look, man, he's offering a legitimate contract. He's even being generous. I'll squeeze a bit more out of him in the negotiations for next year, but if you don't sign this three-race deal immediately, you're out of your mind."

"I want Rachel to read it over first."

"Whatever." Bryan levered himself off the sofa. "I need more coffee."

Cade leapt to his feet. "I'll get it."

The sudden move made Bryan suspicious. "I can get it myself."

"Yeah, but why?" Cade snagged the cup out of his hand. "You get Huntington to let me audition girls for the Hotel Race Babe Contest and have the winners follow me around all season, I'll bring you coffee for life."

Bryan actually smiled as he dropped back into his seat. "Do you ever think about anything else but women and racing?"

"No." Considering, he cocked his head. "Should I?"

CHAPTER THIRTEEN

"I'M GOING TO TELL BAKER I'm switching to them as of next week."

Isabel swallowed her panic. "Bruce, you know we support you no matter what, but we have a lot of money sunk into promoting you through the end of the season. If you go to Baker now, those opportunities will be lost. Plus, you'll have no chance of making the Chase."

"I don't have a chance, anyway."

He was twentieth in points, and he probably didn't have a prayer of making the top twelve in points, but Isabel was trying to find hope. *Any* sense of hope. They'd already shot commercials, bought print and radio ads, used his face and signature on new Blast Energy Drink bottles. They'd launched the new flavor only weeks ago, and it was doing great, largely thanks to the hordes of Bruce Phillips fans buying it.

Losing him now wouldn't just be a marketing problem, it would be a *disaster.*

"Of course you have a chance," she said. "And

even if you don't make it, you're an icon in this sport. So many people buy your merchandise and products. Think how awkward it would be for them."

"I don't know how much more I can take with this team."

Isabel glanced at her uncle, sitting next to her at the kitchen table in Bruce's motor coach. "You're a professional," John said with his characteristic directness. "It's hard to take unprofessional behavior. But we're behind you. The thousands of CATL employees, the ones who smile with pride as they wrap those labels with your face on them around the drink bottles, are your biggest fans. We *know* you can make it to the end of the season and go out like a champion."

Okay, so it was largely a bullish speech. But they were grasping at straws.

"You've established so many lasting relationships in racing," Isabel added. "Don't you want to walk away from this one knowing you did everything the right way? I'd hate to see you burdened with regrets in the twilight of your team's journey."

Obviously amused, Uncle John raised his eyebrows.

Dang. Over the top again. When she was faking sincerity, she often didn't know where to stop.

And she was definitely faking it this time. She wanted to whap Phillips in the back of the head for putting them all through this mess. She got that his job was hard right now. She realized it was uncomfortable to race every week with guys you weren't going to race with next year. But the driver and crew chief of a team were the leaders. It was their responsibility to set the tone for everybody else.

In her book, Phillips was letting them all down. He could make these last months something special, or at least tolerable.

She thought Bruce was a better man than this. Certainly a better driver.

Phillips heaved a giant sigh. "Well, maybe…"

Isabel and her uncle talked to him for another hour or so, soothing him and assuring him that he could survive this crisis. Of course, once Ricky's story hit the Internet and airwaves, Phillips's team was going to be royally pissed, so he'd have a lot of explaining to do. But sometimes a public fight brought things to a head so that everybody could air their grievances and move forward.

Other times, the whole thing blew up into a bigger mess.

For her part, she'd done all she could do to protect CATL. She'd eaten nothing all day, it was way past lunch and she was starting to get light-headed.

"Roger told me you stopped by his party last night," her uncle John said as they headed toward the hospitality village, where CATL had set up a tent to serve barbecue and give out free product samples to fans.

"He and his family were great. It was fun."

"Relationships are everything in this business. Roger is a good man to have on your side."

"Yeah, but I didn't just go for business. I like the Cothrens."

"They're great people. Just make sure you don't get too close. As you can see from Bruce's situation, things change in an instant in sports."

She suddenly thought of Cade and could have kicked herself for even hinting about personal relationships. "What do you do when you start to lose respect for the people you're in business with?" she asked, in an effort to steer the conversation back to a professional topic.

"You mean Bruce?"

Her face heating, she glanced over at him. "I know I shouldn't judge."

"You have to remember something important, sweetie. Bruce is a racer."

"Yeah. So what?"

"Racers instinctively know when a team isn't working. They know when the chemistry is off. Remember, these guys think at 180 miles an hour, so slow them down and they really catch a change in temperature or tension. They're always charging full steam ahead, and when they don't think the people around them are doing the same thing, they get antsy.

"Guys like Bruce also remember the old, scrambling days. When you raced on the weekends for the purse just so you could get your car back on the track the next weekend. They didn't pay light and heating bills. They sacrificed their jobs. They didn't sleep."

"All so they could race," she said. She'd seen that passion in the eyes of so many drivers over the past several years. It was amazing to witness the highs of glory and heartbreaking when dreams ended. The image of Bryan Garrison winning the season opener in Daytona, then the NASCAR NEXTEL Cup just three years ago, came to mind. The smiling, fist-pumping driver of that year had turned into a quiet, scowling, sometimes morose team president.

"Those days are hard to forget," her uncle continued. "They're always on edge for the next race, the next season, the next hot team. Very few ever feel comfortable. It's their nature."

"The boardroom isn't so different."

"In some ways." A couple strolled by dressed head to toe in Roger Cothran gear, including their faces painted exactly like the flames on his car. "But other times it's a whole different world."

Shaking her head, Isabel smiled. It was a different world, all right. A world containing a magician with pale blue eyes and a killer smile. He had to be a magician, since only something supernatural could have her risking her career, her sanity and the respect of her family.

As they drew closer to the hospitality tents, they passed a group of women who were laughing and jumping with excitement.

"He signed my hand!" one of them screamed. "Cade Garrison actually touched me!"

Not so long ago Isabel would have either rolled

her eyes or laughed at a comment like that. It happened every weekend, after all.

Today, with her thoughts and emotions tuned to Cade, with the memory of last night so vivid, she narrowed her eyes as she passed by the group. They were all young and voluptuous. They all had ridiculously perfect hair and bright smiles. That was what he expected, what he was used to.

Could she really compete with women like that? Was she crazy to even try?

You've already questioned your sanity once today. Isn't that enough?

The smell of barbecue drifted through the air, distracting her from anything more personal than her stomach growling. She linked arms with her uncle, and they wound their way through the barricades to enter the hospitality village. Their tent was halfway down the aisle on the left, and they were pleased to see the umbrella tables full of fans eating barbecue or people standing in line to get free samples of CATL products.

With a little maneuvering, they managed to get plates for themselves. They huddled in the corner and watched the buzz of activity. The expectation in the air was contagious. After their stressful morning, and what would undoubtedly be a stressful week, the excitement was a refreshing change of pace.

As they tossed their empty plates in the trash, the crowd around them started to mutter. The sound spread through the tent, then the muttering turned into a buzz. People craned their necks. Several rushed toward the exit.

Was there a problem?

Isabel angled her head to try to catch something coherent from the conversations around her. She heard *oh, my* and *you're kidding*.

Could there be a fire?

She mouthed the ominous words at Uncle John, and he shook his head in denial, but they both moved toward the exit. If there was a problem, they needed to help get everyone out of the tents.

Once they made their way through the crowd, they spotted Vincent and Susan standing at the railing that separated the outside dining area from the walkway between the tents. They'd all been so busy the past few days, she hadn't seen her friends since they left the airport.

"What's going on?" Isabel asked.

Vincent grinned.

Susan crossed her arms over her chest. "What is it about them that they live for adoration?"

Isabel stepped up to the railing. "Who?"

Susan pointed to the crowded walkway. "Them."

Craning her neck, Isabel finally spotted the… problem. Cade and Derek Foster, another hot, young driver, were walking through the hospitality area. They were surrounded by a few security people and hoards of fans. They made slow progress, but they were moving along.

Were they nuts?

If the crowd surged, or got too excited, they'd be overrun. Trampled.

"Vincent." She grabbed his arm. "Go help. Get them out of the walkway."

Uncle John chuckled. "They'll be fine, Isabel. They're probably just on their way to a sponsor appearance."

Her heart pounding, Isabel pressed her lips together. "Right. Of course, you're right." Still, she watched them closely as they walked by. And she saw somebody she knew. Somebody they all knew.

"That looks like Candy," Susan said.

"It *is* Candy," Isabel said. Their colleague, who was supposed to be sticking close to their NASCAR Busch Series driver today, was following behind Cade and Derek with her autograph book held out like a star-crazed fan. "Vincent," she said through clenched teeth, "go get her."

"On my way," her buddy said, heading into the fray.

A few minutes later, Vincent returned with a red-faced Candy, clutching her autograph book tightly in her hands. Her gaze darted from Isabel to her uncle, then back. Uncle John, thankfully, said nothing. The reps were Isabel's responsibility, after all.

Embarrassed for herself, as well as Candy, Isabel still faced her without flinching. "We need to talk." She led the rep around to the back side of the hospitality tent, so they could have some privacy. Only the catering staff was milling around. "You want to explain—"

Candy burst into tears. "You're going to fire me, aren't you? I *should* be fired. It's just I love him so much, and he wanted— And I— Oh, my mother is going to *kill* me."

Good grief, the girl was going to hyperventilate. And who exactly did she love? Cade? Derek? Either one wasn't a good thing. Falling for a driver was forbidden.

You oughta know.

Isabel ignored her conscience and focused on Candy.

"My…b-boyfriend and I b-broke up," Candy said, hiccupping her way through her confession.

Boyfriend? Not Cade or Derek, then. So what was she doing chasing after them?

"I kn-know I was supposed to be with Tad," Candy continued, her baby-blue eyes wide and watery. "I was, I just— My boyfriend just—" She stopped, gasping for air.

Isabel felt panic churn inside her. She was no good with crying girls. "Calm down. It's okay."

Candy cried harder. Several members of the catering staff stared at them.

Watching a bubbly, blond cheerleader have a complete breakdown was not on Isabel's agenda for the day. She weakly patted her shoulder and hoped she'd find a way to pull it together.

Candy was their newest rep—and their youngest. She was just out of college, but she'd done a great job so far, her natural effervescence and sweet smile aiding her whenever she made a mistake. And though Isabel was only a few years older than her, she felt as if she'd been through several more layers of life than Candy had.

Eight months ago Candy's biggest ambition had been shaking pom-poms on the football sideline. The innocence and vulnerability that she didn't even know she had were things Isabel had lost long, long ago.

"I'm not going to fire you," Isabel said, though she could have bitten her tongue off for making such a rash promise.

It was apparently a good instinct, though, because Candy lifted her head. "You're…y-you're not?"

"No."

"But you're Sca—" She clamped her hand over her mouth.

"Scary Isabel. Yes, I know."

Candy's face paled. She obviously didn't realize Isabel knew about her office nickname. She threw her arms around her. "I'm so sorry. I'm a mess. I love him, and he—" She started crying again.

Isabel stiffened for a moment at the unprofessional hugging, then she simply held on. She'd had some recent experience with being a mess over a guy. "What happened?" she asked once Candy's shaking had stopped.

Candy straightened and cleared her throat. "My boyfriend broke up with me two weeks ago, and I'm a wreck." She let out a watery laugh and dashed away the tears rolling down her face. "As you can see. He's *it* for me, you know?"

Isabel blinked. "I know."

"And he loves Derek Foster, so when Tad and his guest said they wanted to relax in his coach—"

"Tad's guest?"

"His *female* guest."

She could hardly expect her reps to follow their drivers into their motor coaches when they wanted privacy with their dates. "Right."

"Tad told me to come back an hour before the race, so he could walk through the garage area and wish his teammates good luck. I found myself with a few hours of nothing to do."

Isabel sighed. "And your boyfriend loves Derek Foster."

Candy nodded.

"Did you get his autograph?"

Looking pitiful, Candy shook her head.

"You know, technically, he's your *ex*-boyfriend."

Candy closed her eyes. "I know."

Isabel sighed again. Guilt. What a horrible and powerful thing it was. Candy's boyfriend was a fool. He'd broken up with this sweet and beautiful girl— for what? Freedom? Somebody else? Plain stupidity?

And did it really matter? Isabel was Candy's boss. Not her friend or confidante. She should only be concerned with her job performance.

So the reasons why she asked a passing waiter for

a napkin, which she handed to Candy for her tear-stained face, were tied to emotions she didn't want to examine too closely. "What's the deal with this guy? Why did he break up with you?"

She hiccupped. "He says he needs some space. He loves me, but he wants to be sure."

"Uh-huh."

"He wants us to date other people for a few weeks, and if we don't feel those sparks with anybody else, he thinks we should get married."

Prepared to call the guy a major player, Isabel halted her runaway judgment. It wasn't a bad plan. It was practical and sensible, which appealed to Isabel. Marriage was for a lifetime, after all.

But for a girl like Candy, *sensible* was a betrayal. A bone-deep humiliation. And didn't every woman—even Isabel—sigh at the idea of a guy who threw caution aside, jumped in with both feet, plus flowers, champagne and a sparkling diamond, and declared his undying love? By comparison, let's-test-the-waters-and-make-sure-our-love-is-real sounded really cold.

"Have you dated anybody else?" she asked Candy.

"No."

"Has he?"

Her lower lip trembled. "Yes."

Ah. "So you figured you'd risk your job to show him how invaluable you are?"

A tear spilled down her face. She pressed her lips together and nodded.

The pain on her face was more than Isabel could stand. She leaned toward Candy. She wanted to shake her. "Are you crazy?"

"Uh, well—"

"Don't chase this guy. You're smart and sweet and cute."

"Cute?"

"Newborn-puppy cute. *Adorable* cute. And this guy is a complete and utter idiot if he doesn't grab you with both hands and run to the altar."

"But—"

"Go out with somebody else. Do it quickly and often. If your guy doesn't come crawling back on his hands and knees within twenty-four hours of finding out you're going out with other people, then he's a bigger idiot than is already apparent."

Candy's eyes brightened. "You think so?"

"Yes." She paused and reached out, squeezing Candy's hands. "You deserve a guy who loves you with every part of him. This is your chance to find out if that's true."

Candy said nothing for a minute or two, then she balled up her napkin and rolled her shoulders. "You're right."

"Maybe."

"Not much gets by you, does it?"

"No."

"I won't get distracted by my personal problems again."

"That would be a good idea. And next time you

have *nothing to do,* you might want to call me. I'll find something for you to do."

"You're Scary Isabel again."

Isabel smiled. "Yes, I most certainly am."

HOURS LATER, SWEAT-SOAKED from the summer sun, after talking to hundreds of fans, as well as a handful of reporters about Bruce's story, and networking with other sponsors around the hospitality tents, Isabel and Susan walked toward the garage area. There they'd give their best wishes to their drivers, then head to the CATL suite. The sun was hanging low in the sky, the race was due to start in less than an hour, and they were dragging. Once the on-track action began, all the business and networking stopped. It was time for sponsors to enjoy the race just like the fans.

Thankfully, their race experience involved an air-conditioned suite and free food provided by the expert track catering staff.

Thoughts of fans brought back the memory of Candy, which reminded her that she should have been tougher. She should have been Candy's boss, not her buddy. A few weeks ago she would have been.

Cade had changed her. The simmering feelings she had for him made her kinder, more sympathetic, less professional.

Ugh!

She'd risen to the top of her profession so quickly

because she put her job first, because she never made a move without considering the impact on her company and the marketing team she and her uncle were so invested in.

"He's ruining me," she said to Susan.

"Who?"

Isabel cut her gaze toward her friend.

"Oh. Him."

"Him, all right. I'm losing my edge. I'm turning into a soft, mushy, no-edge…thing."

Susan angled her head. "You mean a marshmallow?"

"That's it! I'm turning into a marshmallow."

"*You* are not a marshmallow."

"Not yet, but it's only a matter of time."

"Let's just enjoy the race. I heard they have barbecue ribs in the suite."

"Yeah." Thinking of room service and a hot bath, Isabel trudged alongside Susan as they made the rounds by the Phillips and Cothren haulers. Once the drivers were called to introductions, they started toward the suite.

But just outside the door, Isabel stopped. "You go ahead. I'm going back to the hotel."

Susan laid her arm across her shoulders. "Come on. You'll feel better once we sit down and eat."

The emotion of last night with Cade, the crisis with Bruce, the way she'd handled Candy all came crashing down around her. She was drained. Done. Over.

She pulled away from Susan. "I have to go."

"What if Bruce or Roger wins?"

"You go to Victory Lane. You and Uncle John can handle everything."

"Are you okay?"

Tears were building behind her eyes. "Yes," she said, though clearly she wasn't. "I'll call you later. Just—" She swallowed an embarrassing swell of emotion. "Can you handle this tonight?"

Susan nodded, her eyes still focused intently on her face. "Sure. You rest."

Isabel let out a weak laugh. She had to rest. Scary Isabel, who never let anything or anybody affect her or her job, had to rest. "Yeah." She backed away. "Call me if you need anything."

"Okay."

Isabel fled the track. By some miracle she found her rental car without encountering anybody she knew. Clearly, Susan wouldn't be calling her for anything tonight. She knew Isabel was useless.

Unimportant.

Insignificant.

Some part of her managed to pull herself together long enough to get to the hotel. She stumbled through the door of her room and felt instantly better in the silence. After a day of noise and activity, the setting sun peeking through the curtains was plenty of stimulation.

She stood at the window and stared out at the crashing waves. The water plunged over the beach, then slid back, cleansing the sand, leaving it pristine and glistening in the moonlight.

It should be so easy.

But maybe a shower would be the next best thing. As she dropped her clothes on the bathroom floor, her cell phone rang. She closed her eyes against the intrusion. If it was work, she wasn't answering.

Wrapping a towel around herself, she snagged the phone and checked the number on the screen. *Cade.*

The urge to beg him to come over, to hold her until the weird emptiness inside her went away was nearly overwhelming.

"Hey, are you at the track?" he asked.

She could hear the faint roar of engines in the background, telling her he must be there, though he must be inside somewhere. "No, I'm at the hotel. It's been a long day."

"So Vincent said."

"When did you talk to him?"

"I passed him as he was heading to the suite a few minutes ago. He told me Bruce's story hit the wires."

Knowing how Cade felt about Bruce changing teams and not wanting to relive the wild day, Isabel simply said "Mmm-hmm." She turned on the shower and her tension eased a bit from the sound of the streaming water. "Can I call you back in twenty minutes? I feel like I have half the track as an extra layer of skin—and that's on top of the sweat."

"My charming Izzy, you do know how to seduce a man."

She winced. "Sorry. Too much information, I guess."

He laughed, and the sound of *that* sent the rest of her tension into retreat. In fact, she was already warmed from the inside out. "While you shower, why don't I head your way?" he said. "We could have a beer in the bar."

She paused as she was pulling the band out of her hair. "We can't have a beer in the bar, Cade," she said quietly.

"Why— Oh."

"My uncle is here, plus other—"

"I *remember.*"

She swallowed. The resentment in his voice brought tears to her eyes. She leaned her head back to blink them away. What difference did one night make, and did it really matter that they couldn't be together in public?

You're tired. You're just tired.

But she wanted to see him. She *needed* to see him. "Come here." She pressed her lips together, realizing how commanding—and perhaps desperate—she sounded. "I mean, why don't you come to my room? I'll order beer from room service."

Okay, so maybe that still sounded desperate. But then she was.

"I'll be right there," Cade said.

She signed off, then jumped into the shower before she could question her invitation. Her aunt would have dropped her jaw in horror. Completely unladylike. Way too forward.

Isabel, having no intention of dropping her jaw or

being worried about being ladylike or forward, smiled as the shower spray pummeled the top of her head. She felt as if she were washing away the entire, long, nerve-racking day. There was something amazing and rejuvenating about visualizing all the bad stuff circling, then sliding down the drain.

When she stepped out of the shower and looked at herself in the mirror, though, she realized mascara was smeared all over her face, and she looked like a stunt double for a drowned rat. That didn't work into her plan at all.

She quickly dried her hair and dabbed on some makeup. By the time she heard Cade's soft knock on the door, she looked decent. In fact, she had a nice flush to her cheeks, but that was probably due to anticipation rather than cosmetics.

Since she was wearing only a bathrobe, though, the effect might be lost on Cade.

Taking a deep breath, she opened the door.

"Hey, I didn't—" Cade stopped, his gaze sliding from her face down her body to her bare feet. He closed the door behind him, then leaned heavily against it.

"You didn't what?" she asked, licking her lips.

His gaze connected with hers. "I didn't come up here for a beer."

She laid her hand on his chest, then wrapped the other one around the back of his neck. "I didn't ask you up here for one."

CHAPTER FOURTEEN

"MOM, HOW DO YOU PREHEAT an oven?"

"Cade, honey, are you *cooking?*"

"No, I thought I'd stick my head inside and end it all."

Actually, that wasn't a bad idea. He'd gotten a recipe from an online site, printed it out, bought all the necessary cooking pans and ingredients and now he was stuck on the first line of the recipe. This dinner was doomed.

"That's not funny, dear. What are you cooking?"

"Chicken."

"Why are you cooking chicken?"

"'Cause my date won't be seen with me in public."

"That's not funny, dear."

He'd been completely serious, though he could see how his mom wouldn't think so. "I don't have time to be funny. She's coming at seven."

"Who?"

"A woman."

"Cade Michael."

"A special woman. You've never met her. Please, Mom, I'm in trouble here."

His mother didn't hesitate. "I'll be right there."

Before she disconnected, she told him how to preheat the oven, so he was at least able to move to step two while waiting for her to get to his house. He'd managed to rinse the chicken and pat it dry before grinding to a halt when he read he was supposed to grease a thirteen-by-nine-inch pan.

The pan he had, a brand-new one from the kitchen supply store. Grease he had. For his car.

He glanced from the chicken to the pan and back again. He was pretty sure that wasn't what the recipe meant. Knowing he was beat, he did what any calm, intelligent, desperate bachelor would do.

He opened a beer and waited for his mother to come save him.

Since his parents—correction, his mother's—house was only a few streets over, she was there within minutes. "How special?" she asked as soon as she walked into the kitchen.

Cade set down his beer and thought about Isabel, flushed and still warm from her shower, inviting him into her room two nights ago. "Very."

His mother smiled. "Finally."

His stomach jumped at the hope in her eyes. Maybe he should warn her not to plan how she'd spoil her grandchildren just yet. He'd managed to get pretty physical with Isabel, but understanding the emotional side of her was going to be a much bigger challenge. She didn't trust him—or maybe anybody.

Not to mention she was risking her job by seeing him, and he was risking possible sponsorship and his family's support and respect, and he was pretty sure she didn't think he was worth the gamble.

Plus, their first official date was never going to happen if he didn't get this chicken cooked. "You know how to roast a chicken, right?"

"Of course I do."

With his mom's help, they managed to easily follow the recipe. The grease they needed turned out to be the spray stuff he used to keep steaks from sticking to the grill. Once they'd seasoned the chicken and put in the oven, they chopped the potatoes and other vegetables and added them to the pan a few minutes later.

"You've got something besides beer to serve, I hope," his mother said as he unwrapped the roses he'd bought at the florist.

"She likes beer."

"Not with roast chicken, she doesn't. I can bring you a bottle of wine from my cellar. What kind of plates are you using?"

"Plates?"

"Oh, Cade, surely—"

"I'm kidding. I have plates, Mom."

She took the roses from him and examined them critically. "Do you have something to put these in?"

He pulled his newly purchased vase from its box,

filled it with water, then dumped in the flowers. For some reason, they didn't look nearly as good as the ones on display in the shop.

Shaking her head, his mother rummaged through the kitchen drawers until she found a pair of scissors. She cut the roses in several different lengths, then arranged them in the vase. Now they looked perfect.

He kissed her cheek. "That looks great."

"You're welcome, and I'm glad you called me. These days you usually call your sister when you need something."

No way he could talk to Rachel about dinner with Isabel. She was one of the main people they were hiding from.

But he also realized by turning to Rachel so often, he'd neglected his mother. She *wanted* to be needed. She no longer had him and his siblings or her husband to take care of, which was why she was so invested in planning Thanksgiving.

She was lonely.

"If this chicken turns out as good as it smells, I'll call you every time I make dinner," he said lightly.

"No, you won't." She patted his hand. "I've shown you how to do it for yourself. You won't need me next time. That's a mother's job."

"I'll always need you, Mom."

She turned away, placing the flower-filled vase in the center of the kitchen table, then fiddled with the adjustable light switch on the chandelier. "I love you more than anything, Cade," she said, still staring at the table arrangement and gripping the back of one of the chairs. "You and your brother and sister. I know the divorce has been hard on you. I know you don't really understand what your father and I have been through." Her voice caught. "Why we gave up."

He started toward her. "Mom—"

She held up her hand. "I need to say this." She clenched her hands in front of her. "You shouldn't—" She stopped and pressed her lips together, obviously trying to pull herself together before continuing. "You shouldn't give up on love because your father and I divorced. You should believe in love and happily ever after. You should search for it with the whole of your heart.

"If this girl is the one, then hold on to her, cherish her. There are so many pieces of yourself and your life you have to share. Don't give it all to racing."

"Yes, ma'am." His heart pounded. He swallowed. "Why *did* you and Dad—"

"I can't talk to you about that. I don't think it's proper for a parent to discuss the details of their personal relationships with their child."

Why? Cade wanted to argue, though he kept silent. He respected his mother's wishes. Also, he realized something very important in that moment.

She still loved her husband.

And that didn't seem to be a problem he could solve in the few remaining minutes before his date. Actually, it didn't seem like something he would *ever* be qualified to solve. He didn't even have a clue how to begin.

"I should go get that wine." She crossed the kitchen, then stopped briefly, smiling at him over her shoulder. "I may even have some champagne."

ISABEL PULLED HER CAR down Cade's driveway leading to the drive-under garage.

"The only person who uses my front door is my mother," he'd said when they talked earlier. "All my friends come in the back."

The only other time she'd been to his house he'd said the same thing when she'd pulled up to the front. Of course then he wasn't in much condition to argue about which door she helped him through, since he probably couldn't have found any of them on his own.

She drew a deep breath as she exited her car. The anticipation of seeing him had overridden her nerves, but her emotions were also at war with her sense of preservation. She shouldn't be getting closer to Cade, she should be running the other way.

Crazy as she was, though, she smoothed her palms down her silky silver dress and headed toward the deck stairs. She didn't often wear heels, so her steps were a bit slow and unsteady, but she took a moment to glance to her left and watch the sun glistening off the lake, the horizon shaded in orange and red, the trees framing the perfect portrait and promise of a summer sunset.

The wealth and privilege of that kind of view was unreal to her. Uncle John and Aunt Emma had a lake house, and she'd spent many summer weekends there skiing and swimming. But their place was a basic two-bedroom with a bathroom and small kitchen. Nothing like…

She glanced back at Cade's house, then way, way up to the roofline of the three-story brick-and-stone palace. Nothing like *that*.

Starting toward the door, she decided she definitely preferred viewing the house from the back. The deck and view were premium, of course, but the majestic front of the mansion, alongside all the other mansions and the neighborhood security station she'd driven by to get to his place, were even more daunting.

She didn't belong here. She was so far out of her element she'd need a map to find her way back to real life.

Enjoy him while you've got him.

That was her new motto. She was throwing herself into this relationship—as much as she was capable of doing, anyway. Until the risks outweighed the rewards, until he got tired of her, until they both realized long-term wasn't ever a possibility, she was in.

She knocked on the door, and he appeared seconds later.

"Hey," he said, "I thought I heard a car."

He wore black dress pants and a charcoal shirt

with a pressed collar. His wavy hair was swept off his forehead, dipping sexily over one eyebrow. His smile was bright and welcoming.

But it was the look in his eyes that stopped her heart—the hungry, needy look she was sure she'd see in her own reflection if she could. No matter how impractical, wild or temporary their connection was, it was powerful.

"Hey," she managed to say.

"You look—" his gaze swept her "—amazing."

"Thanks."

Susan had—reluctantly at first—helped her with her makeup and arranged her hair in a sort-of-casual, sort-of-messy updo. Vincent had spent his lunch hour consulting with his boutique-saleswoman network to get her plunging neckline dress and sparkly stiletto sandals just right.

Cade wrapped his hand around her wrist and tugged her inside. Pulling her against him, sliding his hand through her hair, he kissed her as if it had been two months instead of two days since he'd seen her.

Her head spun as they separated. "Susan isn't going to be happy you messed up her lip gloss so quickly."

He ran his tongue across his bottom lip. "Tell her I lost all control over the cherries."

"Cherries? I smell chicken. Did you—"

She stopped as she glanced around the kitchen. Lit candles on the table highlighted two place settings and an over-the-top romantic pink-and-red-rose centerpiece. Other candles flickered in glass containers on the curved bar, where a platter decorated with fresh parsley rested next to a silver bucket filled with champagne and ice.

She blinked. "Wow."

He embraced her from behind and kissed her neck, and she noticed soft music playing in the background.

"I figured we should move beyond the generic hotel room."

She still couldn't drag her stunned gaze from the scene before her. "Yeah."

"You wore a dress."

"Yeah."

"You want some champagne?"

"Yeah."

He smiled. "Coming right up."

When he popped the cork, she managed to shake herself out of the trance. She didn't have an appointment to rush to, a problem to solve. He didn't have to practice, qualify or race. They had the whole night together.

After he handed her a glass of champagne, he slid his hand down her bare back. "Why don't we drink this on the deck? We've still got a few minutes before dinner is ready."

She followed him outside, and they leaned against the railing as they looked out on the lake. "How did yesterday with the guys go?"

"Great. Boating, beer and football. What else

could a guy ask for?" He dragged his finger across her cheek. "Besides a beautiful woman."

She smiled over the rim of her flute. "You keep flattering me, you just might get lucky."

He choked on his mouthful of champagne.

As she patted him on the back, her grin widened. "Good. Now you're as off balance as I am."

He coughed, then shook his head, obviously trying to clear it and his throat. "Why are you off balance?"

"First date. Hot guy." She angled her head. "I'm wearing a dang dress, Cade."

"You don't wear dresses?"

"Not even to church. In fact, I wore a tuxedo suit to the NASCAR banquet in New York last year."

His eyes brightened. "I think that excites me. Was it really low cut, so you could see the swell of your—"

She lightly slapped his chest. "You have a dirty mind."

"And that's a bad thing?"

"You'd better behave. I'll sic Mrs. Fitzgerald on you."

"She already has it in for me."

"Maybe not." She sipped her champagne. "She said you asked her to switch the historical society meeting to tomorrow night for a very important date."

"I'd forgotten all about that goofy meeting when I asked you out for tonight. I was afraid if I changed the date, you'd bail."

Would she have used that as an out? A way to escape the emotions and vulnerability he stirred in her?

"See what I mean?" he said, looking away.

She inched her way between him and the railing, making sure she faced him. "I wouldn't have bailed. I'm in this. It's crazy and risky, but I'm here, and I'm not going anywhere." *At least not until you get tired of me.* She slid her hand up his chest, then wrapped it around his neck. "Mrs. Fitzgerald was impressed by your concern for your 'special girl.' She thinks you may have substance, after all."

"I'm so relieved," he said sarcastically.

But he did look relieved. She'd thought he was the self-assured one. Was it possible he had feelings he wasn't familiar with or didn't understand just like her? Was it possible this relationship meant more to him than just another conquest, another good time?

The stove timer beeped, and he captured her hand, leading her back inside, where he pulled a perfectly browned roasted chicken surrounded by colorful vegetables from the oven.

She refilled their champagne glasses, then sat at the bar and stared at him in amazement. She'd smelled the chicken earlier, but she'd pictured foil-covered take-out containers warming in the oven. "You cook."

"I guess I do." Laying the oven mitts on the counter, he turned toward her. "Mom helped, but I could do it on my own next time."

"You cooked for me."

He rounded the bar and sat next to her. "You're important to me. I wanted to show you."

She braced her hands on either side of his face and kissed him. "Thanks."

He slid his arms around her waist, then pulled her toward him, bar stool and all. "The chicken needs to rest for fifteen minutes. You could do that again."

She did.

Well, *they* did.

When they finally managed to separate, her heart was racing and she was gasping for breath, yet she'd never felt more comfortable in her life.

First dates were supposed to be hesitant and awkward, but she realized that somewhere between their zero-to-sixty first meeting, the awkward aftermath, then jumping into the sack more than a year later, she and Cade had become friends. The foundation for their intimacy was still forming, but it wasn't made of sand.

Framed by the lovely bouquet of roses and dozens of flickering candles, they sat at the kitchen table and enjoyed their dinner. They talked about Davidson business and the upcoming historical society fundraiser. Isabel tried to impress upon Cade that the houses and artifacts he was now in charge of saving weren't just falling-down eyesores or rusty relics. They were memories and symbols of the past, like racing trophies or wrecked pieces of cars that his family saved for their museum.

Cade admitted he'd hung several pieces of favored

race cars in his basement pool room, and he never walked through the GRI museum without stopping by the trophy case to remember where he'd come from and the family history of success he needed to live up to.

They talked about racing—the possibility of Bruce Phillips's midseason defection, which they thought was likely, and finally Cade's sponsorship opportunities.

"Are you gonna tell me what you think I should do?" he asked as they worked together to rinse the plates and load them into the dishwasher.

She pressed her lips together. She was often outspoken and used to being in charge, but she wasn't Cade's business manager. "What does Rachel say?"

"We've agreed not to talk until tomorrow."

Isabel fought against giving advice she knew was sound and being too intrusive in his life. What if she recommended the deal and it all went badly? Would he blame her? "She wants you to form your own opinion."

It was smart. Something Isabel herself would do. She didn't know Rachel Garrison well, but she was respected by everyone in racing. She always had her brother's back.

"If you grip your glass any harder, it's going to break," he said.

"It's not for me to—"

"I'm asking your opinion."

She shifted her gaze to his. "Why did you hit Parker Huntington?"

"That isn't—" He stopped and turned away.

"My business?" She ignored the pang of hurt. "You asked my opinion, and I'm willing to give it. Why did you hit Parker Huntington?"

He said nothing for a long moment, then looked back at her, his eyes flashing with heat. "Because he deserved it."

CADE HAD NEVER SHARED his true feelings about Huntington with anyone else. Not his friends. Not anybody in his family. Definitely not Rachel.

"Let's go outside," he said to Isabel.

By now it was completely dark except for the light of the half moon. He'd certainly made mistakes in his life. Would signing another deal with Huntington be one of them?

Maybe.

"He went after my sister," he said to Isabel as he gripped the deck railing.

"Went after?"

"He was always coming on to her. He has this look in his eyes."

"You didn't hit him because he looked at your sister." She leaned next to him. "That may have been the last thing he did, but something else happened before."

As usual, she was right. A lot had led up to his and Huntington's final confrontation. A lot was still left to be dealt with. Some within himself. "Did you know my grandfather raced stock cars?" he asked, staring at the lake.

"I've heard."

"Three generations of racers—that's my legacy. And I'm the last. At the moment and maybe forever. Bryan was supposed to be the one, not me. *He* was supposed to make sure our generation made it to the record books. All I had to do was smile for the cameras, throw out a joke or sound bite." He closed his eyes against the responsibilities weighing him down, commitments he knew he wasn't fulfilling. "I was supposed to have fun. Nobody was supposed to rely on me."

He pushed away from the railing. "Huntington said I wasn't good enough to call myself a Garrison." He swallowed. "Maybe he's right."

She laid her palm against his cheek. "He's wrong."

Her unwavering confidence triggered something inside him he hadn't felt since before Bryan's accident. In all the time that he'd driven his brother's car, he'd never once truly thought he belonged there.

"I'm tired of being compared to everybody else in my family."

"Yeah, I'll bet you are." She paused, searching his gaze. "But here's the thing…the thing that no fan, no sports writer, no team member or family member may ever get. You can only be you. You can try to live up to the past. You can even try to copy your grandfather, your father or your brother. But I'd rather see you follow your own path, do things your own way, meet your own goals. There's more to you than just being the youngest Garrison. You don't have to let that—or racing—be your whole identity."

Would his family agree? They hadn't told him which records to break, but they expected premium performance. They wanted his best, and they put pressure on him just by existing. "Racing is the only thing I know how to do."

She smiled gently. "Other than make a seriously good roasted chicken."

"I could always be a chef."

"I think so."

He narrowed his eyes. "Huntington better not criticize my cooking."

"He'd have me to answer to."

"You'll defend me?"

"Absolutely, though I don't think you have to worry about him criticizing anything. I imagine he regrets his words almost as much as you do your punch." She angled her head. "You actually have a lot in common with Parker."

"*Parker,* huh?"

"His father and my uncle have been friends for years. They tried to throw Parker and me together more than once."

Cade clenched his jaw. Another reason to resent Mr. Too Perfect.

But comparing romantic pasts wasn't something

he wanted to dive too deeply into. Especially since his was pretty crowded. "But you didn't stick."

"We're casual friends, and because we are, I know he used to race motorcycles."

"I've heard."

"Not stock cars, so he doesn't have any right to give you critiques, but he does understand the racer mentality. He just doesn't seem to communicate it very well."

"By telling me I suck."

"Exactly. He's just a little too smart for his own good."

"That Harvard degree."

"And some inbred arrogance. Still, his father and grandfather built Huntington Hotels to incredible success, and now he feels the pressure to follow in their footsteps. Extend the legacy. Sound familiar?"

"A little." He'd never really thought of himself and Huntington as similar on a personal level. He wasn't sure whether he felt more or less comfortable. "Are you telling me I should accept his sponsorship?"

"The three-race deal definitely. After that it's for you, Rachel and Bryan to decide."

"He's not giving me any guarantees about next year, you know. He wants serious performance."

She waved that aside. "You'll meet his requirements, and even if you don't, he'll offer a deal. His legacy is at stake. He wants the best."

Cade shook his head. But *was* he the best? "I appreciate your confidence in me, but—"

She poked him in the chest. "I'm not blowing up your confidence because we're sleeping together. I'm not playing games and telling you you're the best because you cooked me dinner."

Planting her hands on her hips, she paced away from him, and he watched, fascinated, as she worked herself up into a lather over him. Was it any wonder he was completely bonkers over her?

"You asked my *business* advice, something I take very seriously, something I've been considering carefully, and here it is." She stopped and faced him, looking like a slightly-bent-out-of-shape foil star. "Sign the deal. Parker Huntington is a highly respected guy. The hotel chain is solid. They pay their bills. They follow through on their commitments. My only caveat is that you confront him about the past. You need to tell him you're not willing to accept his driving advice. He's not a coach or adviser. He's a *sponsor.* He should act like one."

He pulled her into his arms. Avenging Angel Isabel was an amazing sight. "You and Rachel are eerily alike. I'm wondering if I should be worried about that."

"You should be *honored* by that."

"Uh-huh. If we keep dating, are you going to get as bossy as she is?"

"Depends on how often you screw up."

"Okay."

She pressed her lips to his throat, sending his pulse shooting somewhere near the stars. "Can we have one, last, super gushy moment?"

"Sure."

"Parker was a big, fat idiot to open his mouth about your driving."

"And you're going to tell him so?"

"First chance I get." She leaned back. "What's for dessert?"

"You. Or maybe a movie?"

She kissed him. "How about both?"

CHAPTER FIFTEEN

NESTLED AGAINST CADE'S shoulder as they watched the movie credits roll across the TV, comfy in the sweat-pants and T-shirt she'd borrowed, Isabel lifted her head. "So I guess you're building a car for Indy this week."

"Yeah. We've spent the past few weeks working on one for Chicago, so we'll have to put that aside and start on a whole new car—one that will make the race and finish in the top ten in less than two weeks."

"Huntington wants you in the *top ten?*"

"He'll accept top twenty, but he wants ten."

"Man, he doesn't ask for much."

"Earlier you told me I'd have no problem with his requirements."

Yeah, but *top ten?* At *Indy?* "Of course you won't," she said quickly. "Just do your best. Setting the bar so high is probably a mind game for Parker, to see how you'll respond to the pressure."

"I can handle it. This is what I wanted—back in the Cup series. No better place to prove I belong there than Indianapolis."

"True. It'll be crazy this week for me, too. I'm

leaving in the morning for Dallas. I have to do some training for the western regions PR reps. They're doing a special promo for the NFL."

"And you've been a rep for both."

"Yeah. It's an honor. Usually this is something my uncle does. He's coming with me, but I'm leading the workshops."

"Readying you to take over his job."

She glanced at him, recalling all she was risking. The weight threatened to overwhelm her, so she did something rare—she pushed the confrontation with herself aside. "That's the plan," she said lightly.

"So when are you coming back from Dallas?"

"I'm not. I'm going straight to Chicago for the race weekend. Hopefully, I can keep Bruce Phillips content with his team for another week."

"You will."

"He thinks his team is giving up on him, already moving on to next year."

"Maybe they are. His finishes haven't been too great since he announced he was leaving. It's hard for guys to bust their butt every week for a guy who's chosen somebody else over them. Their morale and confidence is low. After that article, I'm sure it's worse."

"But he signed a contract. All this switching and bailing mystifies me."

"If the team's chemistry is damaged beyond repair, sometimes it's better to just move on."

"For everybody but the company who put twelve million dollars into that team in the first place."

"Yeah, it would be bad for CATL. But you need to be prepared for it. Bruce won't leave midseason unless he has somewhere to drive the last half of the year. Five or six months out of a ride would seem like five years by the time Daytona rolled around again. But if he can get somebody to put him in a car for the rest of the season…"

Isabel sighed. "He'll be gone."

"Yep. So I'll see you in Chicago?"

"Sure." She stretched. "Oh, can you get me Derek Foster's autograph?"

"Uh, *hello?*" He shook his head at the quick change of subject. "Is that a Derek Foster T-shirt you're wearing? Did Derek Foster fix you roasted chicken?"

She rolled her eyes. "Not for *me*. A rep in my office needs it."

Cade's gaze sharpened. "You sure about that?"

"Yes." She sat up. "You're not…jealous, are you?"

"Insanely."

Her whole body flushed from head to toe. "No kidding."

He stroked her cheek with the pad of his thumb. "Do you remember the last time we lay on this sofa together?"

Oh, yeah. Nineteen months, nine days, three hours ago. After those shooters, she would be surprised if he did, though. "Do *you?*"

"I remember every moment."

"But it wasn't enough to last."

"Were we ready for it to last?" he asked, cocking his head. "I wasn't."

"Me, neither. It seemed too impulsive. We didn't even know each other."

"No, we didn't. I felt awkward." He shook his head. "*Me,* who's supposed to be used to one-night stands. You pulled away, and I let you. I was in a different place in my life then. Before the fight with Huntington, I was too focused on myself. I was *too* sure of myself. Knowing how quickly you can lose everything was a real eye-opener. It made me realize I have to fight—though not literally—for everything I want." He paused, sliding the pad of his thumb across her cheek. "And I want you."

She was scared, literally *scared,* to take a chance with him. She hadn't been afraid in a long, long time. And though this fear was different from wondering if her family would, again, be evicted from their ramshackle home, or if she'd get slapped or yelled at that day, there was still the possibility of pain on the other side.

But she managed to swallow her doubts and pull him close. "You have me."

"SO THAT'S THAT," Cade said, laying the pen beside the stack of papers he'd just signed.

His father clapped his hand on his shoulder as he rose from his chair at the conference table. "It's a good deal. You'll make the most of it."

"Just think, little brother," Bryan said with a wry smile, "you burned a bridge and still managed to cross it."

"So, is my Busch pit crew doing double-duty for Indy?"

"Yes," Bryan said. "We can't start hiring a Cup crew until there's a team for them to work on. If you get the finishes Huntington wants, and you guys are happy with each other, then we'll make sure you have a full team for next year."

"You'll back three Cup teams?" Cade asked, wanting to be sure he understood how close he was to getting back what he'd lost.

Bryan nodded. "If Huntington comes through with a good offer, we'll have the money to make it happen."

"The car we were building for Chicago will be set aside for Charlotte or Homestead," his father put in. "In the meantime, the engineers and shop guys are going to be working overtime building you a car for Indy."

"Two weeks isn't much time," Cade said.

"It sure isn't," his father said. "I suggest you spend a lot of time at the shop, offering to help. These guys need to know you want this, and you're worth putting in the extra effort."

"Yes, sir," Cade said.

He could do that. With Isabel out of town all week, he'd have time on his hands. He'd have to let their last, smokin'-hot kiss early that morning carry him until Friday, so he'd need a serious distraction in the meantime.

He should probably be focused on his car regardless of her plans, but with two amazing opportunities dangling before him—three NASCAR NEXTEL Cup races and the lovely Isabel—he was bound to have a hard time focusing on just one.

"Remember Indy is a flat track," his dad said. "It's hard to pass. Qualifying will be important, not just to get you in the race, but for position."

Cade was well aware of how many teams showed up at the hallowed track in Indianapolis. A lot of them would be going home before the race even began. "What happens if I don't make the race?"

His father and brother exchanged a look. "You will," Bryan said. "We'll build you a car to get there."

"You also need to spend some time this week with Kevin," his dad said.

Cade stiffened. "I've raced at Indy before. Last year, in fact."

"And finished thirty-second," Bryan said.

"Kevin has raced there since stock cars first hit the track in '94," his dad insisted. "Talk to him about his setup and strategy. You might learn something."

Cade wasn't opposed to learning, but it would be nice if his family thought he *might* know what he was doing. "Yes, sir."

"I've got a sponsor meeting," Bryan said, glancing at his watch. "We'll talk later?" he said to Cade.

Legendary driver Kevin Reiner aside, Cade had another in-house expert. His brother had won at Indy, but they never talked about racing anymore. At least not track essentials, the line to run, the pacing, when to sit back, when to be aggressive, who to run with. Cade figured it was too painful for Bryan to talk about, so his offer to *talk later* was an empty invitation.

He nodded, anyway. "Sure."

His father scooted out just behind Bryan, so Cade was left looking across the conference table at Rachel, who'd been uncharacteristically silent all morning.

"So we're back with Huntington," he said when she just stared at him.

"Something's going on with you besides a sponsorship," she said, narrowing her eyes.

He ignored the path that led to. "I don't trust him, Rach."

"You shouldn't. He's not a friend, a teammate or a family member. He's your sponsor, so he wants you to succeed, but he's a *business* associate. What you need to remember is that you carry *his* dream, *his* company logo on your chest. He has to trust you a lot more than you trust him."

"You sound like—" He cut himself off from mentioning Isabel's name just in time.

"Who?"

"Bryan."

"Something's going on with you besides a sponsorship," Rachel repeated.

"I'm just worried. I've got to come up with some serious performances or I'm right back where I started."

She jumped to her feet. "Aha! *You?* Worried? No way. You're keeping something from me, Cade Garrison."

"I'm not," he lied.

"I used to diaper your—"

"Oh, please. No, you didn't. We're only two years apart."

She stared at him as if her will alone would get him talking. As if the fact that she managed not just his career, but his entire life, would guilt him into a confession of every thought rushing through his mind at that moment.

In the past he would have spilled everything. But he couldn't tell her about Isabel.

"I feel you distancing yourself from me," she said finally when the silence lengthened. "What's going on?"

Inwardly, he cringed. Now he wasn't holding back, he was pulling away. "Nothing."

She sighed. Clearly, she didn't believe him. "Whatever."

"What's my schedule like for the next two weeks?"

"Full, as always."

"Can we put off some stuff? I really need to spend some time at the shop."

"I'll make it work."

"Don't you always?"

She rose, then walked toward the door. She was clearly ticked, but he didn't see any way to change her mood without telling her what she thought she wanted to know, but really didn't.

Turning in the doorway, she looked back at him. "Even if you don't…*make the most of it,* I'm here. We're all here to back you up. We're your family."

Okay, that hurt.

Though he had plenty else to do, Cade sat at the conference table for a few minutes, trying to set aside the guilt of lying to his sister. Without her, he couldn't get through a single day. She managed *everything.*

She would tell him he was making a mistake with Isabel, though.

Because he was?

No. He refused to believe that. Yes, they were both gambling, but Isabel wasn't just a fling. She wasn't a temporary distraction. She was different from all the other women he'd known in his life.

And if she was as special as he thought, why shouldn't he take risks to pursue her? The reward of finding someone like her was worth everything.

The fact that she didn't seem to feel the same way was only a minor setback.

With those kinds of positive thoughts, who needed a dedicated, stellar engineering crew to build him a perfectly balanced, perfectly tuned racing machine?

Apparently, he did, since he spent the rest of the day sucking up to everybody he could find working in the race shop. Over the next two weeks, he did anything and everything anyone connected with Garrison Racing asked him to do.

He crawled under the car. He crawled in the car. He welded the chassis. He talked to the engineers. By phone and e-mail he consulted with Huntington and the GRI marketing team about the paint scheme and colors. He had lunch catered twice, which he assured his brother was coming out of his own pocket and not the company's. He met with Kevin. He even talked to Shawn about the setup on his car, which used to be Cade's car, but he guessed it was time to grow up and realize the number 86 was lost to him forever and he'd better starting working his butt off to build a new legacy with a new number. They'd been given permission by NASCAR to use 82, so Cade tried to visualize that number as a blur when he crossed the finish line first at Indy.

In Chicago he barely saw Isabel. She spent most of her time chasing after and settling the nerves of the new diva in town—Bruce Phillips. Cade wanted to say something to Phillips, like "grow up" or "give her a break, man," but he knew Isabel would stroke out. Besides, he wasn't in much of a mood to give out advice. Especially to a guy who would soon be driving for those cheating Bakers.

Despite Isabel's advice to settle the past with Parker Huntington, Cade still hadn't talked to him.

But he had talked endlessly about the fund-raiser for the Davidson Historical Society. Mrs. Fitzgerald had softened toward him somewhat—obviously Isabel had been right there, too—since she accepted his suggestion that they have the black-tie event the Wednesday before the Charlotte night race in October. That way, he could invite a lot of NASCAR-related people who'd be only too happy to fork over the $150 price per head to save that falling down eyesore of a—

He winced, remembering that description had led to the single steely glare he'd received from Mrs. Fitzgerald at last week's meeting.

According to Mrs. Fitzgerald, "for a $150 a person, we're saving an amazing property with important historical significance to our community."

Made perfect sense to him. Now, though, he had to actually find people at the track who *did* care about saving the past. Some of the old-timers lived there, at least in their minds, so it should be a piece of cake.

On Friday afternoon, as he and his team rolled his brand-new red-and-gold number 82 toward pit road for qualifying at one of the most revered tracks in the country, he swallowed his nerves, knowing he'd done everything in his power to make sure he'd perform well this weekend.

"Good luck, Cade!" Derek called with a wave as he passed.

Cade gave him the thumbs-up and managed a smile.

"Don't get worked up," Sam said with his usual gruff bluntness. He, along with the rest of his crew, was doing double-duty this weekend. Tomorrow they'd be over at the smaller track next door, qualifying and racing their NASCAR Busch Series car.

"I'm not getting worked up," he said to Sam.

"This is a primo ride. You're gonna be fine."

"I know. I'm not nervous."

"Uh-huh. Well, you clutch that helmet any tighter, you're gonna break it."

"Give it to me," Rachel said, walking behind them and obviously overhearing.

She gave him a tight smile as their hands brushed. She'd spent the past two weeks working like crazy, too. She'd run interference between GRI and Huntington's management teams, worked with the PR reps and marketing staff and organizing all the press interviews.

But she was still ticked at him.

She knew he was holding out on her, and as often as he reminded himself that his love life was his business and nobody else's, he knew that if Isabel had any other kind of job, he would tell Rachel what was going on. He would probably be asking for her advice on a daily basis. But after surviving the Huntington scandal and just now possibly getting his career back on track, she wouldn't be in the mood for giving advice. She'd call him crazy. She'd be even angrier than she was now.

Really, he was protecting her from the truth.

Ignoring that self-serving delusion, he kept walking toward the line of cars ready to qualify. They'd be going out tenth, so at least he'd get it over with quickly. But he'd also have to wait until the entire field made their runs before he'd know if he'd made the race. There was no easy way.

He wished he could see Isabel. Her smile might give him that extra rush of adrenaline.

But he also realized he couldn't have what he wanted, at the moment he wanted—not all the time, anyway. He winced as he thought of pushing her to see him and kiss him before the race in Daytona. He'd stressed her out for his own selfish ends.

He wanted her happy. Lately, nothing in the world seemed to matter more.

The TV cameras and reporters surrounded him and his crew as they stopped at their spot in line.

"Do you think you have a car good enough to get in the race?" Jenna from the Associated Press asked, while the other print and online people stood by with their minirecorders.

"The guys at GRI have been busting their butts for the past two weeks to get this car ready. We'll make it."

"How does it feel to be working with Parker Huntington again?"

"It's great. Mr. Huntington is a long-standing supporter of NASCAR, and I'm honored to have him as part of my team."

"Is there any remaining tension after the falling-out you had last year?"

"We've moved beyond the past. Huntington Hotels wants the best." He grinned. "That's why I'm here."

That got a laugh from most of the reporters, and they quickly moved on to another driver.

"I think some of 'em were disappointed you didn't call Huntington a name," his rear-tire changer said with a laugh.

"Or call him out for the *Great Rumble in Davidson*," his front-tire changer added.

"Hey, let's show some respect for this sponsor we only have for three races," Sam said, sweeping a glare across the group.

They all continued to move toward the exit of pit road, waiting for the official to tell them it was their turn. Cade saw Bruce Phillips's car pull onto the track and wondered if Isabel was in the car with him, holding his hand.

Apparently, his ego was happy since he wound up second.

"All right, buddy," Sam said. "It's time to show 'em what we've got."

Cade climbed into the car and tried to pretend this was any other race, any other qualifying. As the crew rolled the car to the on-deck position, Bob leaned into the car and tucked a folded piece of paper just inside his left glove.

Curious, Cade glanced at him, but Bob just smiled. There wasn't time to question him, since the official gave him the signal to pull onto the track.

It took a full lap to get up to speed, but by the time

he'd crossed the start-finish line the second time, the scoring tower had him in fifth. Fifty-two teams had shown up to qualify, so there were still forty-two teams to go, but when Cade slid out of the car, Sam was smiling. He was confident their time would get them in the race.

All they had to do now was wait.

The problem was, where? Their rented hauler barely held the cars and equipment. Their Busch car hauler was at ORP. Cade didn't even have a place to change out of his uniform.

The crew rolled the car into their garage stall, then decided to walk back to pit road and wait in Kevin Reiner's box, so they could see the TV coverage and the scoring tower. Cade assured them he'd catch up in a few minutes.

When he pulled off his gloves, he palmed the folded piece of paper Bob had given him. He knew without asking that it was personal. From Isabel? A fan?

Bob said nothing as they walked toward pit road, and Cade accepted high-fives from several drivers and crew members along the way. It felt good to think he could still compete on the same level as these guys.

When he passed a pair of NASCAR Busch Series drivers, though, he realized if he did get to compete in the NASCAR NEXTEL Cup Series next year, he'd miss the Busch guys. Especially the drivers who were just starting out. They were hungry and hopeful. They'd sweated and sacrificed, and still only a lucky few had made it to such a prestigious rank in racing.

As much as Cade complained about the pressure and high expectations in his family, their backing was invaluable. His last name was a commodity he couldn't ever take for granted.

Before he reached the pits, he ducked between two haulers to check out Bob's gift. He unfolded the paper and found six words written on it in bold red ink.

I knew you could do it.

There was no signature, but he knew it was from Isabel. Reminding her he wasn't in the race yet would just earn him a head shake. Her unwavering confidence put a spring in his step as he continued to Kevin's pit space.

His father and brother were there, sitting on the box, watching the monitors next to Kevin's crew chief. They all watched the track and talked to the other teams around them. The top thirty-five in car owner points—guaranteed to make the race that week—were mostly comfortable. Others were confident and hopeful. Others sweated it out.

There were sponsors who paid just for the outside chance at the exposure of this race, and there were sponsors who expected to see their cars in front and battling for the lead all day. It all fed the drama of racing.

At the moment, as he watched yet another car

qualify ahead of him, Cade would rather avoid drama, but he couldn't imagine giving up the racing, so he forced a smile at his teammates and pretended he was confident of their chances.

Many sponsors hovered in their team's pit, so at least he didn't have to deal with his own sponsor at the moment.

As soon as that thought slid through his mind, though, he saw something that made him let out a silent moan, even though his heart jumped.

Parker Huntington and Isabel were walking toward him.

When they reached him, Huntington gestured to the woman at his side. "Cade, do you know Isabel Turner?"

Oh, yeah. Pulse pounding, Cade forced himself to simply nod. "Sure. Hey, Isabel."

She gave him her distant, professional smile, though her eyes were bright. "Nice run."

"Sam seems to think it'll hold," Cade said.

"If the practice times are any reflection, you should wind up in the top twenty," Huntington said.

"Your practice speeds were great," Isabel said. "Fifth in the last session. Did you have to make many adjustments for qualifying?"

"We took out a little—"

"Ah, Cade," Huntington said with raised eyebrows. "Isabel works for the competition. You probably shouldn't be revealing our setup."

"Isabel wouldn't—"

Cade stopped before defending Isabel's integrity. Supposedly, they barely knew each other. He certainly wouldn't talk in detail about his car with any other PR rep.

Isabel had warned him there would be moments like this. Times when they had to deceive the people around them, not just by omission, but by outright lying. Cade hadn't anticipated a problem. He figured it was like telling your aunt Melba that she looked great in that fuchsia polyester sweat suit when she really resembled a giant panda in a fuchsia polyester sweat suit.

The reality of pretending was much different. He felt cheated. And angry.

How long could they go on like this?

He'd agreed to Isabel's "secret affair" terms, but now he realized he didn't like them at all. Did being a mature, responsible adult involve accepting the parts of his life that didn't appeal to him?

If so, let the child live forever.

CHAPTER SIXTEEN

ISABEL WATCHED CADE'S face flush. Was he angry or embarrassed that his boss had reprimanded him in front of her?

Probably both.

"The car feels great, so we should run well Sunday," he finally said vaguely.

"Well, good luck," she returned, then clamped her jaw shut. The tension between her and Cade was so pervasive she had no idea how Parker didn't sense it. But then he knew the professional Isabel, not the moony-eyed nut she'd become recently.

How could she be in a relationship with somebody when she wasn't sure she liked the person she'd turned into? Was she just scared, or was she really screwing up her life?

After a few more minutes of awkward small talk, she managed to escape. She spent the rest of the day and late into the night at a CATL fan club function with her uncle and Bruce Phillips, who was still overwhelmed with doubts about his team. She and her uncle had done all they could to prop him up and assure him he'd survive, but neither of them were confident about him staying. Still, every week they bought benefited their marketing plan.

When she climbed—alone—into her hotel room bed after midnight, she lay awake a long time thinking about Cade, where he was, what he was doing. She'd left him a message on his cell phone that she was going to be working late, but he hadn't called back.

Was he angry? Disappointed? Or had he just shrugged and gone on with his schedule?

The uncertainty nagged her, making her restless and unable to relax. She was used to running her personal life the way she did her business life—with commanding efficiency. Hence the reason she rarely dated.

Before Cade, she'd been happy with that arrangement. These days, doubts battered her constantly. She didn't know how *she* felt, much less how he did. She didn't know how to act when they were alone together, and she sure as hell didn't know how to act with him in public.

Predictably, she didn't get much sleep, so the next day she slugged through her schedule—most of which involved watching over and catering to Bruce. She propped herself up with coffee and willpower, which she should have plenty of without Cade around, but she found instead she lacked it completely. She checked her cell phone and BlackBerry a thousand times each, wondering if the silence from him meant he was pissed at her or just busy.

When Candy bounced toward her, waving an autograph from Derek Foster that was personalized for her boyfriend, she actually grabbed her arm and demanded to know who'd delivered the autograph.

Candy blinked. "He said his name was Bob."

Isabel fisted her hands at her sides. She was almost desperate enough to ask when and where she'd seen Bob, what direction he'd gone in and if he'd said anything about Cade.

Almost, anyway.

"He's Cade Garrison's assistant or something." Candy glanced at the autographed picture. "It's authentic, right?"

"Sure." She patted Candy's arm. "I'm glad you got it."

"You got it for me, didn't you?"

Distracted and wondering if she should swallow her pride and chase Bob down, Isabel nodded. "That's what friends are for."

Candy gasped. "We're actual *friends* now?"

"Uh, yeah."

"Can I tell other people at the office that we're friends?"

"Sure, whatever." It couldn't hurt to casually wander around and be on the lookout for Bob. She started to walk away. "Hey, I'll see you later."

Candy grabbed her close for a hug. "You're the best."

Isabel pulled back, then eyed the junior rep,

"Don't go spreading it around that I let you hug me, though, okay?"

"Oh, I won't."

Before they parted, Candy assured her that the autograph would mend her relationship fences. And while Isabel thought it was pretty pathetic to bribe a man to take her back, she wasn't exactly in a position to give out healthy relationship advice.

Her search for Bob came up empty, so she trudged back to Bruce's hauler. Back to work.

She didn't even get to see Cade run in the NASCAR Busch Series race, but heard he finished second. Two of the other drivers in the points in front of him wrecked early, so he moved up to third in the standings. After all his ambition to get back in a NASCAR NEXTEL Cup car, there was a real possibility of him winning another NASCAR Busch Series championship.

Of course she would have loved to talk to him about it, but—oh, yeah—he wasn't answering her messages and wasn't around. Well, he was *around,* somewhere in the vicinity, just not *around* where she could see him and talk to him. How was she supposed to be a girlfriend if—

Girlfriend? Oh, no. No, she wasn't a girlfriend.

She was a temporary, attraction-of-the-moment… girl. Woman. He was the guy she was sleeping with. Secretly. Very secretly.

The emotions didn't go beyond that. She wouldn't let them.

Her uncle insisted on taking the reps out to dinner

that night. He knew they'd all been working crazy hours and still making the company look good every week. He also wanted to remind Isabel that if your people weren't happy, the company didn't move forward.

The training for VP continued.

But instead of being encouraged and feeling appreciative, she was nauseous.

She fell into bed—again, alone—and examined the complexities of her life. Since she'd done that all day, the review took about ten minutes, so she decided to check her cell phone for messages.

She had one. From Cade.

She'd turned her ringer off during dinner and had forgotten to turn it back on, so *naturally,* that was the time he'd called. Holding her breath, she listened to the message. It was brief.

I miss you. Call me.

Heart pounding, she dialed his cell. "Where the hell have you been all day?" he asked the moment he picked up.

"*Me?* I've been trying to call you for two days. Where've you been?"

"Running my butt off between two teams. I don't know how these guys run both schedules."

"It's tough. That's why so few do it."

"It would be easier if I could see you."

She lay back into her pillow and smiled for the first time all weekend. "Yeah, I know the feeling."

"Bruce driving you crazy?"

"I went past crazy weeks ago. Now I'm holding on for dear life."

"Me, too."

"Not with the race. I heard you finished second, and tomorrow you'll—"

"I miss you."

Oh, my. She snuggled down deeper into the covers. "I miss you, too."

He sighed. "Then what are we doing, Izzy?"

She clutched the receiver. "What are we—"

"*Doing.* Why are we hiding? I hated yesterday, lying to Huntington."

"It wasn't exactly fun for me, either, but that's what we have to do. That's the cost of being together."

"I don't like it."

"Me, neither." Panic rose in her chest. She had to talk him down from the ledge. He'd dump her, or maybe he'd demand more. Either one wasn't something she was ready for. "You weren't angry earlier because Parker corrected you in front of me, were you?"

"No. I just don't want to hide anymore."

"We don't have a choice."

ON RACE DAY, ISABEL reported to Bruce's hauler as usual. She brought ham-and-cheese croissants that she bribed the hotel's chef to cater for her at the last minute. The team loved them; Bruce frowned.

"I need to talk to you alone for a minute," he said after his team had dug into the warm breakfast.

This can't be good.

Clutching her foam coffee cup, Isabel followed Bruce to the back of the hauler. He closed the door, then leaned back against it. "I'm leaving," he said. "I'll do it Monday, so they'll have all week to find somebody to put in the car for Pocono."

Oh, a whole week? Isabel bit her tongue to keep from letting the snarky comment escape. Buying herself some time to formulate a professional response, she sank to the sofa. "Baker's going to put you in a car for the rest of the season," she said, knowing, as Cade had suggested, that was the only way Bruce would make this move.

"Yes. They're restructuring so my team for next year can work together this season."

And with Bruce's past champion's provisional, they'd automatically qualify for every race. She'd never begrudged that rule, but now she suddenly did.

"What about *this* team?" she asked, glaring up at him.

"They have Busch drivers. They can pull one of them up."

Isabel could see all her coddling and assurances hadn't done any good. Even as she and her uncle had talked to him in Daytona about sticking out the rest of the season, he'd been planning this move. He hadn't listened to a word she'd said. She'd spent the past month kissing his butt for nothing.

Even though she was furious, she kept her cool. Burning bridges wouldn't benefit her or CATL. They still had to work with him. "Have you told the people at TR Motorsports?"

"No, I thought it was best to wait until after the race."

"Still need those tires changed, don't you?"

She regretted her harsh words the moment she said them, but Bruce didn't seem offended. In fact, he relaxed and walked toward her. "You're great, Isabel. You and CATL have been so amazing and professional." Shaking his head, he sat next to her. "I'm a driver, and I'm not racing here. I'm just riding around." He paused and glanced at her. His eyes were stark. "It's killing me."

She bowed her head.

Dating a driver had changed her. Hadn't she been moaning about that just last week? Maybe some of those changes had been positive.

Fifteen years down the road, if Cade was in Bruce's situation, would she resent him changing teams so he could still be competitive? Finishing in the fifteenth to twentieth position was fine for her and her company, but obviously not enough for Bruce.

"I'm trying hard to hate you," she said, realizing they'd somehow moved passed the client-driver relationship in the past few minutes.

"I'll bet. But I can still compete with these young guys. I think I can win another championship, and this is my only chance to find out."

She lifted her head and managed a smile. "Yeah, maybe it is."

"Can we still be friends?"

"Sure. Come February you belong to us again, remember?"

"I can't wait."

"And I need you to sign a thousand Blast bottles before you go."

Rising, he laughed. "I can manage that."

Isabel stood and shook his hand. Despite the past few weeks of tension, she respected Bruce. He'd been a wonderful representative for CATL and would no doubt continue to do so after the rest of this season played out.

"Can you manage something for me?" he asked.

"Sure."

"You got any more of those ham-and-cheese pastry things?"

ISABEL PACED THE SUITE during the race.

She couldn't appreciate the grilled shrimp and tornados of beef over rice served to the guests. She probably could have used a glass of wine, but she didn't have one. She longed to scream at the top of her lungs, but she didn't do that, either.

The suite's view, high above the track, allowed her to see the entire two-and-a-half-mile asphalt surface, an advantage over the fans in the grandstands. Still, the refined atmosphere set Isabel further on edge. She'd rather hear the growling engines and deafening shouts from the crowd.

Then maybe nobody would talk to her.

Or expect her to talk back.

Maybe, if Bruce finished well, he'd reconsider leaving. She'd already done some Internet research to learn who the TR Motorsports NASCAR Busch Series drivers were, and both of them had little experience. The good-to-decent finishes the Blast car had been getting with Bruce were likely to come to an end, and that was if the guys at TR decided to pull one of them up to the NASCAR NEXTEL Cup car.

They could hire somebody brand-new, or decide to give auditions to several drivers, rotating them for the rest of the year. Any promotions CATL had been planning would most likely have to be canceled.

With all this in mind, she nervously glanced at the various TVs around the suite, then at the track. By midway through the race, she was exhausted and had nearly worn a hole in the carpet. Vincent brought her a diet soda at one point, but none of the other reps approached her. That "Scary Isabel" thing worked in her favor again.

Though she'd managed to smile and make small talk with a few of their VIP guests, she mostly plotted, planned and cursed silently. She told no one about Bruce leaving. Monday would be soon enough to share the grim news.

"Crash, Turn Two!" the network announcer shouted.

Isabel stopped pacing. *Please don't let it be Bruce. Please, oh, please.*

When she glanced at the TV hanging above the

buffet table, she saw the wreck was in the middle of the field. Running up front, Bruce hadn't been impacted. But of the three cars spinning on the track, one of them made her gasp.

"That's Cade Garrison's number 82 Huntington Hotels Chevrolet sliding to a halt against the outside retaining wall," the announcer continued as Isabel leaned closer to the TV, as if she could get to him. "Pauley and Lipperman have recovered enough to drive away on their own, but Garrison will need assistance to get off the track.

"Garrison's window net is down, and the safety crews have arrived. The rest of the field will pit."

"What happened?" Vincent said from behind her.

Needing to see the replay, Isabel continued to stare intently at the TV. "I don't know." She was ashamed her mind had been on work and not how Cade would do in this all-important race. She'd just never dreamed he'd have any trouble.

His head high and his helmet dangling from his right hand, Cade climbed into the back of the ambulance for the required trip to the infield care center. She was proud he controlled his emotions. He had to be furious.

After she watched the slow-motion replay several times, she realized Chance Baker had tapped Cade and spun him around, causing the wreck.

"Who's got a headset?" she asked, turning to face the crowd that had gathered behind her.

Somebody handed her one, and with the pit road

chatter in her ears and the TV coverage giving her the visual, she got the full story. The guys in the broadcast booth admitted Baker had hit Cade, though perhaps not on purpose. Pauley and Lipperman's teams were ticked by their damage and also pinned Baker as the cause. During the caution and track cleanup everybody held their breath, waiting for Cade to be released from the infield medical center so he could give his version of the incident.

They all knew about the animosity between the Bakers and the Garrisons. Chance Baker dating Bryan Garrison's ex-wife Nicole was the latest, but not necessarily the most bitter. It had started with Mitch failing to win the season opener in Daytona, and all the little digs along the way had added up to a legendary rivalry.

Personally, Isabel had found Chance and Nicole a little too smiley, perfect and self-involved for her to hang out with, but that had been the extent of her dislike. For Cade, she knew the anger, understandably, ran much deeper. And now that she knew Bryan better and had seen pain and anguish cross his face more than a few times, she found herself much less sympathetic toward the Baker family's actions. Bryan's pain wasn't all in his leg. It extended to his heart. And that she related to better than most.

Was the tap personal?

If so, why *this* race? Why now?

"You're showing you care," Vincent said quietly in her ear.

She faced him. "About what?" she asked coolly.
"Cade Garrison."

Of *course* she cared about Cade and his family,
the incredible pressure on him and his future. That
punk idiot Chance had *hit* him. Was she supposed
to be neutral about that? Thanks to Bruce, she was
going to have to work with the Bakers next year.
Was she supposed to calmly nod and go with her
job like normal?

Ah, yes, Miss Neutral Professional, you are.

To her horror, she found tears stinging her eyes.
"Create a distraction," she said to Vincent as she
slipped into the bathroom.

Leaning over the sink, she drew deep breaths and
tried not to think about the disappointment and anguish Cade must be feeling. Her heart raced and her
fingers tingled. The urge to *run,* not walk, out of the
suite and find him nearly overwhelmed her. He
needed her, dammit. He needed her to hold him and
remind him that everything would work out. He
needed to know his dreams of running in the
NASCAR NEXTEL Cup Series next year would
come true.

You're his secret *girlfriend. This is the price you
pay for lying.*

She glared at herself in the mirror. She was doing
all she could. She was managing. Just because she
wasn't rushing toward him at this very moment
didn't mean she didn't care.

She pulled lip gloss from her pants pocket and

ignored the annoying internal doubts. Even if she was his real girlfriend she couldn't get to him right now. She couldn't bust her way onto the track.

You could be there when he's released by the doctor.

But she *couldn't* be there, and the barrier troubled and depressed her.

She did the only constructive thing she could. She e-mailed Bob's BlackBerry with her own, asking him to let her know Cade's prognosis ASAP. Then, hoping her emotions were firmly under control, she pushed open the bathroom door.

Vincent stood just outside. "Are you okay?"

"No." She rolled her shoulders back. "Any word on Cade?"

"Not yet. Any minute, though." He cupped her elbow and steered her back into the main room. "I'm here, you know."

"Yeah." Her heart heavy, she glanced at him. "And that's a lot more than I'm doing for him."

They stood in the back of the room, the track laid out before them through the windows. The cars were still rolling around at caution speed. The TVs in the corners of the room showed the on-track action silently. They were obviously in a commercial break.

The green flag flew a few minutes later. The race rolled on. Bruce Phillips was still in sixth. Isabel leaned her shoulder against the wall, where she could see both the TV monitors and the track, trying to pretend it all meant nothing to her.

"Let's go live to the infield care center," the play-by-play announcer said. "We have a comment from Cade Garrison."

"First of all, are you okay?" the pit reporter asked as Cade stepped in front of the cameras.

"I'm fine. My team did an awesome job, and the Huntington Hotels Chevy was great. We were strong and moving up. Too bad we didn't get to show those guys what we had."

"Obviously, you're done for the day."

"Yeah. Too much damage. And we weren't racin' for points. We were just trying to keep our nose clean and get a top-ten finish, and our car was good enough to do that."

"Have you seen the replays of the on-track incident?"

Cade angled his head. "No, but I bet you guys can give them to me."

The slow-motion clip of the wreck rolled across the screen.

"Do you have a comment about Baker's actions?" the reporter asked when it was over.

Cade shrugged. "Guess somebody's threatened by me being back in the Cup Series." He grinned and stared straight at the camera. "Sorry, Chance, old buddy, I'm not goin' anywhere."

THE "I'M NOT GOIN' anywhere" clip played on every sports-media outlet in the country for a week. The Garrison-Baker rivalry was analyzed endlessly. The tap-and-wreck slow-motion replay was shown hundreds of times on TV and discussed for technique and motive.

After a solid month of not being able to sneeze without a reporter there to record it, Cade was beyond ready to move on.

But then that wasn't the worst of the developments in his life.

At first, he'd thought the wreck would bring him and Isabel closer. She'd been sitting on his doorstep when he got home from Indy at nearly 1:00 a.m. She'd offered him a cold six-pack of beer and a silent hug that made all the anger and frustration fall away.

But Monday brought more stress and drama. His and Isabel's relationship got even more complicated, which he didn't think was possible.

Bruce Phillips announced he was leaving his current team for Baker, so she spent every waking moment meeting with his TR Motorsports team and executives at CATL, trying to decide who would be his replacement. When the team pulled up one of their Busch drivers, she ran interference between him and the media, plus she trained him on the art of dealing with the bright spotlight of the NASCAR NEXTEL Cup Series. Cade rarely got to talk to her, much less see her.

Then, in the weird, wild world of the modern media, the wreck story morphed into something entirely different. And untrue.

Despite the fact that the wreck had occurred in a

car sponsored by a hotel, some goofy reporter, who was either a conspiracy theorist or had been driven crazy by a deadline, decided there was a tie between Bruce, Cade and Chance, because Go!, Cade's NASCAR Busch Series car sponsor, and Blast, Bruce's former NASCAR NEXTEL Cup sponsor, were competitors.

Were drivers simply spinning out of control— Phillips breaking his contract, Chance hitting Cade and Cade hitting his sponsor? Or was there a deeper reason for recent events? Had Bruce Phillips actually been fired because the people at Blast weren't happy with him? Had Bruce been unfairly compared to Cade, who executives at Go! bragged about daily? Was there an energy drink war in NASCAR?

Since CATL made Blast, the whole thing made it harder than ever for Cade and Isabel to hook up. Rumors of them being seen together would fuel a story already burning out of control. His love life was dictated by news stories and marketing strategies, and Cade had absolutely had enough.

Weeks flew by with them barely catching a moment here or there together. Their romantic date after Daytona seemed another world away. Finally, the first week of September, with the racing world embroiled in the debate about who would make the Chase for the NASCAR NEXTEL Cup, Cade convinced Isabel to be seen with him in public. On Tuesday night, he would head to Midtown Sundries with Jay and Dean, she'd come with Susan and Vincent, and, if the stars and planets aligned, maybe they could join their groups.

Since this was *his* life he was living, though, the plan didn't go smoothly.

Tuesday morning, Rachel stuck her head in his office. "Parker Huntington's on the phone. He wants to know if you're free tonight."

Cade started to shake his head but stopped just in time—the glare from his sister jarring his memory. He was supposed to have invited Huntington for a beer weeks ago. They'd spoken little since the wreck at Indy, though Huntington had assured Cade he didn't hold him responsible for his lousy finish. More important, though, they were supposed to have settled the past. Both Rachel and Isabel had advised him to.

He was meeting Jay and Dean at seven. "Can he meet me for a beer at Sundries around six?"

"I'll check." She left but was back in a couple of minutes. "All set," she said.

His sister seemed to be the only person lately who wasn't driving him crazy. He smiled at her. "Thanks, Rach."

"You look exhausted. Why don't you go home early?"

He shook his head. "Everybody else is just as tired."

"But you have to deal with the pressure on camera, in print, everywhere."

"The press calls Bryan just as often. I'm fine."

Rachel sighed and walked into his office, settling

into one of the chairs in front of his desk. "But you look sad. And worried. Not just tired." Her gaze flickered to his. "What's wrong, Cade?"

"After all we've been through over the past few weeks, you actually need to ask?"

"I'm talking about more than racing or the press or sponsorship issues. I can't remember the last time you went on a date."

Me, neither. But even if he had gone out recently, his sister wouldn't approve of the woman he saw. "I date," he said, trying to sound confident instead of disappointed. "I'm going out tonight, in fact."

"To meet Parker. That's work."

"I'm meeting Jay and Dean afterward. We'll find some women to hook up with."

Rachel waggled her finger at him. "Be sure that you do. I want to see you smiling tomorrow morning."

"I thought you wanted me to be more responsible. You said I was a degenerate."

She flipped her hand dismissively as she rose. "That was months ago."

During the afternoon, Cade somehow managed to focus on work instead of anticipating seeing Isabel. Maybe because part of him didn't believe she'd actually show up. A work-related crisis had come up at the last minute dozens of times over the past several weeks, causing her to cancel their plans.

When he arrived at Midtown Sundries, he dropped into an empty booth and asked for a beer. Alone and silent after the waitress delivered his order, he sipped from the bottle and realized Rachel was right. Something *was* wrong. He used to be fun. He used to smile. He used to get into trouble. He used to hang out with his friends. He used to flirt with women.

These days, he worked constantly, worried about the future and mulled over his *feelings*. He stressed out over events that hadn't even happened yet. He hadn't seen Dean and Jay in two weeks. He was apprehensive about everything.

Especially Isabel.

He wanted her so much he was willing to accept her on any terms she offered. He absorbed every scrap of affection they shared. He hung on her every word. He was proud of every smile and moment of pleasure he made her feel. He was depressed when he couldn't see her. He felt lousy when they argued.

And so he'd become convinced this was God's way of punishing him for being an uncommitted, freedom-loving, never-settling-down bachelor. Who knew the Man Upstairs had such a biting sense of humor? Cade had fallen hard for a woman who didn't want him. Well, she wanted him sometimes. Just not as much as he wanted her.

It'll pass.

It *had* to pass. Didn't it?

"You look terrible," Huntington said as he slid into the booth.

Cade scowled at his beer and said nothing.

"Not even a witty comeback? You've been bursting full of those the past few weeks. Are you sick?"

"Look, I'm here to apologize. I don't have to be happy about it."

"I called you and asked to meet," Huntington reminded him as the waitress set down a glass of deep red wine, which he must have ordered as he came in.

"Yeah, but Rachel has been on me for weeks about apologizing and settling the past."

"She's a smart woman."

Cade finally looked at Huntington directly. He examined his expression for *that look,* the one he always got when he talked about Rachel, or when he looked at Rachel. But he found Huntington's face blank. Those eerily piercing green eyes of his watched Cade with passive interest. "So, I'm sorry," Cade said abruptly.

"For?"

"Hitting you. What else?"

Huntington surprised him by toasting him with his wineglass. "With an offer that gracious, how could I not accept?"

Cade shoved his beer aside. "Look, I've had a really lousy few weeks, so I'd appreciate you not—"

"I should add that I'm sorry about the arrest and probation. I understand you're serving on the local historical society, though. That should be some consolation."

Ugh. Those historical society meetings. At least he only had them once every other week now. Mrs.

Fitzgerald had decided that since their event was sold out, she could give them all a break from the weekly schedule.

Another part of his life that Isabel had encompassed. She'd suggested asking NASCAR's hottest drivers—that would be him and Derek Foster—to auction off a dinner date. Each ticket sold would be entered into a draw, and two winners would be selected the night of the black-tie event at the Visual Arts Center.

Tickets sold like crazy.

"It's okay," Cade said neutrally. "I guess I should explain that before I slugged you, I had some anger issues."

"With me?"

"I didn't like the way you looked at my sister."

Huntington's neutral expression didn't change. "No kidding?"

Cade noticed he didn't promise not to look at her again, but then that might be an extreme compromise. Rachel was a beautiful woman, and Huntington would hardly be alive if he didn't notice her. "And I got tired of your driving advice," he added.

"I agree I overstepped my bounds there. I tend to overmanage. I don't relate as well as I should to employees. Or so my father says."

Cade couldn't relate to some of the things his father and brother said. Isabel had told him Huntington was a good guy and that they had similar backgrounds. She was right, as usual.

Huntington sipped his wine. "I do have some experience in racing."

"I've heard, and I respect that. I can be more open." Cade glanced down, then back at Huntington. They'd danced around the issue, they'd found some common ground, but they hadn't hit the core of the problem.

Remembering the moment, the words Huntington had said, he clenched his jaw, then forced himself to relax. "Do you really think I'm not good enough to call myself a Garrison?"

Huntington winced, his sophisticated demeanor finally broken. "It was a lousy, stupid thing to say." He leaned back and shook his head. "You weren't living up to your potential, and I thought it was my duty to save you from yourself."

"I've won a Busch championship, and I placed third the year after that. After I was promoted to the Cup series, I finished seventh. I gave my speech at the Waldorf-Astoria in New York. I may be from the North Carolina woods, but I've been around. I know what's at stake."

"Of course you do." Huntington shook his head. "But my perception was different. I realized you had more talent than I could ever dream about, and I thought you were throwing it away on parties and women. It was driving me crazy."

Thinking about maturity, Isabel and God's revenge, Cade could almost agree.

But he was a fun guy. He liked socializing. He

enjoyed his friends. He wasn't about to pretend—for Huntington or anybody else.

Even Isabel? his conscience asked.

Even her.

Starting tonight he was going to find his old rhythm. He wasn't going to wallow. Or worry. He was going to make things happen. In both his personal and professional lives.

"I won't let you down, Parker," Cade said finally, lifting his fist.

At the same time, Parker held out his hand as if preparing for a handshake.

Cade shook his head. "Dude, you need work." He wrapped his hand around Parker's, closing it into a fist, then he punched his own hand forward so that their knuckles connected briefly. "Try it," he added with a smile. "It'll get you a hell of a lot further in the garage than your Harvard MBA."

Parker glanced at his hand. "You think so?"

Cade laughed. "Yeah."

"What do you think about this whole Bruce Phillips situation?" Parker asked, leaning forward, the light of a genuine race fan in his eyes. "It seems to me the guy made a bad trade. His new Baker team has performed way below par, while that young guy TR Motorsports pulled from the Busch Series is kicking butt."

"Chemistry is a big aspect of racing," Cade said.

From there, they launched into a debate about the news stories of the day. They discussed who they thought would make the Chase, who was running well, and who was struggling. They theorized about who was changing teams, and the impact of the Car of Tomorrow on the strategy and competition. They even discussed promotional ideas for next year.

"So, this may actually work out," Parker said, echoing Cade's own thoughts. "If you finish well at Charlotte and Homestead, that is."

Cade raised his eyebrows. "You're not seriously trying to put the hammer to me now?"

"Just a little. I'm your boss, you know."

Cade shook his head. "No, you're not. I answer to my brother and my father. But since you sign the big checks…"

"*If* you finish well at Charlotte and Homestead."

"…I'll cut you some slack. You could even stay and hang out with me and my buddies. They'll be here any minute."

Another sponsor would make Isabel and her friends coming by look even more legit. Wouldn't she be proud he'd offered a concession to Parker and helped their cause at the same time?

Parker nodded. "I'd like that."

Cade gestured toward the wineglass. "They're gonna rag you about that."

"I can take it."

Cade slid out of the booth. "Then let's go outside. My volleyball team won the championship, so we have an honorary table."

"Sure. Let me get my bottle from the waitress first."

Cade's gaze dropped to Parker's half-empty glass. "What bottle?"

"The one I brought." Parker rose and craned his neck, clearly looking for their waitress. "Beer connoisseurs are abundant, but the wine list here leaves a great deal to be desired."

Cade tried not to let his jaw drop, but it just did. "Who brings their own drink to a bar?"

"I do."

Cade sighed. "If we're gonna be friends, you really need to cut back on the uppity, Mr. Sophisticated stuff."

"I'll do my best. Can I ask you a favor?"

"Sure."

"Please don't call me Mr. Huntington in front of the press. It makes me feel like my dad."

CHAPTER SEVENTEEN

ISABEL WALKED INTO Midtown Sundries flanked by
Susan and Vincent, who looked like an honor guard.
They knew she was on the verge of bolting, and they
were determined to force her to follow through
meeting Cade.

"It's not that I don't *want* to see him, you know,"
she said to them as they moved through the crowded
foyer, heading for the patio.

"We know," they said at the same time.

"You're worried," Susan added.

"You're scared," Vincent said.

"I have a right to be both," she said, glaring from
one to the other.

"You never used to be scared of anything," Vincent said with a disappointed shake of his head.

Susan bit her lip. "She always has been a wor-
rier, though."

"No, I'm *not*," Isabel said, walking ahead of
them, then turning around and stopping to block
their path. "I'm a doer. I *do* things, not worry about
them."

Vincent crossed his arms over his chest. "At the moment, you seem to be stalling."

"I am *not*."

Susan tapped her foot. "You're already here. There's no point in trying to escape."

"I thought we were supposed to be discreet," Isabel said, deeply insulted her friends thought she was trying to escape.

Besides, she'd tried that as they got into the cab, so the element of surprise was long gone.

"You guys are rushing toward him as if he's going to write you a check when you get there," she continued.

Her friends stared silently at her, then exchanged a look with each other. Moving forward, they scooped her underneath her arms, lifted her off the floor, then continued their progress toward the patio.

Isabel kicked her feet. "Have you lost your minds? Put me down!" Hearing muffled laughter from around her, her face burned. She lowered her voice. "This is ridiculous."

They ignored her and talked to each other.

"Do you think he'll introduce me to some of his luscious fan club members as a reward for bringing her?" Vincent asked.

"Wouldn't it be great if Rex could get on with GRI? Then we could all double-date." She paused. "Or maybe it's triple-date."

Isabel rolled her eyes. They didn't give a hoot about her. They were only concerned with their own love lives. These people were supposed to be her friends. Clearly, she needed to make getting new friends a priority.

And if she had to watch Susan and Rex, the jack man she'd hooked up with in Daytona and had been dating exclusively since, she was going to throw up. Happy people were a pain in the butt.

Especially since she couldn't see the man she wanted without causing an international scandal.

Or getting fired.

Or jeopardizing his sponsorship deal.

"Hey, guys!" Susan said with ridiculously overt surprise and cheer. "What're you doing here?"

They're always here, Isabel wanted to say. But only after she threw her friend a disgusted glare.

Susan and Vincent set her on her feet, but she didn't turn around. She'd actually rather crawl under the table than face anybody sitting at it.

"It looks like you had some trouble getting Isabel away from the office," somebody at the table said. Maybe Jay or Dean? It wasn't Cade.

How could she face him? He'd immediately assume she had to be dragged and bullied into keeping their date.

Which she did.

When had she ever run from honesty? When had she ever been afraid to face a situation that could get messy or hard?

Ah, that would be now.

She was cranky, exhausted and humiliated. She

was ninety-nine percent sure being here was a mistake.

Susan poked her side, so she grudgingly turned.

And all her negative emotions melted away the moment she saw Cade.

A beer bottle in one hand, he was leaning back in his chair and smiling up at her. He wore a navy-blue polo and worn jeans, his dark hair swept off his face in wavy disarray and his blue-eyed gaze fixed on her face. "Hey, Isabel," he said.

"Uh, hi," she said lamely.

With a rush of happiness, she remembered the last time she'd touched him. Last Saturday night during the Bristol race, they'd sneaked off to his motor coach. They'd made spaghetti and watched the race on TV, while still able to hear the cars roaring around the track just outside their door.

Early Sunday morning she'd tiptoed to the door, but he'd obviously woken when she slid out of the bed, because he leaned over her shoulder as she turned the doorknob.

"Dream about me, okay?" he'd said.

Even though the hoarse intimacy of his voice had sent warm tingles through her body, she'd glanced at him and said, "In between marketing plans? You bet."

He'd smiled and kissed her neck, but she had to have hurt his feelings. He'd been trying to push them closer, deepen their relationship, and she was constantly pulling away.

She wanted that moment back. She wanted the opportunity to say something weighty and special, not blow off the emotions with humor. Not hide behind work and the fear of depending too heavily on him.

"You guys want to join us?" Jay asked.

Isabel dragged her gaze away from Cade and started to respond, but Susan jumped in first.

"We'd *love* to," she said, and promptly dropped into an empty chair across from Dean.

Vincent already had his eye on a doe-eyed brunette near the end of the table, so Isabel didn't see the point in—

She halted her thoughts as she saw somebody else at the end of the table. Parker Huntington. What was *he* doing here?

"Are you gonna sit or pace?" Cade asked.

"I—" She slid into the empty chair next to Susan, putting her directly across the table from Cade. "I'm sorry. I've had a long week at work. It's making me nuts."

Cade nodded as if he understood. Since things had been just as crazy for him lately, he certainly had to. So why was he calm as he introduced her to the other people around the table, most of whom worked for GRI? Why didn't he look like one sharp comment or movement would send him scurrying under the table, curled into the fetal position?

Isabel accepted a beer from Dean and tried to relax and make small talk. After a while, she did so genuinely. The night was miraculously cool for early September. She was sure she hadn't felt a decent breeze not drenched in humidity in six months, and, as usual, Cade and his friends were charming and funny. Nobody, not even her, could stay cynical and moody around these guys.

Cade lightened her, she realized, watching him laugh over some story Dean told. He reminded her not to take everything so seriously, not to work to exhaustion without having some fun in between.

As the night wore on, she managed to work her way around the table so that she sat next to Cade. Beneath the table, she slid her hand down his jeans-clad thigh. "Why did you publicly challenge Baker Dunlop when you came out of the infield care center?"

"What?"

Obviously, whatever he'd expected her to say the first time they could talk privately, it hadn't been that. "I've been meaning to ask you for weeks, so now I really want to know. Do you really think he hit you on purpose?"

"Hell, yeah."

"I do, too. But why—"

"You do?"

"Sure." She angled her head. "It was obvious, but I want to know why he did it. I get the rivalry between your families and everything but— Why are you looking at me like that?"

"You're on my side."

"Of course I am."

He smiled. "You look good there."

For now, anyway.

She shook aside the negative thought. She was going to enjoy herself if it killed her. "So why did he hit you?"

"To rattle me. He knows I'm in a shaky situation with NASCAR and my sponsor. He knew I wouldn't retaliate."

"But you did. You were just clever about it."

He leaned close to her. "You know what I thought when that reporter asked me how I felt about Baker hitting me?" He dropped his gaze to her lips. "I asked myself, *What would Izzy do?*"

"You did?" She paused and considered what he'd said. "And you figured I'd say something challenging and snarky?"

"Wouldn't you?"

"Oh, yeah."

"Playing by the rules doesn't have to be completely boring."

"But we're not playing by the rules." Nervously, she licked her lips, then glanced down the table. Everybody was talking and laughing. Nobody even seemed to notice she and Cade were next to each other. Even Parker. Maybe she'd been paranoid for no reason.

And maybe he'd catch on thirty seconds from now.

"They didn't drag me here," she said, shifting her gaze back to Cade.

"Yes, they did."

She flushed. "Okay, maybe a little. There's just so much at stake. And what were you thinking, inviting Parker?"

"I thought you'd be happy. He's a sponsor, too. More cover for us."

"It's still a huge risk. If he finds out about us, he might decide you, Mr. Never-Met-a-Scandal-You-Didn't-Like, are a fifteen-million-dollar risk he's not willing to take."

Cade sipped his beer. His eyes darkened. "I could do without the lecture."

She bowed her head. She was doing this all wrong. He just wanted to be with her. He wanted to have a good time. He *deserved* a good time. They both did.

She had to relax and let the stress and secrecy and worries go. She was among friends. Parker was too busy flirting with the wide selection of women that tended to follow Cade and friends around to pay attention to anything else.

"I'm not trying to be difficult," she said finally to Cade.

"You just are."

"Yeah." Her heart sank. "Yeah, I guess I am."

"Stop it," he whispered, leaning closer.

She glanced at him. "What? I'm not—"

"I'm not going to desert you because you're difficult. My feelings for you won't change because your job sucks right now and you're with twelve different crises at once." He lifted his hand as if he was going to cup her cheek, but he dropped it back to the table, knowing he couldn't touch her. "Lean on me," he said, his gaze burning into hers. "Turn to me. Please."

She closed her eyes. Their secret affair had morphed into something much more serious than she'd planned. This wasn't just physical. Or casual.

"I will," she said, looking at him and feeling the weight of the emotions in his eyes. "I am."

Under the table, he laid his hand over hers. "When we leave here, you're coming with me."

She swallowed. "Okay."

"You're staying the night."

"I can do that," she said with a calm nod, though her heartbeat sped up.

"I've missed you."

"Me, too. I—"

"You two seem pretty intense," Parker said, standing behind them and laying an arm across each of their shoulders. "Are you bringing about world peace?"

Startled from their intimate conversation, Isabel squeezed Cade's thigh, hoping he realized the regret she felt before she returned her hand to her own lap. "We were actually talking about Thanksgiving. Cade's mother apparently has big plans for the holiday."

Cade picked up the pass she tossed him and brought Parker up-to-date on his mother's angst over china, silverware and crystal. Color schemes and place cards. One-hundred-percent family participation and following a dress code she'd designated.

"She's actually having a seamstress make a custom-designed tablecloth," he said in disbelief. "She calls me for my opinion about themes and whether fall leaves, mums or daffodils will work better with the china. It's completely weird, and *I'm* the one she wants advice from?" He shook his head. "I have no idea what she's talking about half the time."

"Is this the first holiday since their divorce?" Parker asked.

Seeming lost in the past, Cade nodded. "Yeah."

"My mother did the same thing the first Christmas after my parents separated when I was fifteen. My dad had this whole sixties-era bachelor pad with psychedelic colors and his twenty-five-year-old girlfriend in a miniskirt, and my mom tried for a Norman Rockwell holiday."

"My dad has a disco ball and a bearskin rug," Cade said.

"And a girlfriend half his age?" Parker asked with a knowing look in his eyes.

"Yep. But it's Mom I'm worried about." Cade dropped his gaze. "She misses him. She misses him more than any of us, especially her, want to admit."

I'm in love with him.

Isabel actually looked around, wondering where the bizarre thought had come from. Certainly not inside her own head and heart.

But with dread creeping into her stomach, she

knew it had. As he sat next to her, asking her to lean on him when she was tired and weak and angry. As he worried about his heartbroken mother. As he risked his career and a lucrative sponsorship deal to be with her, she knew she loved him.

Oh, boy. *That* wasn't good.

Love was messy and complicated. Emotions were unstable. She was used to counting on herself, relying on concrete facts and hard work to make her life meaningful and successful.

In her experience, love couldn't be counted on.

"Are you okay, Isabel?" Parker asked. "You look pale."

Her heart fluttered in panic. "I'm fine." She looked briefly at Cade. "I'm just—"

"Isabel."

Isabel glanced across the table to see a CATL rep staring down at her with her arms crossed over her chest.

"How interesting to see you here," she said, angling her head. Her gaze flicked to Parker, then Cade. "You're certainly hanging with a new crowd."

"I—" Usually ready to speak to members of the press, corporate CEOs and NASCAR big shots, Isabel froze. She panicked in the face of some newbie PR rep whom she'd never liked very much and frankly didn't think was too great at her job.

She glanced to her left, where Cade's friend Jay was sitting. She wrapped her arm around his. "Yeah, well, Jay thought it was time I met some of his friends."

Nobody's going to buy this. You're an idiot. Stop talking.

But she didn't stop.

"And I guess Parker came with Cade, right?" she asked, looking at the two men on her other side with pretend confusion.

Talk about confused. Jay stared at her as if she'd grown two heads. "What are you—"

She patted Jay's arm. "It's okay, honey. Kristie works in my office."

Jay looked lost.

Parker looked amused.

Cade looked pissed.

Isabel ignored them all. Instead, she watched Kristie. She had no intention of introducing Miss Nosy to the assembled group, much less inviting her to join them. Hopefully, she'd move along quickly.

"So, I guess I'll see you at the office," Kristie said finally.

Isabel gave her a fake smile. "Sure."

Just as she was about to breathe a sigh of relief, another figure approached the table. One that was much more dangerous. One that was bound to worry even Cade.

"Hi," Rachel Garrison said. "Mind if I join the party?"

"ISABEL TURNER ISN'T dating Jay. What's up?"

Cade leaned against the bar and ignored his sister, who'd dogged his heels the moment he'd left the patio. "Can a man get a beer around here?" he asked bartender.

"There's a whole bucket of them on the table outside," his sister reminded him.

"Make that two," Cade told the bartender.

Rachel grabbed his arm; he shrugged her off.

When he had his beers, he twisted the top off one of them and drank deeply. Fueling his temper with alcohol was probably a bad idea, but at the moment he just didn't give a damn.

Isabel and Jay. What a joke.

He knew she was covering for them. He knew she was trying to protect him. But with the fury boiling inside him, he couldn't see past her arm wrapped around his friend's. He couldn't forget the panic in her eyes, or the humiliation that washed over him while he mutely sat back and let her lie for them.

Why did it hurt so much? Why couldn't he get his brain to realize she was only denying him so they could be together? They *had* to lie. They'd *agreed* to lie.

So why did it feel so wrong? *Why did it hurt so much?*

"Give me one of those," Rachel said, holding her hand out.

He handed her a beer, and they drank silently together, leaning back against the bar.

"Mom's a mess," she said after a few minutes.

"I know."

"Dad's a mess."

"But he'll always have his disco ball."

Smiling, she shook her head. "There's always that."

"I don't really have to wear a suit jacket to Thanksgiving dinner, do I?"

"If you ever want to have a meal after that in the house, you do."

"We always play football in the yard after lunch. How am I supposed to do that in a coat?"

"So take it off. Wear the damn jacket, Cade. It'll make Mom happy."

"No, it won't."

"For that day it will."

"Should we talk to her?"

Rachel sighed. "I've tried, but I think it's just part of the process. She's trying to establish new traditions. To make the present different so she doesn't miss the past so much."

Saddened, but knowing he couldn't solve his own problems much less his parents', Cade slumped against the bar. "So I'm wearing a coat."

"You're wearing a coat. And Dad's going to Hawaii."

"Seriously?"

"Yep. Him and Desiree," Rachel said.

"Desiree?"

"Desi for short."

"Love it."

Even with the awkwardness of his dad and his

too-young girlfriend, Cade thought Thanksgiving at the beach sounded like a great idea. For one, Isabel would look great in a bikini.

Speaking of that…what were they going to do about Thanksgiving?

They couldn't be together openly. His sister would freak. Her uncle would freak. And introducing his super-secret girlfriend on the first Thanksgiving after they'd become a split family seemed like undue punishment for Isabel.

But he still wanted her there. He wanted to enjoy the brief time off from racing, the special, relaxing moments that every other couple had. He wanted to brag about her and show her off.

Dude, she's never going to go for it.

Rachel nudged him. "So Dad's into the beach, and Mom's into china. What're you into?

A forbidden brunette. "I'm into not screwing up," he said.

"Are you a mess?"

"I'm not really sure."

"I'm here if you need me."

"I know." He put his arm across her shoulders. "Let's go back to the party." He paused. "But no flirting with Parker."

"Oh, gee, and that was my primary mission."

"Don't encourage him. He already likes you too much."

"Naah." She bumped her hip against his. "He's too much of a suit."

When they rejoined the group, Cade worked his way through the crowd. He avoided Isabel. He wasn't angry at her; he was angry at their situation. And with Rachel there, plus that girl from Isabel's office lurking around, pushing their luck didn't seem smart.

He wasn't going to ignore her all night, though. In fact, he intended to give her his *exclusive* attention when they got to his house later.

"Hey, Cade, I haven't seen you around much lately."

He turned to face Lila, a woman he'd dated briefly last year. She placed her hand on his arm and stepped close. She smelled alluring and looked as good as ever. Dating her had been fun and uncomplicated.

But she wasn't Isabel.

He stepped back. "I've been working."

She smiled, not seeming at all insulted he didn't return her come-on. They caught up on mutual friends and recent events. She didn't challenge him or try to pull away from him. She didn't frustrate him.

But she didn't have warm brown eyes, either. Or a sense of humor as sharp as a razor blade. She didn't make his chest grow warm when she smiled. She didn't need him to prove to her that there was more to life than work. She didn't need him to show her that families stuck together, trusted one another and leaned on one another, no matter how difficult the situation.

She didn't need him to love her.

Of course, he didn't know how to love somebody not related to him, so he didn't see how he was going to convince Isabel of anything. It was hard to love a woman who was usually running as fast as she could in the opposite direction.

After Lila moved off, he leaned back against the patio railing and watched everybody else have fun. He'd thought falling in love—when it happened somewhere way in the future—would be exhilarating. He didn't plan on a roller coaster of sailing when they were together and sinking when they weren't, when the doubts and fears kicked in.

So maybe he wasn't in love. Maybe this tightness in his chest would go away.

"You seemed awfully close to that blonde earlier," Isabel said as she strolled by.

It's not going away, you idiot.

Didn't he *have* to be crazy in love when a woman could make biting comments like that, and he still wanted nothing more than to breathe the same air she did? He sipped his beer and pretended indifference. "Jealous?"

She glared silently at him.

He *wished* she was jealous. "Don't worry," he whispered, "you'll have me all to yourself later."

Clearly nervous, she glanced around. "You can't expect me to—"

"Oh, I do."

"But your sister."

"She's not invited."

"My fellow rep."

"Neither is she."

He walked away before she could argue further and he lost his temper completely. Wasn't he worth a little risk? It wasn't like he was asking her to shout his name from the top of the Empire State Building.

His mood continued to sour. He snapped at Jay when his friend suggested they head to a bar in Charlotte. He left soon after.

The cab dropped him off at home, and he stormed into the kitchen. He started to reach for another beer, then changed his mind and grabbed a bottle of water instead. He needed a clear head to reason with her, to make her see that they couldn't go on like this. They were going to have to make some hard choices.

Half convinced she wouldn't show, he waited for her on the front porch. When her cab pulled into his driveway twenty minutes later, he let out the breath he'd been holding, but he didn't let the troubling look on her face sway his determination.

He might be the driver on the track, but he was letting her steer the direction of this relationship, and he didn't like it one bit.

He slid the cabbie some money, then snagged her hand and led her into the house.

In the foyer, he closed the door, then turned and pinned her against it. "You're *mine*. Not Jay's. Not even CATL's." He kissed her, pouring all the frustration at not being able to show her openly how

much she meant to him. He unleashed the disappointment he'd felt the moment that girl from her
office had spotted them. The moment she'd denied
him and made everything they were together seem
wrong and embarrassing.

She softened beneath his hands as she always did.
She clung to him and returned his affection as if
she'd longed for his touch all night. He wanted to
hold on to *this* moment, when everything was right
and sweet and perfect.

"Say it," he said against her lips, his breath
rushing out in gasps.

Her eyes glittered as she stared up at him. "I'm
yours."

CHAPTER EIGHTEEN

"THAT'S THE KIND OF woman he should be with," Isabel said, thinking of the flirting blonde. "One who looks like a lingerie model and agrees with every word that comes out of his mouth."

"Of course he likes that, dear. He's a man," Mrs. Fitzgerald said as she stuck another silk rose in the arrangement they were assembling for the historical society fund-raiser later that week.

She'd taken her landlady into her confidence about Cade and had just told her about the evening last month at Midtown Sundries. She loved Susan and Vincent, but their opposing opinions were wearing on her. She needed a new perspective.

She and Cade couldn't go on dating in secret. She lived in fear of somebody finding out, and the deception was wearing on him to the point that any day she expected him to give her an ultimatum—him or her job. And she had no idea which she'd choose.

"But he cares about *you*," Mrs. Fitzgerald continued. "He appreciates the challenges you present. Even if he doesn't like them all the time."

"I don't want to be a challenge." *I want to be the love of his life.*

"Relationships are hard sometimes. Especially the important ones."

"But *nothing* about us is easy."

Mrs. Fitzgerald peered at her over the top of her wire-rimmed glasses. "The chemistry between you seems pretty intense."

Isabel felt her face heat. Talking about her sex life with her landlady wasn't a direction she was ready to take. "Yeah. It's…good. But lately he's angry all the time."

"Not at you."

"It's not me. It's the situation."

"I believe so, yes."

Isabel shook her head. "The situation sucks."

"I completely agree." Mrs. Fitzgerald stepped back and admired their project. The silk arrangement stood a good two feet tall and was plush with several different varieties of greenery, plus roses, lilies and gardenias. "That's perfect."

Isabel glanced around the town hall conference room they'd taken over for the fund-raiser preparations. "Now all we have to do is make nine more."

The black-tie event was in three days, after qualifying on Thursday night. They were doing the decorations themselves to save money and funnel more funds into the restoration project. All the committee members had recruited family and friends into helping out the cause. Cade had even drafted Jay and

Dean to help him build a couple of trellises to place behind the buffet tables. They were at the venue now working on the finishing touches.

"I thought I'd find you here," Isabel's uncle said as he walked into the room.

"Hey, Uncle John." Isabel wound her way through the empty pots and bags of Spanish moss as she walked toward him. She kissed his cheek. "Have you come to help?"

"I can't. I'm on my way to a dinner meeting with the accounting team."

She smiled. "Aha, trying to squeeze a few more marketing dollars from the budget?"

He didn't return her smile. "Something like that. Can I talk to you for a few minutes?"

At the tight expression on his face, dread moved through her stomach. "What's wrong? Is Aunt—"

He grabbed her arm. "She's fine. It's a…work thing."

It obviously wasn't a good work thing, though. Isabel headed to the door. "I'll be right back, Mrs. Fitzgerald," she called over her shoulder.

"Okay, dear."

"You've certainly been working hard on this project," he said when they reached the hallway.

"It's important to Mrs. Fitzgerald. And the community."

"And to Cade Garrison?"

Isabel's gaze shot to her uncle's. She swallowed. "Sure. He's on the committee."

"Stop it," he said, his tone abrupt, his eyes dark and angry. "You're through lying to me about him."

She stiffened. "I wasn't aware I'd ever lied to you about him."

"You're seeing him. *Dating* him. Kristie Tidwell told me she saw you out with him and his friends."

Panic bubbled in her stomach, but she kept her tone calm and controlled. "What I do with my personal time is none of her business. And she didn't see anything inappropriate."

"*I* saw you."

Dizziness washed over her. "Where?" she whispered. "How did you—"

"I followed you after work on Friday. You went to his house. You didn't knock on the front door as if it was a business appointment. You drove into the garage under the house. Are you going to tell me nothing inappropriate happened there, too?"

She literally had to brace her hand against the concrete wall to keep herself upright. "You *followed* me?"

"I had to know for sure. I didn't believe Kristie at first. But then I started putting together some things, the way you and Cade act when you're together. The way you've canceled plans with your family lately for other vague things you don't want to talk about. You even admitted to me several months ago that you were attracted to him. So Friday I followed you."

She was pretty sure she knew the betrayal he'd

felt. She was feeling it now. He'd followed her as if she were a teenager breaking her curfew. And yet, if she hadn't been breaking the rules, he wouldn't have found out anything.

He paced away from her. "Your personal time may not be any of your colleagues' business, but it is *mine*. It is when the man you're spending your personal time with is a NASCAR driver. Reps don't date the drivers. Especially not drivers for the competition."

"So if he drove for us, I could see him?"

He whirled. "Don't get smart with me, young lady."

"*Young lady?* I'm not fifteen."

"No." John closed his eyes briefly. "No, you're certainly not. You're a grown woman, one who's done something incredibly stupid and unprofessional. Unethical." A muscle ticked along his jaw. "It's not like you. What were you thinking? You'd jeopardize your career over some guy?"

Deny, deny, deny. That had been her plan if her uncle or anybody else confronted her. She couldn't lose Cade or her job. She'd been so sure she could escape if she played it cool. She was clever and quick.

But she was so damn tired of pretending.

Uncle John had saved her from poverty, neglect and abuse. She couldn't lie to him. She owed him… everything.

Feeling her throat start to burn, she pressed her lips together. "He's not just some guy."

"You're in love with him."

Silently, she nodded.

John pulled her into his arms. "Oh, baby. I'm sorry. I'm so sorry."

She clung to him, but she didn't cry. Later, she was sure the tears would fall, but right now she was too numb to think straight, much less feel anything.

"I can't change the rules for you. They're NASCAR's as much as they are mine, and they're in place for a reason."

"I know."

"Business reputations and millions of dollars are at stake."

"I wouldn't do anything to jeopardize—"

"Of course you wouldn't." He sighed. "But you don't just represent the company. You represent me." He squeezed her briefly before leaning back and meeting her gaze. "You're going to replace me soon."

She nodded. "I can't see him anymore," she said, surprised her voice didn't crack as the dreaded but inevitable words escaped.

John braced her face between his hands, then kissed her forehead. "No, honey, you can't."

CADE BRUSHED A SPECK of lint off his tux as he exited the limo. He longed to turn around and see Isabel behind him, one of her long, lean legs peeking from the folds of a silky cherry-red dress.

Instead, Dean clamped his hand on his shoulder

as they walked toward the entrance of the Visual Arts Center on the Davidson College campus. "Hey, if we gotta get trussed up in these penguin suits, at least we're arriving in style."

"We're bound to impress the ladies like this," Jay added. "You think we'll score, don't you, Cade?"

"Ah, well, most of the people attending will be college professors and local people who support the historical society." His friends looked so disappointed, he added, "But I'm sure you guys can find a babe or two."

When they entered the room, the party was in full swing. Uniformed waiters walked around with trays of champagne. Bars were set up in each of the corners. Artfully arranged food was spread out over long tables. The flowers, swags of red-and-silver fabric, candles and sparkling tablecloths Isabel and Mrs. Fitzgerald had worked on all week made everything look inviting and luxurious. They'd also draped his trellises with greenery and tiny white lights.

The huge room had turned intimate. It glowed not just from the styling but from the people who wandered around with plates and glasses. They smiled and laughed. They scooped up the food and gushed over one another's formal duds.

"Hey, man, this is cool," Jay said.

Smiling with satisfaction, Cade nodded. "Yes, it is."

While they wandered off—presumably to find babes—he accepted a glass of champagne, then spent several minutes looking for Isabel. She and Mrs. Fitzgerald had probably been here for hours. They'd been obsessing about details until late last night.

Then he saw her.

She wore a silky, halter-top gown—in gold, not red. It dipped low between her breasts and showed off her golden brown shoulders. She was smiling at a couple as they filled their plates.

"She's a remarkable young woman," a familiar voice said from behind him.

Cade turned toward Mrs. Fitzgerald. "You look lovely, ma'am." And she did, in a powder-blue suit with a jeweled trim.

"Thank you, Mr. Garrison, so do you. A man always looks more distinguished in formal wear."

Better than his usual jeans and T-shirt, he guessed. "Is there anything I can do to help you?"

"No, thank you. The catering staff has taken over. All we have left to do is enjoy ourselves."

If he could get to Isabel, he was sure he could do that. He took a step in her direction. "It was nice to—"

"Are you sure you know what you're doing, Mr. Garrison?" she asked in that steel-toned voice of hers.

"Ah…" He was pretty sure his tie was straight. Was he holding his champagne glass wrong? "With what?"

"With Isabel. The two of you are taking some pretty big risks."

How did she know? Was the gig up? He resisted the urge to glance around to see if everybody was staring at him.

You're losin' it, man.

Nobody at this party cared about his love life. Though, there were a few NASCAR people around. A couple of executives had bought tickets. Derek Foster was coming to help him draw the names of the date winners. Isabel had invited Ricky Jones from NASCAR.com and asked him to cover the party.

Had he gotten another one of his insider scoops?

"I know everything," she said, as if reading his mind. "She told me," she added.

Either this woman was a downright scary mind reader, or the paranoia over this secret keeping was finally pushing him over the edge of reason. He shook his head to clear it. "Why?"

"She's under a lot of pressure, and she needed somebody to talk to."

Not me. He clenched his jaw. Why couldn't she rely on him? Was he so terrible as a boyfriend? Was he such an idiot he couldn't offer advice and sympathy? Hell, he was caught up in all this, too. He was the only other person who truly did understand. "She could have talked to me."

"She wanted somebody objective."

"You're not objective."

Her eyes widened. "I beg your pardon."

"You don't like me."

"That's not true, Mr. Garrison. I think you're a re-markable young man."

He simply stared at her.

She cleared her throat. "I might have been a little hasty in my original judgment of you. All I knew was that you'd assaulted someone, and you drove a race car for a living. But you've done wonderful work on the committee and with this fund-raiser. I'd also like to think that some of the reasoning behind our efforts has rubbed off on you."

"The Cotton House isn't a crumbling eyesore. It's a piece of history."

She smiled. "Exactly. I'm sure you heard the property sold this week."

"I did."

"To be used as office space by a group of attorneys, one of which happens to be your personal lawyer."

He stiffened. "They needed new offices, and we needed a buyer. I know you wanted a family, but—"

"I wanted it to be loved, and I thank you very much for making that possible."

"You're welcome."

She patted his hand, the only slice of affection she'd ever revealed. "But back to Isabel. I only brought her up because I'm concerned about both of you. You're putting your careers in an extremely precarious position. Are you sure you're making the right decision?"

"I'm sure."

She nodded. "Good. I thought so." She angled her head. "But she's not so confident, is she?"

"No."

"Her job means a great deal to her. It's her foundation, and you're putting that in jeopardy." She glanced behind her briefly, as if checking to see if they were being overheard. "Do you mind if I make a suggestion?"

He shrugged. "Why not?"

"I think you should push her for a commitment."

He'd been wanting to do that for weeks. He needed to know how she felt about him. He needed some hope that their relationship could work out. He'd fully expected Mrs. Fitzgerald to say something like *give her some time and space, everything will work out, blah, blah, blah.* "You do?"

"I do. There's too much at stake for a simple fling." She raised her eyebrows. "You're not having a fling, are you, Mr. Garrison?"

"I was. I mean, we agreed that's what we were doing, but—" He peered into those piercing blue eyes and swallowed hard. "No, ma'am, I'm not."

"Then tell her." Mrs. Fitzgerald turned and waved. Isabel waved back, then headed toward them.

"What are you doing?" Cade asked Mrs. Fitzgerald.

"You're not going to shout across the room at her, are you?"

"No, ma'am, but—"

"Then there's no time like the present."

But before Isabel reached them, Ricky Jones stopped her. They talked for a minute, then started moving toward him and Mrs. Fitzgerald together.

Great.

Even before Mrs. Fitzgerald's pep talk, he'd envisioned this party as a romantic night for him and Isabel. He knew they couldn't act like a couple, but because they were both working on the committee, they had a legitimate excuse to be around each other for once. Doing that while tripping over the motorsports press wasn't his idea of a good time.

Introductions were made, and Cade fought the urge to pull Isabel to his side. He couldn't show anybody how he felt about her. He couldn't touch her or smile intimately at her.

Mrs. Fitzgerald was right. It was time, long past time, that she made a choice.

He made inane small talk with everybody for a few minutes and nearly kissed Mrs. Fitzgerald when she said to Ricky, "Mr. Jones, I'd like to introduce you to some more members of our committee. Would you come with me?"

Smart guy that Ricky was, he understood this was a command, not a request.

He nodded. "Yes, ma'am." He waved at Cade and Isabel as he walked away.

"You look beautiful," Cade said softly.

Isabel's startled gaze met his. "Thanks. You look… nice, too."

"What's wrong?"

"Nothing."

"You're jumpy. Your hands are clenched." Her eyes were blank and emotionless. "You look scared."

"I'm fine. I really need to get back to—"

He grabbed her hand and led her through the nearest door, which happened to be the one into the service hallway. She was obviously too shocked to protest, because she said nothing. They walked to the end of the hall and stopped at the emergency-exit door.

It wasn't a very romantic location, but then he wasn't too confident about this being a romantic conversation.

"We can't go on like this," Cade said.

"I know."

"You do?"

"We're both on edge all the time. You're angry. I'm nervous."

He cupped her face in his hand. His gut was tight, and he had control of his emotions by a thread. "I'm not angry at you. It's just that things have changed for me." He stroked her cheek. "This isn't a fling anymore for me. It hasn't been for a while. I want us to be together. Openly." He swallowed his anxiety and plunged ahead. "You've got to decide whether I'm more important than your job."

Her eyes, so distant before, finally fired. "The choice is easy for you. You don't have to give up anything."

He took a step back. "You want me to give up racing?"

"No, but can't you understand that what you're asking me to give up is just as important?"

"I do understand, but you can do your job outside of NASCAR. I can't."

"I've built my career at CATL." She shook her head, and his heart pounded. "I was going to wait until tomorrow to tell you. I wanted to enjoy tonight, but—" She looked sad. Resigned. "Uncle John knows about us."

"Oh, man." He dragged his hand through his hair. "Since when?"

"He came to see me Monday night."

"And you didn't say anything." She'd been distracted, though. In hindsight, he could see she'd been acting different all week. She hadn't argued with him when he asked her to stay overnight at his house. She hadn't reminded him once that they had to be discreet tonight. And she'd clung to him a little longer each time they hugged.

Like she was saying goodbye.

"You're choosing your job."

"Yes."

Dread filled his stomach. He'd half expected her answer, but he hadn't anticipated the stabs of pain that consumed his body. She didn't want him. Not enough.

Panicked, he grabbed her arms. "Don't. We can—" *What? We can work it out? We can change the rules?*

"You can work for me."

"What?"

"If Parker and I sign the new sponsorship deal, we'll need a new marketing plan."

"And you'll give your girlfriend a sympathy job to keep her occupied."

"That's not what I meant. We need you." As he said it, he realized it was true. "Rachel has a hard-enough time running the office with a small staff. She can't take on more responsibility."

She shook her head. "I've worked my whole career for CATL. I've sweated and bled to get where I am. I can't abandon that. They're going to make me a vice president!"

"But I love you."

She seemed just as shocked as he was by his confession. He hadn't meant to throw it at her like that. None of this was going the way he wanted.

She closed her eyes, and when she opened them again, they were filled with tears. "It isn't going to work. I can't give up my job."

"Why?" He grabbed her hands and squeezed them. "I'd do anything for you. I can make you happy."

She shook her head and pulled away. "I can't rely on somebody else to make me happy."

"You could rely on me, if you let yourself. Trust me."

She continued to shake her head. "I can't let Uncle John down. He saved me."

Cade wanted to argue, to keep her with him, but he knew she was gone even before she started backing down the hall.

"I have to go," she said, lips trembling but eyes determined. "I'll talk to you later."

"No, you won't," he said quietly as she disappeared back into the main room.

He pressed his back against the wall and slid down it, sitting with his legs drawn up and hands dangling between his knees. He didn't move for a long time, not knowing what to do.

He didn't want to go back to the party and face her or anybody else. He didn't want to go home where he would be filled with memories of her, reminding him how much he'd wanted to have her as part of his life. It wouldn't feel like home without her. Was she really going to go one way, while he went the other?

He wanted to put his fist through the concrete wall behind him, but he didn't do that, either.

Could emptiness fill a person?

Empty was nothing, right? It couldn't fill you. But that's how he felt, anyway—stuffed with emptiness.

After a while, he heard the click of a woman's heels down the hall. His heart leapt as he looked over.

And saw Mrs. Fitzgerald heading toward him.

He managed to push himself to his feet. Despite his personal grief, he had responsibilities toward the committee. "Do you need me to do something?" he asked her in a hollow voice he barely recognized.

She shook her head and pulled him into her arms. "I'm so sorry, Cade."

CHAPTER NINETEEN

EVEN THOUGH IT WAS BELOW fifty and blustery, Cade sat in his mom's backyard by the pool, staring at the plastic cover. After all he'd accomplished in the past five weeks, and the fact that it was Thanksgiving Day, he should be happy. Or at least grateful.

He was numb.

In the Cup races, he'd placed third at Charlotte, then tenth at Homestead. He'd finished second in the NASCAR Busch Series championship, only twenty points out of first.

As of Tuesday, he was a NASCAR NEXTEL Cup driver again. He and Parker had signed the deal with his father and brother by his side, then afterward, they'd held a press conference in the GRI museum. His entire Busch team, plus his crew chief, Sam, were moving with him to the Cup series next year.

Today, his mom, siblings, aunt, uncle and cousins had gathered inside the house, eager to share stories, good food and accomplishments.

He should be thrilled. He'd gotten everything he'd wanted.

He was miserable.

"What the devil are you doing out here?" Bryan called irritably from the door. "It's freezing."

"Just thinking," Cade said without turning around.

"Hell."

The door closed, and Cade breathed a sigh of relief. He was tired of talking to the press, his team, even his family. He wanted to be left alone in lousy, depressed peace.

But just a few minutes later, the door opened and closed again. He heard footsteps on the deck behind him, then a bottle of beer was dangled over his shoulder.

"Take it," his brother said.

He did, but winced when he glanced at the bottle. It was the brand Isabel liked.

Bryan sat in the lounge chair next to him and twisted off the top of his own beer. "You bring a suit coat? Mom won't let you eat without a coat."

Cade nodded. "It's in the living room."

They were silent for a few moments, then Bryan asked, "Who do you think we ought to hire for the new Busch team?"

Surprised, he worked up the energy to glance at his brother. "You're asking my advice?"

"Sure. You're part of this family, aren't you?"

But Bryan had never asked his advice about the business before. "I don't know. Can I think about it and get back to you?"

"Yeah, sure."

Cade stared at the pool again. Okay, he'd gotten even *more* than he wanted. But he was still miserable.

"I'm going over to a buddy's house later for wings and beer," Bryan asked. "You want to come?"

"No."

"You got a date?"

"I've got stuff to do at home."

"You sick?"

"No."

"You look sick."

"Thanks."

Bryan said nothing for a minute, and Cade figured he'd leave. His brother wasn't much of a talker, whereas Cade was—usually, anyway—one of those people who felt compelled to fill silence with talk or laughter.

No such luck.

"Okay, that's it," Bryan said, swinging his legs to the ground and leaning his forearms on his thighs. "You should be dancing from the rooftops. You're back in a Cup car. The press is buzzing about next year. You and Parker Huntington are, somehow, all buddy-buddy. But you haven't cracked a decent smile in weeks. What's wrong?"

"Nothing."

"You're wallowing."

Cade glared at him. "Go away. I don't want to talk to you."

"Oh, no, little brother." Bryan shook his head. "That won't cut it. Nobody around here let's me wallow, so you can't, either. *What's wrong?*"

Though the ink was still wet on the contract, his sponsorship was secure. What did it matter now if he told Bryan the rules he'd been breaking? Especially since he wouldn't be breaking them anymore. And maybe saying the words aloud would make him accept Isabel's decision and move on. "My girlfriend broke up with me."

"What girlfriend?"

"The one I've been seeing in secret since June."

"Huh?" He took a long drink of beer. "Secret? What are you— Who?"

"Isabel Turner."

"The CATL rep?"

"And future vice president."

"Oh, boy." Bryan sighed. Then he smiled. *The jerk.* "Well, that would have added a whole new element to the press conference. Cade Garrison, NASCAR's sexiest bachelor, has finally met a woman who won't fall at his feet."

"I didn't expect her to fall at my feet. I just wanted—"

"For her to quit her job and spend her days waiting quietly in your motor coach and smiling prettily while posing for pictures in Victory Lane?"

"No." Cade jumped to his feet. "I *love* her. I wanted her to be part of our family. I asked her to come to work for us, as a matter of fact. Her career is as important to her as mine is to me, and I thought she could give us a new direction and a fresh strategy."

"Normally I'd remind you that you can't offer jobs to people without talking to me, but since you're such a miserable idiot, I'll let it pass."

"*Idiot?* Hey, you asked me what was wrong, and I'm telling you. What about a little sympathy or—"

"Rachel!" Bryan shouted as he stood.

As Cade turned, his sister burst through the back door and rushed toward them. "Did he spill it?" She yanked Cade into a hug. "I've been so worried. What's wrong? Bryan, what's wrong?" she added when Cade didn't answer quickly enough to suit her.

"He's in love."

"He's—" Her jaw dropped. *"What?"*

"It gives me a sick kind of pleasure to realize you didn't know anything about this, either," Bryan said.

"You two are in on this together," Cade said slowly. Obviously his misery had slowed his response time. Bryan didn't initiate conversations. Rachel, who'd tried endlessly to get him to confess some deep-seated problem, had put Bryan up to his beer-bonding visit.

"I had to know what was going on," Rachel said, brushing his cheek with her lips. "You were sad and dark and quiet." She narrowed her eyes at him. "Still are, in fact. I should have known it was a woman. You're a mess, brother dear. All that talk about Mom and Dad and their problems, when it was really you all along who—" She gasped. "Isabel Turner."

Bryan toasted her with his beer bottle. "Oh, she's good."

"It's her, isn't it?" Rachel asked, grabbing Cade by his elbows.

It was with a weird relief to admit the truth to the one person he'd been so determined to hide from. "Yeah."

"Oh, good grief. You can't date a rep. And she works for the competition. The Go! people will go nuts, and even though they're not your primary sponsor anymore, they did agree to a partial sponsorship for next year. Your car will carry their special paint scheme at the Bristol night race, in fact. And if NASCAR found out, they'd totally lose it. Big conflict of interest and business ethics and all that." She paused, angling her head. "Still, if we could lure her away from CATL, we could really use her on the team with us. She's savvy and certainly wouldn't take any crap from you, which I could use on occasion. You might lose your "sexiest driver" title, since the public likes a single guy for that, but Derek Foster is cool, and he'd be glad for the exposure. She could stabilize you, and I'd love to hear her ideas about the Huntington Hotel publicity…"

"I think we've already been through this," Bryan said, leaning close. "And with far less words."

"Shh," Cade said, watching Rachel run on with such energy and concentration. He couldn't take his gaze off her. "I've been struggling with this for months. She's going to solve it all in ten minutes."

Finally, Rachel fell silent. She planted her hands on her hips. "*You* love her. *I* think she's great. Do you think she's great, Bry?"

"Definitely."

Rachel glared at Cade. "So what's the problem?"

"She broke up with me."

"So get her back."

"Oh, yeah. Just get her back. What great advice." He smacked his palm to his forehead. "If only I'd thought of that."

"What have you done to get her back?" Rachel rolled her eyes. "Besides wallow in misery."

"Well, I— I've been busy."

"See, *he* wallows, not me," Bryan said, looking triumphant.

"Shut up!" Cade and Rachel said to him.

"It doesn't matter how I feel," Cade said, turning back to his sister. "She doesn't want me. She chose her job instead."

"Well, *duh,* her job is her life, her self-worth. She's a strong woman, and she's not going to give that up without a fight."

"I didn't ask her to give it up."

"Yes, you did." Rachel flicked her fingers through his hair, then smiled when he winced in confirmation. "She works for her family, too, Cade. It makes everything more complicated. You don't just work for your boss, you love him."

As he searched his sister's gaze, a wave of acceptance and love washed over him. Different from what he felt for Isabel, but just as important. "I've got to get her back."

Rachel smiled. "Yes, you do."

"Hey, dude," Bryan said, "not that I should be offering relationship advice, but diamonds usually work." His eyes darkened with understanding and a hint of the pain he must have experienced on his own. "I called you an idiot because I knew you were on the verge of giving up. Don't."

"I won't."

"Good grief, we're about to have the blessing," their mother said as she flung open the door and shouted in their direction. "What are you three doing out here?"

Cade stared at his siblings for a moment, and maybe, just maybe, the heaviness in his heart lifted a fraction. "We're coming," he called to his mom.

"Don't forget to grab your coat," Bryan said to Cade, smoothing his own lapel.

"Don't whine," Rachel said. "I had to wear a dress."

When they reached the door, Cade kissed his mother's cheek, with Rachel and Bryan following. Whatever personal drama they had to deal with, it was Thanksgiving. Their dad wouldn't be at the head of the table, determined to convince somebody that the leg he preferred was a portion none of them wanted, but they were mostly together.

And Cade was grateful, even if he couldn't be happy without Isabel by his side.

"Cade's in love," Bryan said as they headed toward the dining room.

Even as Cade groaned—it was possible his aunt or one of his cousins had the tabloids on speed dial—his mother clapped her hands. "Oh, honey, really?"

She hugged him—even before he'd grabbed his dinner coat.

"Who is this girl?" she asked, looping her arm through his. "You need to bring her out to the house so I can meet her." Her smile lit up the already perfectly decorated table, with its orange swirl-and-dots china, Le Pois silverware and dark orange tablecloth. "*Love*. My little Cade. Finally. It's amazing. But, honey, if you want a spring wedding, we've got to get to work. The best planners and venues are booked nearly a year in advance. I just read this great article about theme weddings. Maybe we could borrow the Cothrens' yacht. Rachel, make sure you clear his calendar...."

Cade pulled his brother to a stop and let his mom and her obsessive planning drift away. "What are you doing, telling her? What if I can't get Isabel back?"

"Have some faith, man." Bryan winked. "And better you than me."

"ISABEL, CAN I TALK TO you in my office a second?" her uncle asked.

Isabel set down the handful of silverware she'd been using to set the table. "Sure."

"John, now? It's Thanksgiving," Aunt Emma said

from the other end of the table, where she was setting out plates. "We're eating in twenty minutes."

"It's important, Em. I won't take long."

Aunt Emma shook her head in mild exasperation. "Well, go on, then."

Isabel followed her uncle down the hallway to his office in the front of the house. The living-room fireplace also backed up to that room, and the gas logs were crackling behind the glass when they entered.

She used to lie in front of that fire and do her homework, while her uncle did paperwork.

"Close the door behind you," he said.

As she did, she swallowed her nerves. She was numb and miserable these days, so the least little thing set her off on a crying jag. She knew her work had suffered, but she couldn't have cared less.

She wasn't herself. She wasn't complete without Cade.

She had to tell her uncle she'd made a mistake. She'd assure him she loved him and appreciated all he'd done for her career, but the motions she was going through now weren't living. She wasn't good to him, CATL or herself like this.

These realizations didn't ease her trepidation, though.

"You share my blood, Isabel," he said, staring out the window. "Sometimes that's a good thing." He turned his head toward her. "And sometimes not."

"How's that?"

"I've taught you to be competent, resourceful and

self-sufficient. I've taught you the value of good business relationships and how to succeed." His eyes softened. "I should have also taught you that there are times to chuck that all for love."

"I—" She goggled at him. "There are?"

"Absolutely." Smiling, he walked toward her, laying his hands on her shoulders. "If you don't tell Cade Garrison you love him, I will."

Tears sprang to her eyes. Scary Isabel had turned into Crying Isabel lately, so it was a familiar sensation. "Oh, Uncle John, I've made such a mess of everything."

He drew her into his arms and held her close. "No, I have. I was blind and selfish not to encourage you before. My other kids never showed any interest in my business. They wanted to be doctors and lawyers." He sighed in mock disgust. "You were special. You were like me, and I didn't want to lose you."

She managed a watery smile. "I didn't want to disappoint you."

He leaned back and looked at her directly. "You could never do that, sweetie. I'm your father."

Nodding, she knew the life she'd led before finding this wonderful, generous, loving man was truly gone. "You certainly are."

He held her close again, and Isabel felt the last few months of secrecy, uncertainty and fear lift off her shoulders.

After a while, she grinned. "Uh, Dad?"

"Yeah, sweetie?"

"Can you teach me how to make your lasagna?"

He kissed her forehead. "For you, anything."

DESCENDING ALONE IN THE Waldorf-Astoria hotel elevator, Isabel smoothed her hands down the sides of her red satin gown. In the heart of Manhattan and among the black-tied racing elite, she'd stand out, but they only gave out the NASCAR NEXTEL Cup once a year, so she had a reason to go all-out.

Plus, after months of hiding and sneaking around, she wanted to be noticed, and wearing Garrison red seemed like a good start.

She moved through the crowd gathering in the main lobby for the cocktail hour. She spoke to several people, but she didn't see any drivers. They were probably waiting until the very last minute to show up.

"Does this thing get bigger every year, or is it just my imagination?" Ricky Jones asked as he squeezed by her.

"It gets bigger every year."

She headed toward the back of the room. Maybe she could spot Cade from there when he came in. She was anxious to find him.

She was unemployed.

Cade had broken through the wall she'd built around her heart. He'd healed the hurt and trust issues she'd been carrying around since childhood.

She loved him, and she wasn't going to let anything stand in the way of their happiness.

Part of her was nervous. She'd barely seen him in the past month and hadn't talked to him at all since the night of the historical society fund-raiser. How would he react to her tonight?

He had to be hurt and disappointed. But she knew he loved her. He'd been proving that to her every day for months. She had faith in that love, and she was going to apologize and make things right, no matter how long it took to win him back.

She was concentrating so hard on finding Cade to tell him all this that she nearly bumped into Susan.

"Have you seen him yet?" Susan asked.

"If I'd seen him, I wouldn't be standing here talking to you, would I?"

"Hey, don't snap at me. A few weeks ago you weren't so sharp when I held your hand for five hours while you cried over him, then I fed you ice cream."

"I know. I'm sorry. You've been great. I'm just—"

"Anxious?"

"Yeah."

"Excited?"

"That, too."

Susan sighed. "Oh, it's so romantic. Like Romeo and Juliet."

Isabel looked askance at her friend. "They *died* at the end, you know."

Susan crinkled up her nose. "Oh, right. Yuck.

Anyway, I came over to tell you something big. Guess who I saw talking to your uncle—*er,* I mean, your father? Are you really changing your name to Bonamici?"

"Yes, and who did you see with him?"

"Vincent."

"Well, isn't that interesting." She studied Susan. "Are you okay with that?"

"Are you kidding? After all the crap *you've* gone through this season? I wouldn't have your job. No thank you."

"Vincent can handle it."

"Sure."

"Where's Rex? I thought you two were supposed to hook up here."

Susan narrowed her eyes. "Flirting with some secretary from Baker. What a jerk. What did I ever see in him?"

And yesterday she was in love. Tomorrow she'd probably be in love—with somebody new. Isabel shrugged. "I had no idea. You'll find—"

Susan pointed toward the doorway. "Ooh. There he is!"

Dizzy, Isabel stared at Cade, his shoulders looking broader than she remembered them, his dark hair just touching the collar of his crisp white shirt, his smile bright. "Wow."

"He does fill out a tux well, doesn't he?" When Isabel didn't move, Susan poked her in the back. "What are you waiting for? Go get 'em."

"Go get 'em?"

"Oh, you know what I mean."

After a quick hug, Isabel wound her way through the room toward Cade. Her heart felt as if it was about to jump out of her chest.

"I heard CATL's losing you," Roger Cothran said, pulling her from her self-obsessed thoughts.

Though she wanted to keep moving, she stopped in front of him. "Yeah, they are."

He smiled. "How about coming to work for me?"

"Well, I—"

"Sorry, man," Cade said as he walked around Roger, "she's already got a new job."

"Damn."

His eyes, looking bluer and more beautiful than she remembered, focused intently on her face. "That wasn't the greeting I was looking for."

"I wanted to tell you about quitting."

Cade slid his arm around her waist and tugged her toward the doorway. "And I want to hear it."

"Bye, Roger," she said with a wave over her shoulder.

Roger stared curiously after them, but he was a pretty smart guy, so he'd figure it out quickly.

Now that Cade was next to her, touching her, her heart pounded even harder. She didn't question whether he'd changed his mind, but the realization that her whole life was about to change, that after all they'd been through, they could finally be together, was heady.

"Where are we going?" Isabel asked when they got in the elevator, which was blessedly vacant. "Not that I care, I was just curious."

As Cade pushed the button for the twentieth floor, he squeezed her waist. "You'll go anywhere with me?"

She grinned. "Oh, yeah."

"My room. I thought we'd have our own private cocktail party."

Her heart jumped. "Okay."

The elevator dinged and they walked out. When he opened the door to his room, she saw candlelight flickering in the sitting area. An ice-filled champagne bucket sat next to the sofa, and what looked like five dozen roses rested in a crystal vase on the coffee table.

"Wow," she said, glancing back at Cade.

He grasped her hand and led her to the sofa. "It looks much better with you sitting in the middle." He sat next to her, holding her hand between both of his and looking at her as if he couldn't quite believe she was next to him.

She was past awe. She wanted to jump into his lap. She wanted to kiss him until neither of them could breathe. But they were all dressed up, and he'd gone to so much trouble to set a romantic scene. Maybe they should talk first.

She cleared her throat. "So, how did you find out about my job?"

"Are you kidding? The second I got here your uncle cornered—"

"You mean my father?"

His eyes widened. "Father?"

"It's a new thing. I'll tell you about it later. He cornered you?"

"Yeah, in a dark ally and threatened to fit me with cement shoes if I didn't remember every day for the rest of my life that you're his perfect princess."

"It's that Italian blood."

"I can take it." Cade cupped her chin, rubbing his thumb across her bottom lip. "It's a big sacrifice you're making for me." He paused, angling his head. "You *are* making it for me, aren't you?"

"Only for you. And it's not a sacrifice, it's just a job."

He raised his eyebrows. "Since when?"

She wrapped her arms around his neck, bringing them closer, so she could feel the rush of his heart against hers. "Since I realized I love you more."

He kissed her, and she felt the weeks of pent-up worry and tension flow out of him. "I was so terrified when I got here. I had no idea how I was going to talk you out of your job and back into my life."

Her throat tightened. "I never should have walked away from you. I was scared of letting you mean too much to me."

"I know working for me isn't exactly your dream, but if you could believe in me the way I believe in you, we can make it work."

"I trust you with everything in me, and I'd love to work for you."

He leaned his forehead against hers. "Is that why you wore a dress? A red dress?"

"Yep, and I hear you're going to be back in red yourself. Congratulations."

"Honestly, I haven't been too thrilled about it until now. I couldn't be happy about anything without you. But *with* you…" He grinned, then dropped to one knee in front of her.

"What are you—"

He pulled a robin's-egg-blue box from his coat pocket. "I love you, Izzy. Marry me."

Astonished, she stared at the sparkling, pear-shaped diamond. "I— Wow, I—" She swallowed. Hard. "I thought we'd just date, you know, in the open this time like regular people."

"I need a commitment."

"We could live together."

"No way. My mom would never go for that."

"In that case…*yes.*"

His eyes lit up. "Really?"

"Yes, Cade, I'll marry you."

He slid the ring on her finger, then pulled her into his lap and kissed her. She found the security and belief in love that had eluded her for so long in his arms. Loving Cade made her complete.

"Do we have to go back down to the party?" she asked when he shifted his kisses to her neck.

He grinned. "Maybe later."

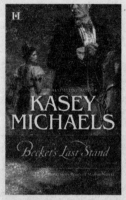

REQUEST YOUR FREE BOOKS!
2 FREE NOVELS PLUS 2 FREE GIFTS!

Silhouette®

SPECIAL EDITION®
Life, Love and Family!

YES! Please send me 2 FREE Silhouette Special Edition® novels and my 2 FREE gifts. After receiving them, if I don't wish to receive any more books, I can return the shipping statement marked "cancel." If I don't cancel, I will receive 6 brand-new novels every month and be billed just $4.24 per book in the U.S., or $4.99 per book in Canada, plus 25¢ shipping and handling per book and applicable taxes, if any*. That's a savings of at least 15% off the cover price! I understand that accepting the 2 free books and gifts places me under no obligation to buy anything. I can always return a shipment and cancel at any time. Even if I never buy another book from Silhouette, the two free books and gifts are mine to keep forever.   235 SDN EEYU 335 SDN EEY6

Name	(PLEASE PRINT)	
Address		Apt.
City	State/Prov.	Zip/Postal Code

Signature (if under 18, a parent or guardian must sign)

Mail to the **Silhouette Reader Service™:**
IN U.S.A.: P.O. Box 1867, Buffalo, NY 14240-1867
IN CANADA: P.O. Box 609, Fort Erie, Ontario L2A 5X3

Not valid to current Silhouette Special Edition subscribers.

Want to try two free books from another line?
Call 1-800-873-8635 or visit www.morefreebooks.com.

* Terms and prices subject to change without notice. NY residents add applicable sales tax. Canadian residents will be charged applicable provincial taxes and GST. This offer is limited to one order per household. All orders subject to approval. Credit or debit balances in a customer's account(s) may be offset by any other outstanding balance owed by or to the customer. Please allow 4 to 6 weeks for delivery.

Your Privacy: Silhouette is committed to protecting your privacy. Our Privacy Policy is available online at www.eHarlequin.com or upon request from the Reader Service. From time to time we make our lists of customers available to reputable firms who may have a product or service of interest to you. If you would prefer we not share your name and address, please check here. ☐

SSE07

HQN™

We *are* romance™

Sparks will fly, but this catch of the day could be the dish of a lifetime!

From the author of *Fools Rush In*,

KRiSTAN HiGGiNS

Take one lovelorn diner owner

A generous helping of nosy local gossips

A dollop of envy at married sister's perfect life

A splash of divine intervention

Combine ingredients and add one strong-but-silent lobsterman with a hidden heart of gold.

Catch of the Day

Don't miss this delightful new tale. In stores today!.

www.HQNBooks.com

PHKH224